THE PUBLISHER GRATEFULLY ACKNOWLEDGES THE GENEROUS
CONTRIBUTIONS TO THIS BOOK MADE BY THE FOLLOWING GROUPS
AT THE UNIVERSITY OF CALIFORNIA, SANTA CRUZ:

THE ARTS RESEARCH INSTITUTE,
ART DIVISION

INSTITUTE FOR
HUMANITIES RESEARCH

# NEW ORLEANS SUITE

*Music and Culture in Transition*

Lewis Watts and Eric Porter

UNIVERSITY OF CALIFORNIA PRESS

*Berkeley   Los Angeles   London*

Page i. LOUIS ARMSTRONG PARK, 2001.

University of California Press, one of the most distinguished university presses in the United States, enriches lives around the world by advancing scholarship in the humanities, social sciences, and natural sciences. Its activities are supported by the UC Press Foundation and by philanthropic contributions from individuals and institutions. For more information, visit www.ucpress.edu.

University of California Press
Berkeley and Los Angeles, California

University of California Press, Ltd.
London, England

Library of Congress Cataloging-in-Publication Data

Watts, Lewis, 1946–
    New Orleans suite : music and culture in transition / Lewis Watts and Eric Porter.
        p.   cm.
    Includes bibliographical references and index.
    ISBN 978-0-520-27387-0 (cloth : alk. paper) — ISBN 978-0-520-27388-7 (pbk. : alk. paper)
    1. Popular music—Social aspects—Louisiana—New Orleans.
2. Hurricane Katrina, 2005—Social aspects.   I. Porter, Eric (Eric C.)
II. Title.
    ml3917.u6w37   2013
    306.4'84240976335—dc23                                    2012026488

Manufactured in the United States of America

21  20  19  18  17  16  15  14  13  12
10  9  8  7  6  5  4  3  2  1

The paper used in this publication meets the minimum requirements of ANSI/NISO z39.48–1992 (R 2002) (*Permanence of Paper*).

# CONTENTS

# ACKNOWLEDGMENTS

First, we would like to thank the people of New Orleans for their hospitality and their inspiration. We are indebted to the following individuals, who hosted us, showed us around the city, patiently shared their insights about it, made necessary introductions, or were just good company: Ayanna Bassioni, Marcie Blanchard, Keith Calhoun, Alison Davis, Joel Dinerstein, Yolanda Estrada, Rashida Ferdinand, Mark Fowler, Donald Harrison Jr., Herreast Harrison, Cherice Harrison-Nelson, Randell Henry, David Houston, Stella Jones, Laura Lawson, Ronald Lewis, Chandra McCormick, Girard Mouton III, Thomas Neff, John O'Neal, Georgia Ross, Jim Rowell, John Scott, Juan Suarez, Claire Tancons, Eric Waters, Ronald Waters, and Deborah Willis.

Our research and photography was supported by a Committee on Research Special Research Grant and Faculty Research Grant as well as an Arts Research Institute Major Project Grant, all from University of California at Santa Cruz. Together or individually, we have benefited over the years from comments on our project by members of audiences at the Autonomous University of Baja California, Tijuana, the City College of New York, the Fisher Museum at the University of Southern California, Louisiana State University, the University of Nevada, Reno, the Newark Museum, the San Francisco Art Institute, the San Francisco Jazz Heritage Center, Stanford University, the Tisch School of the Arts at New York University, and multiple venues at UC Santa Cruz. Lewis received important feedback on and sustenance for this project by exhibiting his photographs at the Amistad Center for Art and Culture in Hartford, Connecticut; the San Francisco Museum of Modern Art Artists Gallery; the Alfred C. Glassell Jr. Exhibition Gallery in the Shaw Center for the Arts, Louisiana State University, Baton Rouge; Museum of the African Diaspora, San Francisco; the Sesnon Gallery, UC Santa Cruz; the Zokei Gallery and University Museum, Tokyo; Gallery AUBE, Kyoto; the Nathan Cummings Foundation, New York; the Engulfed by Katrina exhibit at the Tisch School of the Arts, New York University; and during Tarell Alvin McCraney's play, *The Brothers*, at the Magic Theatre in San Francisco. We are grateful to event organizers and curators at these places for enabling us to share our work and make it better.

Mary Francis of University of California Press believed in this project from the very beginning and provided necessary advice and encouragement along the way. We have benefited from working with project editor Dore Brown, editorial coordinator Kim Hogeland, designer Lia Tjandra, and copy editor Elizabeth Berg. We received invaluable feedback on our book proposal and manuscript from Bruce Raeburn and anonymous readers for UC Press. Portions of sections 2 and 3 were previously published as part of Eric's essay "Jazz and Revival," which appeared in *American Quarterly* 61, no. 3 (September 2009): 593–613. We appreciate the journal's willingness to let us publish this writing again. Feedback from AQ's editors and readers helped sharpen the arguments presented here. We give special thanks to Girard Mouton III for his meticulous reading of a draft of the book and for his invaluable corrections and suggestions for revision. He and Eric Waters generously shared their wisdom as longtime photographers of African American New Orleans and assisted with identification of the subjects of some of the photographs. We are grateful to Saul Williams for allowing us to include his poetry at the beginning of section 1 and to Charlotte Gusay for coordinating this arrangement. Publication in this format was made possible by the generous donation of subvention funds by UC Santa Cruz's Humanities Research Institute and Arts Research Institute.

Last but not least, we thank our families, friends, and colleagues for believing in us, encouraging us, and giving us the time to get this done.

# PREFACE

## FOUNDATIONS

Edward Kennedy Ellington from the District of Columbia composed and performed music for over fifty years. He made quite a name for himself. Along the way, he transformed American music, especially that which some (though not often Ellington) have called jazz. His grace, charisma, and artistic chops inspired a great many reviews and studies of the man and his music, and many photographs. These representations have made Ellington one of the archetypal figures who, for better and for worse, have helped to generate the layers of cultural meaning—a kind of noise, if you will—that have become inseparable from the sound.

In the spring of 1970 Ellington went to New Orleans, at the invitation of the promoter George Wein, to perform at the first New Orleans Jazz and Heritage Festival. On April 25 he premiered *New Orleans Suite* as a five-movement composition. Through these movements—"Blues for New Orleans," "Bourbon Street Jingling Jollies," "Thanks for the Beautiful Land on the Delta," "Second Line," and "Aristocracy a la Jean Lafitte"—*New Orleans Suite* expressed three objectives that defined many of Ellington's longer works: representing place, representing history, and representing the cultural expressions that constitute places and histories. Ellington recorded these movements a few days later in New York, but he did not stop there. For he was simultaneously working on four additional "portraits" of prominent musical influences and collaborators associated with New Orleans. He recorded these additions—"Portrait of Louis Armstrong," "Portrait of Wellman Braud," "Portrait of Sidney Bechet," and "Portrait of Mahalia Jackson"—on

May 13. These newer pieces augmented and refocused the representational pallet of New Orleans, its history, and its culture by showcasing black and Creole inhabitants (albeit famous ones) and by expanding the references to musical style and genre.

From our perspective, *New Orleans Suite* is not Ellington's best work. As others have pointed out, the suite was hastily composed and inadequately rehearsed. Ellington created the work at a moment of transition in his band, symbolized tragically by the passing of saxophonist Johnny Hodges two days before the second recording session. We agree with those who point out that the individual pieces do not cohere well as a whole, even as we take exception to similar characterizations of other lengthy compositions, like the *Far East Suite*.[1] But, as listeners, we still like most of the individual pieces on *New Orleans Suite*. More important, we appreciate what Ellington tried to represent as an outsider. New Orleans, like the "Far East," was not home but rather a site of occasional visits that nonetheless had deep symbolic significance for him personally and professionally. His suite thus provides a suggestive frame for documenting and expressing our own complex affinities for New Orleans.

Our *New Orleans Suite* expresses our long-standing interest in the city from afar. This interest was refocused by the catastrophic events in New Orleans beginning in the late summer of 2005 and also by the many ways people survived, overcame, and represented those events in the years since. Like Ellington, we have been compelled to survey the history, geography, built environment, and cultural matrix of New Orleans. We give particular attention to its black residents while also seeking to understand the complex and rapidly changing demographic and cultural scene in the city. At its core, this book conveys our impressions of the ever-changing position, role, and meaning of Afro-diasporic cultural expressions in New Orleans and its environs.

Ellington's *New Orleans Suite* provides further guidance as it surveys multiple genres. As put together on the Atlantic LP, the piece starts with the blues, ends with gospel, and has as its climax a celebration of New Orleans's second line culture.[2] The series of rhythmic figures that Ellington uses on the various pieces—waltz, Latin, blues, swing, and so on—evoke a spatial and cultural multiplicity that we also hope to represent. Also inspiring is the composition's evocation of the contradiction that often defined Ellington's work. According to Mercer Ellington, his father's playful deconstruction of a "Second Line" in the suite is an example of the way he was often invested in categories—in this case trying to capture the distinctiveness of a culture and music—that he was also willing to interrogate and even reject. "He was really a glorified anarchist in the way he was so often a part of the very things he sought to knock down."[3]

Building from Ellington's perspective, our *New Orleans Suite* joins the post-Katrina conversation about New Orleans. It pays homage to the city (and region) and its residents; maps recent, often contradictory, social and cultural transformations; and seeks to counter inadequate (and often pejorative) accounts of people and place. We also show how anxieties about the future of the city and its residents after the storm are now foundational to New Orleans cultural life. Yet *New Orleans Suite* is not a book solely about

Katrina. The storm and its aftermath are among the catalysts for this project, and they figure prominently in this narrative. Yet we also try to situate Katrina and its aftermath within a broader history. We consider how the storm was both a transformative force and a vehicle for enabling long-standing processes to come into view.[4]

Although we use modes of expression here that differ from Ellington's, music remains a critical point of entry for representing place, history, and culture. We explore the multifaceted role of music in this region in the past and present, as well as the ways it illuminates complicated social phenomena in this city as it undergoes transitions of both short and long duration. Among these phenomena are the affinities and anxieties embedded in the production and consumption of black culture, which have been all the more apparent locally (as well as nationally) in the wake of Katrina. And as we look to the music, the social spaces it inhabits, the events for which it provides the soundtrack, and the rituals of which it is a part, we examine the linked themes of *diaspora, history and historical memory, transformation, regeneration,* and not least of all, *survival.* For, in the end, this is a story about how bad things have happened to people in the long and short run, how people have persevered by drawing upon and transforming their cultural practices, and what crises can teach us about citizenship, politics, and other issues.

Finally, as a recording that lacks some polish and coherence, Ellington's *New Orleans Suite* cautions us to beware of misrepresentation—especially of being out of sync with one another—as we similarly narrate a story as outsiders that is in thousands of ways each day being narrated from within. While we readily admit to the limitations of our outsiders' perspectives, we also believe our concerns around this question of misrepresentation have made this a better story.


## REHEARSAL ONE
### LEWIS WATTS

There is a long and rich tradition of African American photographers—indigenous, transplanted, and itinerant—providing their own impressions of the city, its architecture, and its people. In fact, photography was first brought to New Orleans by Jules Lion, a free person of color and established painter and lithographer who had emigrated from France in 1837. Lion showed his daguerreotypes in 1840 in the city, in an exhibition at the Hall of the St. Charles Museum. This exhibit marked the beginning of prominent black-created art exhibitions in the city.[5] The tradition has been carried forth by Arthur P. Bedou, Villard Paddio, Florestine Perrault Collins, Marion James Porter, Carrie Mae Weems, Marilyn Nance, Chandra McCormick, Keith Calhoun, Roland Charles, Eric Waters, Girard Mouton III, Deborah Willis, and a host of others who have lived, photographed, or shown their work in the city.[6] Their images have made site specific the black photographic project of, in Robin D. G. Kelley's words, "locating and reproducing the beauty and fragility of the race, the ironic humor of everyday life, the dream life of a people."[7] Such work accomplishes this in the face of the crushing weight of stereotypical images, even as it is sometimes itself complicit in economies of misrepresentation. And it does so in part because of the participation of the subjects who inhabit the frame: men, women, and children who gaze back at the lens and at us with looks that appeal, scold, calm, love, and satirize. In other words, there is a dialogue between photographers and their subjects—people who craft their humanity through action and reaction.

I joined this site-specific tradition in 1994, when, like Ellington in 1970, I traveled to New Orleans on a commissioned assignment. Long before that, the city had been on my radar as a place I wanted to explore as part of my long-standing survey of the African American cultural landscape. I had been working on documenting cultural connections between the U.S. South and the urban West and North and had devoted much attention to people who inhabited built environments, the architectural spaces in which human-created culture was manifest, and the visual evidence of time and migration. I was immediately attracted aesthetically to the city and have since made numerous trips back to photograph. I think my approach has been well suited to documenting the multilayered history of New Orleans. While investigating New Orleans, I have been reminded of William Faulkner's comment about the South: "The past is never dead. It's not even past."[8] I view the city's atmosphere as a palimpsest that reflects its complex history and narratives. The "hothouse" composed of the built environment and the musical, cultural, and spiritual practices in the city have presented to me a compelling and complicated set of aesthetics. In other words, I am drawn to New Orleans as a place that wears its past and present, as well as its heart, on its sleeve.

I was scheduled for a fall 2005 Artist in Residency at the Ogden Museum of Southern Art in New Orleans, but Hurricane Katrina derailed these plans. I was able to get into the city six weeks later, with access to various parts of it made possible by being "embedded" with the National Guard. But most of the residents were still gone. I felt great loss entering the city after the storm because of that absence. I also grieved for the loss of access to the artistic and cultural life of the city that the residency would have provided. My loss, of course, was minuscule compared to what people who lived there were facing, and in the end, post-Katrina visits to the city exposed layers and complexity in New Orleans that were not available to me before. I have been able to see more clearly how much the people and culture functioned as the connecting tissue and activating agents for the visual elements that had originally drawn me to the place. Moreover, I have seen parallels between what the storm did to dislodge so many of New Orleans's African American residents and the demographic changes wrought by urban renewal and gentrification in other places I have photographed and researched, like West Oakland, the Fillmore in San Francisco, and Harlem. The strong feelings that have emerged from making these connections have provided much of the inspiration for my contributions to this volume.

Also inspiring have been the attempts of New Orleanians to keep the "essence" of their city from disappearing in the wake of Katrina. That struggle has indeed been a central element of our observation of place. My research and photographs of New

Orleans before and after the storm have yielded deep relationships with artists, curators, musicians, and other cultural practitioners, who have granted access to cultural practices, ritual, and physical parts of the city that were only partially available to me in eleven years of photographing before the storm. My experience has been that the people of New Orleans are very protective of the image and culture of their city, but for the most part people of all walks of life have been very generous to us, because we both try to approach our research with a personal and professional background that places the specific narrative here in a global context. The collaboration with Eric has also been a great way to open my eyes and rethink my reactions to places and events.

## REHEARSAL TWO
### ERIC PORTER

There is a long history of writing about and otherwise representing music in New Orleans as a means of situating this city in larger narratives concerning diaspora, nation, race, blackness, and so on. People from New Orleans have been invested in this project, and outsiders have too. This work has continued into the post-Katrina present, with many, often elegiac accounts emerging that map this complex cultural terrain and quite often stake a claim for the national and global importance of local expression.

I made several visits to New Orleans during the sixteen years prior to Katrina, beginning with one on the way to a family reunion in Shreveport. I was also interested in New Orleans as a jazz scholar, well aware of the importance of the city to that genre's history and, more generally, to the history of music in the Americas. Important to that story have been the ways that New Orleans's social and cultural environment has informed the complex meanings that accompany jazz and other forms of music.[9]

Like others in the field of jazz studies, I have been interested in understanding music and its meaning in their broader social and political contexts and also in the ways music has been mobilized—by musicians and others—to make social commentary and perhaps even change the world. Following long-standing trends in cultural studies and cultural history, I have tended to look at cultural production as a contradictory site. Genres, communities, and even singular expressions can simultaneously reinscribe power and provide a means of resisting, or at least negotiating, it. Music can express a progressive or even revolutionary orientation or philosophy along one axis of power (say, race) while being simultaneously retrograde on another (say, sexuality). And like many other African American writers, I have understood that trying to say something smart about the music is a project of political and even moral import. Thus New Orleans has seemed to offer a lot when thinking about power and paradox in and through music.

Although I was not able to visit the city until eight months after the storm and what some call the "federal flood," I was, like many, profoundly affected, beginning that fateful August, by the humanitarian and political implications of Katrina and the threat posed to New Orleanians and their cultural scene. I was also captivated by the ways people turned to music for sustenance in the wake of the storm, and how New Orleans culture was mobilized, for better and for worse, by people with varying and sometimes conflicting interests, to rebuild the city and help (or not help) those who were displaced or otherwise affected by the storm.

Responding to Katrina as a scholar quickly became an imperative and, as the complexity of Katrina's aftermath and the representation thereof unfolded, an analytical challenge. Attending an early 2006 symposium at the University of California Santa Cruz, where Lewis and I both teach and where he presented his wonderful photographs, provided the catalyst for writing something about the city in the post-Katrina moment. To make a long story short, Lewis and I talked at the symposium about a collaborative project on New Orleans and, after successfully putting together a grant proposal to fund a visit to the city that May, began this collective effort in earnest.

Admittedly, I initially imagined that my contribution to the volume would be based on a much deeper and systematic engagement with archival sources and a large collection of interviews that I hoped to conduct during lengthy stays in New Orleans, but the profession and life more generally got in the way. I also recognized quickly that a tremendous amount of excellent writing on the phenomena that interested me most was being produced by scholars, journalists, activists, and artists with deeper connections to the city than I could ever have. So my approach has been to rely significantly on secondary literature to develop an understanding of some key phenomena that I witnessed (and was directed to by generous local contacts) during visits to the city in 2006, 2008, and 2010. Others' scholarship has also helped me understand issues I encountered in the myriad media representations of post-Katrina New Orleans over the past seven years. And of course, I have drawn immensely from Lewis's photographs. I have learned much from their content, and I like to think they have enabled me to bring more art to my writing. Ultimately, I hope that my outsider status—my somewhat different investments in the subjects at hand, the experiences I bring as a scholar interested in the broader (even global) implications of local phenomena, my fascination with paradox, and perhaps also a kind of analytical distance—can provide a distinctive perspective on some familiar subjects and maybe even some new insights.

## COMPOSITION AND PERFORMANCE

Our *New Orleans Suite* is composed with our preferred modes of professional communication: analytical writing and photographs. As a "suite," the book's organization follows the logic of two definitions of that term. A suite, of course, is a set of musical compositions designed to be performed and heard in succession. But please consider this a composition that has developed out of a kind of improvisation—a creative exchange between us that proceeded in often unplanned and unexpected ways as we have shared ideas over the phone and e-mail, in conversations in Eric's living room, when sitting in front of a computer screen in Lewis's studio, and most important, while walking and driving around New Orleans together in 2006, 2008, and 2010. The conversations and shared observations have been mutually influential, in terms of identifying the key themes around which this story coheres and in terms of their effects on where we have taken our individual narratives. So, on that note, we also envision this book as a "suite" that is analogous to an integrated set of computer applications that operate as a whole and share data.

We present here groups of photographs and written sections that form two narratives. We intend for these to operate independently but also to represent in tandem New Orleans's cultural history and its recent transformations. At times the mutual influence will be quite subtle, requiring active and creative interpretation on the part of the reader. At other moments the dialogue will be clearer. We also hope to convey in this implicit and explicit dialogue the cooperative process of creating this volume as well as a deeper level of analysis that emerges from such collaboration. One way to think about this collaboration is as a "jam session," where we riff separately and in unison on ideas and variations on themes.

We invite you, the reader, to make your way through this book as you see fit. Some may choose to focus first (or solely) on the photographs. Others may move first to the text. One might, while reading the written sections, go back to individual photographs for illustration of issues encountered there. Or one could, while surveying photographs, check the index for textual references to Mardi Gras Indians, second lines, jazz funerals, and other subjects represented in the images.

But here is what we think it means to read this book from front to back, with the idea of a suite (and a jam session) in mind. The first section of photographs provides a foundation for those that follow. It portrays the *atmosphere* of the city, the cultural practices and environmental conditions that Lewis encountered and was directed to by many friends and acquaintances in visits over the years. Most of the photographs in this section predate Katrina, although he also includes a few post-Katrina images that reflect enduring qualities that have survived the natural and human-made disasters. Eric's written sections 1 and 2 are also foundational. In section 1, "New Orleans, America, Music," he provides a brief meditation on the political, social, cultural, and moral scene one must engage with when writing about New Orleans and its music post Katrina. Section 2, "Reflections on Jazz Fest 2006," conveys some of our impressions of the first iteration of this event after Katrina. The key issue Eric ponders here is the complicated notion that "the culture" can enable the reconstruction of New Orleans, which is a recurring theme in the words and images.

One crucial component of our shared data is the specific destruction wrought by the storm and levee breaks and what many have described as the additional catastrophe caused by the response to the crisis by the government and local elites. Eric tells some of that story briefly in sections 1 and 2, and Lewis expands upon it in the first section of the large group of photographs that follow. There he uses his long-term interest in the "cultural landscape" as a filter for reacting to the specific effects of the storm on the environment. He reflects further upon its impact on local culture and the ways people responded, for better and for worse. Some photos are from several weeks after the storm, while a number were taken during the spring 2006 trip, when Eric was also present. Their shared conversation while traveling through the city on this visit shaped each contributor's analysis of what they encountered and thus also became part of the shared data for the suite.

The large group of photos continues with two sections dedicated to the rituals that have sustained people before and after Katrina, with particular attention to traditional African American practices. The first section, on second line parades and funerals, includes photographs taken before the storm and during several later visits to the city. The second section includes photographs from Mardi Gras in 2007 and 2008. Eric's written sections 3 to 5 follow and provide a parallel take on rituals and transformations to them. Section 3, "Parading against Violence," examines some of the different ways cultural workers and their allies have employed traditional and alternative second line practices in the struggle against criminal and state violence and have, in the process, opened up space for an interesting referendum on who bears responsibility for violence in post-Katrina New Orleans. Among other things, Eric discusses a 2008 Lundi Gras second line that also appears in some of Watts's photographs, providing another set of shared data. Section 4, "Reconstruction's Soundtrack," looks at the ways post-Katrina recordings by local musicians comment on the transformations in the city following the storm, speaking forcefully for an equitable reconstruction of the city and ultimately theorizing New Orleans as a zone of radical potential forged out of the often mundane, sometimes heroic relationships of its citizens and sustained through alliances with outsiders. Finally, section 5, "To Reinvent Life," focuses on cultural shifts that are happening along with demographic transformations and changing spatial relationships in the city. It suggests that future writing about New Orleans would benefit by conceptualizing the city as a node in overlapping diasporas, the site of multiple experiences of displacement in the past and present.

Much of the inspiration for these last two written sections came from encounters during our April 2010 visit to the city, when we witnessed the paradoxical ways that New Orleans was recovering from the disaster five years later. That visit more or less coincided with the Deepwater Horizon oil spill, which has produced a new set of challenges while reminding us that the 2005 storms are part of a much longer history of people surviving and celebrating under difficult conditions.

# FOUNDATIONS

PLATE 1.  Tremé bar, 2001

PLATE 2. Central City, 1994

PLATE 3. After school, Rampart Street, 2000

PLATE 4. Lee Circle, 1994

PLATE 5. Algiers, 2011

PLATE 6. John Scott drawing at a house party, 1994. John Scott was a MacArthur Award–winning artist who lost his house and studio after Hurricane Katrina and died shortly afterward.

PLATE 7. Earl "African Cowboy" Turbinton playing for Adella Gauthier and her daughter at a house party, 1994

PLATE 8. Player piano restoration, Magazine Street, 2001

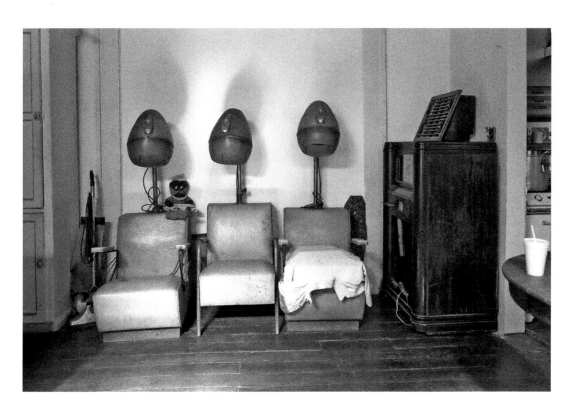

PLATE 9. Magazine Street, 2001

PLATE 10. Rashida Ferdinand's bedroom in her recently reconstructed house, Ninth Ward, 2008. Pictured is her grandmother, Marjorie Belcina Pajeaud.

PLATE 11. Black Madonna, Uptown, 2010

PLATE 12. Sweet Olive Cemetery, Baton Rouge, 2001

PLATE 13. Jessie Hill's grave, Holt Cemetery, 2005

PLATE 14. St. Roch ("patron saint of miracle cures") Chapel, Bywater, 2001

PLATE 15. Altar to Marie Laveau, Voodoo Spiritualist Temple, 1996

PLATE 16. Fats Domino under the freeway, Claiborne Avenue, 2006

# 1

# NEW ORLEANS, AMERICA, MUSIC

. . . How much are we subject
to the metaphors we reference?
If we sing of mighty battles
will we conjure them?
New Orleans
the siege of Orleans
Joan of Arc
in her 12th year
claimed to see God
Black boys
on bottle caps
heard voices
strangled in dance step
Sourced from the broken wind
of overgrown sea
hormones
within the waves
dismantled
more black than white keys
Some songs we cannot sing
until we cross to the other side
New Orleans is at a crossroads
Music is at a crossroads
America is at a crossroads

—SAUL WILLIAMS (2009)

Saul Williams's words, speaking of the power and possibility in creative work, the spirit, the natural world, human identities, and collective sensibilities, come from the liner notes of a 2010 CD titled *Dear New Orleans*.[1] Released in August 2010 to commemorate the five-year anniversary of Hurricane Katrina and to respond to the Deepwater Horizon oil spill, the album was produced by Air Traffic Control (ATC), a nonprofit organization supporting activism, advocacy, and philanthropy among musicians.

*Dear New Orleans* consists of thirty-one tracks recorded by some of the sixty participants in the "artist activism retreats" in New Orleans that have been sponsored since
2006 by ATC and the Future of Music Coalition (FMC), the latter of which addresses
policy, legal, technological, and economic issues on behalf of musicians.[2] These retreats
have brought musicians from across the United States together with local musicians,
organizers, community leaders, tradition bearers, and other artists. According to ATC,
retreat participants' interaction with local artists and activists left them with the "feeling
that their lives have been changed by what they have experienced in New Orleans and with
a sense of empowerment for what they can accomplish through their music and activism." These collaborations have, in fact, led outside musicians to engage in philanthropic
fundraising for and activism on behalf of New Orleans–based community and grassroots
organizations. They have also inspired a number of musical collaborations among participants. These two sets of practices come together on *Dear New Orleans*. In addition to
offering some compelling music, the album raises money for Sweet Home New Orleans,
which supports New Orleans cultural workers, and the Gulf Restoration Network, an
environmental organization dedicated to protecting coastal wetlands and other projects.[3]

As a listener, I like the breadth of this album. The performances on it represent a
range of genres—pop, jazz, country, R&B, folk, rock—and a diversity of inspirations.
Some songs are directly about the city or Katrina. Others are merely thematically connected to New Orleans or the storm. Others simply remind artists of the city or were performed live at retreat concerts. I also like the ways the fusion of genres comes together
powerfully on successive tracks and within individual performances. Listen to the way
jazz pianist Vijay Iyer's mournful, tense original instrumental "Threnody" sets the stage
for "Where Is Bobbie Gentry?," singer songwriter Jill Sobule's haunting follow-up to
Gentry's 1967 number one hit, "Ode to Billie Joe," sung in the voice of the grown-up
ghost of the aborted baby that, according to some interpretations, is the object that the
narrator of "Billie Joe" threw off the Tallahatchie Bridge. And dig Nicole Atkins and
trombone-centric band Bonerama's version of Joe McCoy and Memphis Minnie's "When
the Levee Breaks" (as appropriated by Led Zeppelin). With its loose and bluesy horn
arrangements, its distorted electric guitar and trombone solos, and Atkins's fantastic
rendition of Robert Plant's caterwauling, it is simultaneously a brilliant parody of classic
rock excess and a politically on-the-mark recontextualization of this blues lament about
the Great Mississippi Flood of 1927. And to use a certain vernacular, it absolutely rocks.

As a writer, I appreciate what *Dear New Orleans* represents as it marks Katrina's
fifth anniversary. The producers and musicians framed it as a response to *New Orleans
Times-Picayune* writer Chris Rose's epistolary editorial "Dear America," published eight
days after the storm hit. Rose expressed gratitude to the Americans who reached out
to shelter the displaced and who sent resources or came in person to the city to rescue
and rebuild. His letter was also a statement of local pride—in the place and its unique
culture, and more importantly, in the people. It spoke of the resiliency of New Orleans
residents and what they would offer the nation in the future. "So when all this is over

and we move back home, we will repay to you the hospitality and generosity of spirit you offer to us in this season of our despair. That is our promise. That is our faith." And in response, five years later, "America" wrote back to New Orleans in the liner notes to *Dear New Orleans*, expressing our regret for the "super shitty things [that] keep happening to you" and for only writing when they do. America was thankful, too, for the city's music, even if we could not quite figure out what to make of it. But beyond just a "sorry" and "thank you" that were not quite adequate, America sent back some music "we made while thinking about you"—and some money.[4]

*Dear New Orleans* performs an economy of obligation that has surrounded the city over the past several years, of political and moral failings needing to be rectified. Something we know all about, at least if we are willing to read against our own forgetfulness and many of the accounts offered by the corporate media. We know, then, about the damage caused by the winds and the rain, as well as the more devastating surge of water that overwhelmed the levee system and flooded 80 percent of the city. And the long-standing knowledge that the levees might fail, and the federal government's failure to maintain them despite that knowledge. And the deplorable conditions Katrina victims faced at the Superdome and Convention Center. And the delays in the arrival of active duty troops and National Guard personnel to rescue them. And the rapes and murders. And the exaggerated reports of rapes and murders and the concomitant "elite panic" that made the rescue efforts such a disaster as they put less focus on rescuing victims than on protecting others from them.[5] And the police and vigilante killings. And the cluelessness of President George W. Bush and his mother. And the 1,800 plus officially counted dead in the immediate aftermath and the many more who died later from inadequate medical care, stress, or grief. And the suicides. And long-term and permanent displacement. And the innocent and minor offenders lost for months and years in jails and prisons. And the difficulty people have had extracting money to rebuild from governments and insurance companies. And the toxic FEMA trailers. And the unscrupulous contractors. And the diminishing workers' rights, the scaling back of environmental regulations, and other manifestations of "disaster capitalism," in which elites use a crisis to lessen state protections and further their market-friendly political agenda.[6] And the closure of structurally sound Charity Hospital and public housing projects. And gentrification, planned and unplanned. And high rents. And the failures of the social safety net and the criminal justice system. And the fired public school teachers and a privatized public school system that still fails families without financial means. And joblessness and poorly paid jobs. And ultimately, as many of these phenomena attest, the ways poor people (especially black poor people) have been most dramatically affected by these things while being blamed for their own suffering.

But five years after the storm, this musical exchange also marks an important economy of inspiration and a horizon of possibility rooted in the heroic deeds of New Orleanians who have tried with varying degrees of success to bring their city back as they knew it or wanted it to be. And rooted also in the work of outsiders who have expressed their care for and dedication to the city. As Rebecca Solnit notes, disasters bring out the worst in some human beings but some of the very best in others, especially in a world defined increasingly by "private life and private satisfaction." "Disasters," she continues, "in returning their sufferers to public and collective life, undo some of this privatization, which is a slower, subtler disaster all its own."[7] And there seems something particularly special about the ways many New Orleanians have risen to the occasion of Katrina.

We saw this public response begin immediately with citizen rescuers—the "Soul Patrol" of working-class black men from the Seventh Ward, Cajun fisherfolk from the surrounding countryside, and others from as far away as Texas—who brought their boats or found someone else's and navigated the floodwaters to save people when the government could not or would not. We subsequently saw it in the efforts of those who stayed, those who soon returned, and those volunteers from across the nation and beyond, who quickly began feeding, clothing, housing, and administering medical care to the needy in the wake of government and established aid agency failings. We know this has not worked smoothly. We know about the heroic deeds of local activists but also about the schisms that tore apart some organizations. We know about the activists who moved to New Orleans and acted with grace and virtue but also about those who did not listen to local concerns or acted as if establishing their activist credentials was more important than serving the community in which they settled. And about the artists whose representations have been haunting, beautiful, and inspiring, but who took bread from the mouths of local colleagues. And about the rents that the well-meaning transplants helped raise. And so on.

Ultimately, *Dear New Orleans* begins to map a space of collaborative artistic production and a broader economy of civic engagement in and around New Orleans that remains contradictory and uneven. This space has shifted from the incredible highs and lows, the rawness that defined the immediate post-Katrina period, into something more prosaic. The city is, of course, in many ways still reeling from the catastrophe. The past several years have been extremely difficult, especially for the displaced, the poor, the female, the young, and the elderly, the people who lost family members to the flood and to the state or criminal violence that followed. It is worth noting that Amnesty International reported shortly before Katrina's fifth anniversary that displaced New Orleanians (particularly low-income people of color), as well as some of those who had returned to the city, continued to experience human rights violations because of a lack of access to affordable and adequate housing, racial inequality in reconstruction projects, a lack of reasonable health care, police misconduct, and a dysfunctional criminal justice system. Yet things have been made better for some in the city, and not just for the elite.[8] Optimism and levels of civic engagement exceed that of most places in the nation.

On the cultural front, though many worried that neighborhood-based cultures—Mardi Gras Indians, social aid and pleasure clubs and their parades—would disappear along with working-class black residents of New Orleans, these groups have reconstituted themselves and have played an important role in the reconstruction of the city through their public rituals and explicit activism. Major artists and even some previously underground performers, like transgender rap artists Big Freedia and Katey Red, have received national media attention.[9] So in many ways we see a city whose unique culture is not only surviving but in many ways blossoming despite and in some ways as a result of the disaster that was Katrina. Indeed, New Orleans has much to teach us at a moment when, as Saul Williams puts it, we stand at a crossroads.

My initial reaction to what I saw happening in New Orleans was, like that of many others, one of outrage. The lesson of the storm indeed seemed to be, as Michael Eric Dyson put it soon thereafter, "The deeper we dig into the story of Katrina, the more we must accept culpability for the fact that the black citizens of the Big Easy—a tag given the city by black musicians who easily found work in a city that looms large in the collective American imagination as the home of jazz, jambalaya, and Mardi Gras—were treated by the rest of us as garbage."[10] Moralizing about New Orleans has proliferated. Often called the most African of U.S. cities, New Orleans has functioned in the political imagination post Katrina much like Africa. As V. Y. Mudimbe describes the representational function of Africa, New Orleans often operates as a "sign of something else."[11] Following Paul Theroux's description of contemporary affinities for Africa, post-Katrina New Orleans is often seen as an "unfinished project," where people can ennoble themselves by acting upon it.[12] Over the past seven years this moralistic ennobling has sometimes taken reactionary forms, as in the we-told-you-so accounts of black savagery and the errors of big government in the immediate aftermath of the storm. One infamous example was Representative Richard Baker of Baton Rouge telling lobbyists, "We finally *cleaned up* public housing in New Orleans. We couldn't do it, but *God* did."[13] But we have also seen the righteous performances of the Left, in which the traumatized, displaced, or dead bodies of New Orleanians have been the cudgels with which we symbolically beat down the racial, heteropatriarchal state, the interstitial power of Empire, and other evils. While my affinities lie with the second moralizing project, I recognize that it can obscure and silence some residents of the city, and that it does not always enable a very good understanding of the complexities of people's lives, their cultural movements, or their own analyses of the conditions they face.

One must, of course, try to come to terms with the ways the twin evils of exploitation and neglect have long helped to constitute New Orleans. Outrage remains an important motivation for writing and activism. But moving politically and analytically into the future also requires paying attention to insistent expressions of humanity. Watts's photographs do this. Some evoke the pain and the destruction, but most show "the beauty and fragility of the race, the ironic humor of everyday life, the dream life of a people."[14] In other words, they help us to not be overly consumed by outrage about what happened to this city and its residents in the late summer of 2005 and its aftermath.

Ultimately, the possibilities of political and creative collaboration in the music and the affirmative content of (at least some of) Watts's photos encourage me to examine the ways that New Orleanians have "reinvented life" in the seven years after the storm and the levee breaks. As a writer, I am compelled to frame this story less as an argument for the necessary survival of a special place, as many fine works have done, than as an analysis that builds from the confidence one can find in the activism and cultural acts of New Orleanians in recent years.[15] Even with all the difficulty and contradiction, such expressions perform the ways in which the city and its residents are surviving and have been since the moment the storm hit. Such practices now reflect less what was and what happened and more what is becoming.

To try to tell this story via music is like a dance on bottle caps: staccato, slippery, and precarious. People have long talked about the relationship between music and the social. Some of us have asked how history is sedimented in sound and lyric, how music reflects the complexities of political moments, and how it might point to utopian and dystopian futures. We have considered how music inspires people to imagine a better, or at least a different, world and about how people sometimes use it to try to change the world. But even those of us who are invested in music and social possibility recognize, at least if we are honest, that it is difficult to say with certainty what specific pieces, movements, or genres actually mean and do. Musical expressions are generally quite complicated. They often contain contradictory and ambiguous sentiments created by artists, producers, recording engineers, and businesspeople; and their diverse listeners hear them differently and selectively across time and space. This is true even when talking about music with lyrics carrying a relatively straightforward semantic meaning, let alone when considering music full of complex imagery and innuendo, or without lyrics at all.

Writing about power and possibility in New Orleans music brings with it a particular set of challenges. One stems from the depth of investment that artists, businesspeople, boosters, activists, politicians, and everyday people have in defining New Orleans as a musical city. We are thus faced with the challenge of separating fact from fiction regarding what music actually accomplishes and how it may actually relate—as opposed to mythically relate—to the specific needs, circumstances, and aspirations of the city's residents.

The HBO television series *Treme,* for example, the most prominent dramatic representation to date of New Orleans post Katrina, contributes to this phenomenon by portraying the city's predicament and recovery primarily through the lives of musicians and other cultural workers. As some have argued, such a focus, as well as the narrative needs of television entertainment, leads to a less than adequate treatment of complex social arrangements with deep historical roots that continue to unfold in the present. These include the profound and multifaceted racial and economic marginalization of large segments of the black population.[16] It also potentially reproduces a flawed sense that multiracial musicians' networks—composed of people who often live very difficult lives, to be sure, but who are also cherished and privileged in a symbolic if not financial sense—may be seen as a sufficient reflection of the broader community's struggles for recognition, normalcy, and even survival.

One should instead stay attuned to the way traces of the contradictions that have defined the city's post-Katrina recovery are embedded in New Orleans music and also to the ways that music has served as one vehicle for creating these contradictions. We can examine how post-storm jazz funerals and second line parades have helped heal people and convinced them to stay in or return to the city. We can also look at the ways musicians are participating in progressive political projects. But another part of the story is how the New Orleans tourist economy is fundamentally exploitative in the wages paid to musicians and others and how honoring musical traditions following Katrina has served as cover for draconian political acts and social policies. We also need to contend with the ways that the production and consumption of New Orleans music facilitates an economy of cross-racial and cross-class desire that cherishes traditional culture bearers but can also ignore or breed hostility toward the needs of those members of poor or colored communities who are not engaged in such cultural work and whose presence—their assumed drain on resources, their criminal behavior—is read as a threat to everybody else's good time.

Adding to the challenge of mapping these contradictions is the fact that the fluidity and complexity of music scenes and audiences alike make it analytically dangerous to indulge in neat assumptions about how local music represents particular identitarian or political sentiments. Musical scenes bleed into and inform one another, artists are in dialogue across genres, and audience tastes are hard to pin down. Tom Piazza describes "the surprises that lurk so often around the corners of someone's seemingly straightforward identity. It is a lesson that one has to learn continually in New Orleans." Yet it is precisely this indeterminacy that allows the story of this city to be embedded in the music. As Billy Sothern has remarked, "Here, the cultural synthesis of past and present creates a vibrancy and originality in our music that defies simple categorization, makes life interesting, and locates the culture squarely in New Orleans."[17] And on that last point *Treme* is quite incisive, as its creators represent, on camera and via its soundtrack, the multiple genres and hybrid expressions, the vast array of performance sites and spaces, and the diverse audiences that make up the New Orleans music scene. It is to the show's credit that it showcases, playing themselves or in character, not only prominent jazz and brass band musicians, but also venerable R&B stars like Irma Thomas, ex-underground rappers like the aforementioned Katey Red and Big Freedia and up-and-comers like Ace B (playing Lil Calliope), genre-bending bands like Bonerama, and those, like pop rock vocalist Susan Cowsill, who work in genres seldom included in celebratory genealogies of New Orleans music.

There are clearly modes of writing about music that play into the aforementioned distortions, but some post-Katrina authors have showed us how music can be deployed to explode neat, problematic narratives and assist in the process of remembering complicated histories and understanding the present and future through them. Clyde Woods calls the confrontation between the forces of oppression and social justice that we are forced to confront again in the post-Katrina era "the dialectic of Bourbonism and the Blues." And he shows how various musical expressions, from the colonial to the present, not only can be placed within this dialectic but also bear the traces of this history.

The singing, dancing, and drumming at Congo Square, the blues, second lines, brass bands, jazz, Mardi Gras Indians, gospel, R&B acts, and hip-hop all emerged out of a complicated social and cultural matrix and provided a mechanism from the eighteenth century to the present by which black New Orleanians in particular could challenge in direct and subtle ways the conditions and acts that threatened to dehumanize them.[18] And Ruth Salvaggio shows us how music can disrupt the process of the intentional and unintentional forgetting of the traumas of the past. Building on comments by clarinetist Sidney Bechet, she describes the "long song," which is both carrier of and metaphor for an enduring cultural memory, rooted in the racial and sexual regimes of slavery, that cannot be fully repressed. "It's a song that keeps breaking through the seams of a tidy history built on selective erasures and national amnesia. We can keep tracing this song farther and farther back because it always precedes history. . . . [I]t is a song about a problem that won't go away, about a pain-wracked body that keeps reemerging throughout history, or in sweltering attics after a flood."[19]

As one writes about New Orleans music in the present, one must confront the return of history in often unexpected ways in the post-Katrina moment. Watts's photographs address historical return, and I have found myself looking to them for evidence of the ruptures that expose multiple pasts brought to bear on our present and future. These images ask us to consider multiple layers of local history and the exposure of this history and its contradictions by Katrina. And there are the chaotic aspects of this history, too, evident in photos that show the helter-skelter ways that New Orleanians' life histories were jumbled together inside houses and tossed into the street by the water and reconstruction workers in the weeks after. Sometimes clarity about the past with present-day import can emerge from such chaos. For example, while peering into the bedroom of a busted home in the Lower Ninth Ward in 2006, the elegant framed bed and nightstand, forced upward at a slant by rubble that had floated into the room and settled underneath, reminded me (albeit in a distorted form) of the working-class elegance I came to know as a boy in the homes of grandparents and great aunts and uncles. It was a memory that spoke against the denigration, romantic victimization, and intrusive surveys (yes, we were implicated) of the neighborhood's fate while demanding a different way of telling their story. But the massive debris fields in the Lower Ninth, exposing as they did the complexities of people's lives, also remind the historian (of music; of other things) that to convey the story of history's return is tremendously difficult. But we must try.

So music, for better and for worse, is my vehicle for trying to write about New Orleans as a place and an idea. It is also my analytical and theoretical frame. I try to tread carefully because of the complexities of the scene, the political and cultural noise surrounding the music, the dangers of giving it too much attention, and the scholarly tendency toward distortion. But I enthusiastically take this on because I know that dissonance can be productive and quite beautiful. I am simultaneously jaded and naïve, but that seems the correct perspective when writing about New Orleans, its residents, its culture, and the ways they might help us choose the best direction to go as we stand at the crossroads.

MARDI GRAS INDIAN AFTER PERFORMANCE, JAZZ FEST, 2006

JAM SESSION WITH GLEN DAVID ANDREWS AND OTHER NEW ORLEANS MUSICIANS, JAZZ FEST, 2006

SET OF HBO'S *TREME*, 2010

ACE B (LIL CALLIOPE) AND FRIENDS, NEW ORLEANS, 2011

# 2

# REFLECTIONS ON
# JAZZ FEST 2006

My first visit to New Orleans after the storm and the levee breaks coincided with the 2006 New Orleans Jazz and Heritage Festival. This massive celebration of music, food, and arts and crafts started in 1970 and, in recent memory, has brought hundreds of thousands of people to the city's fairgrounds over two spring weekends. At Jazz Fest and elsewhere in New Orleans that week, Lewis and I witnessed familiar, though locally inflected, patterns of consuming jazz (and other forms of African American–rooted music). We were in differently integrated and not-so-integrated audiences in different kinds of performance spaces, where we saw evidence of nonblack people's (and some black people's) deep respect and collective desire for certain aspects of blackness and their simultaneous anxieties about a threatening black (and particularly poor black) presence.

Acts of identification and disidentification via black music have long histories, which in the United States can be traced back to the antebellum period.[1] Yet such acts in the present must also be understood as part of local, national, and indeed, global cultural economies that are intimately connected to the restructuring of our society. In other words, when thinking about the future of New Orleans at Jazz Fest, it was difficult not to suspect that within the modes (institutional, financial, discursive, and affective) through which this music was cherished lay both hope for the future and the seeds of reproducing older formations of inequality and some of its recent manifestations.[2]

I ponder in this section how what we observed at and around Jazz Fest, amplified by what became apparent in retrospect after learning more about the history of the event, exemplifies just how complicated a notion it is that "the culture" can enable the reconstruction of New Orleans. I try to address some of the thorny issues that have emerged when jazz and other forms of music have been invoked or deployed to rebuild New Orleans, given the competing claims on the city and its musical cultures, the fault lines of race and class in play before and after the storm, the long-standing ways that local musical cultures have reflected social exclusions, and the complexities that emerge when the complicated cultural practices of the past and present collide in the context of disaster. But I try not to be too pessimistic. I also suggest here that we can locate social possibilities in the contradictions of Jazz Fest. This section thus provides a foundation for analyzing in more hopeful terms some of the social and artistic projects considered later in the book.

Wandering through the tents and arenas of Jazz Fest that spring, one could easily get swept up in the grand sense of multiracial communion promoted by the festival organizers. Also compelling was the idea, expressed by musicians and audience members alike, that a shared love for the music and the city could somehow bring them both back. The stated theme of the festival was "Homecoming." There were simply sublime moments offered by local luminaries: Irma Thomas joining Paul Simon to sing "Bridge over Troubled Water"; Marva Wright singing Gloria Gaynor's disco anthem "I Will Survive"; John Boutté's revised rendition of Randy Newman's "Louisiana 1927," a mid-1970s ode to local perseverance in the face of natural disaster and government neglect, especially poignant because of the tradition of Jazz Fest performers using the song to keep the spring rains at bay and new lyrics that spoke of the horrific flooding in the Lower Ninth; and the impromptu Sunday afternoon jam session in the Jazz Tent, which culminated with "What Does It Mean to Miss New Orleans," "When the Saints Go Marching In," and many words of appreciation for local musicians, ordinary folk, and tourists who returned to New Orleans for the first post-Katrina iteration of the event. Such homecoming rituals were played out across town. I witnessed them also at a brass band show at Donna's Bar and Grill and at an art opening and impromptu jam session at an acquaintance's home. These performances affirmed the profound attachments many have to the city that are mediated and consolidated through music.[3]

Culture was also deployed as a more specifically economic resource at Jazz Fest. It was clear that the good feelings of homecoming and multiracial communion were intertwined with the desire to generate capital, as when one performer thanked people for their "moral support" and for their "financial support." Many local musicians were displaced by Katrina and had difficulty finding work in the storm's aftermath. For some of them, Jazz Fest represented a paycheck, either through the few gigs available to them on the festival grounds or for stints in clubs filled with tourists during Jazz Fest season. Perhaps more importantly, Jazz Fest represented the possibility of more paychecks if the crowds and enthusiasm accurately signified the local music industry's revival. More than one musician on stage, and cultural workers I spoke to offstage, talked about the fundamental importance of the music and tourist-friendly festivals to the city's collective spiritual resolve and to its financial health. After all, New Orleans, in this first year after Katrina, had lost most of its convention business as well as other big-name tourist events, such as the Sugar Bowl and the Essence Festival. The featured article in the Jazz Fest program commented that the event "marks a major public celebration of homecoming and rebirth for the city and its music. Musicians and singers like [Irma] Thomas are back where they belong in late Spring. But the festival also showcases the work of an entire community to rebuild and rejuvenate the Crescent City."[4]

Another message in the aforementioned performer's thank-yous was the notion that the tourists themselves were empowered to shape the direction of the city's recovery. As one local writer offered to Jazz Fest visitors, "I hope you'll be able to get some idea of what makes this place so unique, so special, so different, and worthy of saving. Stand up for New Orleans, and do something tangible to help the city. Just coming here and spending time with us certainly helps—not only economically—and it lets us know that you care."[5]

These invocations of culture as a tool for reconstructing New Orleans speak to cultural studies scholar George Yudice's account of the complex ways that "culture as resource" serves and constitutes residual and emergent forms of power and knowledge in the current neoliberal political-economic order. Geographer David Harvey describes neoliberalism as being supported by the idea that "human well-being can best be advanced by liberating individual entrepreneurial freedoms and skills within an institutional framework characterized by strong private property rights, free markets, and free trade."[6] In Yudice's view, culture under neoliberalism takes on a new and pronounced role as a resource in the formation of ideology and identities, the production of social norms, and the consolidation and distribution of resources. Culture as resource also fills the political void caused by the neoliberal shrinking of government and a decline in normative civic participation.[7] This perspective has been commonly voiced in New Orleans after the storm. As local artist and radio producer Jacqueline Bishop put it early in 2007, "In post-Katrina, most New Orleanians are convinced that it is the role of art and artists to rebuild our city, especially since we have no leadership."[8]

We must be attuned, of course, to both the progressive and regressive ways that culture as resource fills the political void. Culture is central to the new economy of the global era and its attendant divisions of labor, as well as to the formation of "communities," which are understood, depending on the context, as economic development projects, marketable commodities, political blocs, or social problems. The creative economy, as Yudice notes, enables the upward flow of capital to a multiculturalism-friendly professional managerial class, while people with lower status and income (particularly members of racially subordinate groups) are often relegated to being low-level service workers or "providers of 'life giving' ethnic and other cultural experiences." Yet, in the void created by the retreat of the welfare state, the "'disorganized' capitalism that spawns myriad networks for the sake of accumulation also makes possible the networking of all kinds of affinity associations working in solidarity and cooperation." And cultural practices, as vehicles for consolidating group awareness, self-worth, and distinction, can also serve as a "foundation for claims to recognition and resources."[9] Voicing and acting upon such "claims to recognition" are, of course, a delicate dance. Such claims can be used to enhance the lives of those on the margins, but they can easily be manipulated to benefit instead the market, the state, or individuals with power. In various ways, they can be redeployed to extract value from, contain and surveil, and even terrorize the communities that produce them.

Jazz Fest fits into a pattern long established at other jazz festivals. As the list of artists mentioned earlier indicates, a wide range of sounds are often sold and celebrated under the rubric "jazz," which in turn signifies an array of musical meanings and functions. When thinking about how Jazz Fest exemplifies the role of culture in the reconstruction of New Orleans, we should consider what literary studies scholar Lisa Lowe has termed the "multiplicity of the festival-object." Examining a 1990 multicultural arts festival in Los Angeles, she identifies competing narratives at work in the exhibits, performances, spatial arrangements, and acts of consumption evident at that festival. The challenge, she argues, is not to "reconcile the narratives or to determine one as dominant." Rather, it is to understand how competing narratives may produce "both a mode of pluralist containment and a vehicle for intervention in that containment," as they simultaneously elide "material differentiations" among racial, ethnic, and immigrant communities and expose cracks in the slick, pluralistic facade.[10]

There is a relevant historical foundation to this, of course—one that emerged during the early twentieth century, wherein deployments of culture set forth discursive, ideological, and transactional arrangements that are manifested somewhat differently in the neoliberal era. Jazz has for about a century been an often exploitative business that is reflective of broader racial, class, gender, and geographic inequalities. Yet it has also been a visible signifier of the possibilities of multiracial democracy in the United States and of black achievement and distinction. Jazz histories, of course, often begin in New Orleans, which, as a port city in a succession of empires and an important crossroads in the southern United States, provided the multicultural milieu that musicians, most notably black and Creole musicians, drew upon as they created a variety of urban and urbane musical styles that they eventually synthesized into something called jazz near the beginning of the twentieth century. New Orleans has since been seen as the "cradle" of a music that was uniquely "American" because of its hybrid composition and also because of the heroism of musicians, such as Buddy Bolden, Louis Armstrong, and Sidney Bechet, who created great art despite, and in the face of, white supremacy. Such perspectives have been voiced both from liberal and radical perspectives, by musicians and others. For some, jazz history and culture affirm the nation's success in overcoming its racist legacy. For others, the jazz world betrays many of the racial contradictions of the nation, while illustrating the need for further struggle.[11]

Jazz Fest's own history reproduces this story while making visible the late twentieth-century institutionalization of "culture as resource" at the local level. The establishment of Jazz Fest, the expansion of Mardi Gras, and the appearance of other high-profile, tourist-friendly urban spectacles that developed in New Orleans after 1970 betrayed a rapidly expanding tourism infrastructure, strategically developed in response to deindustrialization, a declining tax base, and cuts to public infrastructures. As such, these festivals have been "contested terrain," representing at their core the interests of economic and political elites while also providing opportunities to challenge the status quo from below at the levels of meaning making and the distribution of resources.[12]

The first New Orleans Jazz and Heritage Festival, where Ellington's suite premiered, was held from April 22 to 26, 1970. Musicians appeared at several venues in the city, but the main site, where a "Heritage Fair" consisting of crafts, food, and local music was held, was Beauregard Square, alongside Rampart Street in the Faubourg Tremé. This site, of course, was previously known as Congo Square, the legendary place of Sunday marketplaces during the eighteenth and early nineteenth centuries, where slaves and free blacks gathered to market, drum, and dance. In other words, Jazz Fest's original site represented, at least potentially, and among New Orleanians who did not identify with General Pierre Gustave Toutant Beauregard and the Confederacy, the possibilities of Afro-diasporic music for enacting social change.

The story goes that the roughly 350 performers, staff, and volunteers outnumbered the audience members at the daytime performances in the square at the first Jazz Fest (although more attended evening concerts at other venues), but the event quickly grew. The festival moved to the New Orleans Fair Grounds Race Course in 1972, in order to accommodate an audience that reached 50,000 over the course of four days. In 1976 the schedule was expanded to include two weekends. At its apex, in 2001, before a post-9/11 decline in tourism, 664,000 people attended Jazz Fest, pumping $300 million into the local economy. Although the scope of what has become an internationally famous and massive music, arts and crafts, and culinary festival has changed dramatically since 1970, the original gatherings can be seen as a product of a number of forces that continue to define Jazz Fest's programming, the festival's economic role in and around New Orleans, its racial politics, and the celebratory narratives that surround the event.

The 1970 event came together after pianist and impresario George Wein, who was performing in the city in late 1969, was asked by local businessman Durel Black to take over the city's jazz festival, which had run for two seasons. Wein, of course, was one of the most prominent live music promoters in the world, having established the Newport Jazz and Newport Folk Festivals as well as other ventures. According to Wein, the emergence of such a jazz festival in New Orleans was only possible because of the changes wrought by the civil rights movement. Wein had been approached by local boosters in 1962 about organizing a major jazz festival in the city, but they eventually came to the shared conclusion that a big-time jazz festival would not work in an unreconstructed, segregationist city whose hotels would exclude black guests, whose audiences might well be segregated, and whose cultural gatekeepers would frown upon mixed groups on the bandstand. A second attempt to mount a major festival with Wein at the helm was canceled after American Football League athletes, no doubt buoyed by the recent passage of the landmark 1964 Civil Rights Act, organized a boycott of New Orleans in early 1965, after African American players arriving for the league's all-star game were refused service by taxi drivers, hotels, and other businesses. A smaller event did go forward but received little attention within or outside of the city. The New Orleans International Jazz Festival finally did get off the ground in 1968, although the invitation for Wein to produce it was rescinded. The job instead went to Tommy Walker's Entertainment Attractions. In Wein's view, the issue was that he was married to an African American woman. Others claimed that Wein had demanded too much compensation. Willis Conover produced the 1969 festival, before Wein was brought on board the following year, in his own account at least, because of Conover's disagreements with festival board members and because the racial climate loosened up to the point where his mixed marriage was less of an issue.[13]

According to various origin stories, Wein brought to the festival not only years of promotional experience but also the ethos of eclecticism and the commitment to blurring generic and aesthetic boundaries that had defined his Newport projects. In large part because of the influence of Allison Miner and Quint Davis, the young local producers Wein's company hired to help run the festival, The New Orleans Jazz and Heritage Foundation, the nonprofit organization that owns Jazz Fest, was from the beginning invested in highlighting the local and "giving back" to the community, even as it sought to create a festival with popular appeal. The foundation's articles of incorporation defined a mission of promoting New Orleans jazz, folk, blues, gospel, Cajun, and soul music; employing musicians from Louisiana to perform at the festival; promoting New Orleans as a tourist destination; bringing favorable attention to the city generally while helping the business community; and working with business and civic organizations for the "economic betterment" and "cultural advancement" of the city.[14]

The initial presentation of high-profile traditional and modern jazz artists, black and nonblack popular musicians, gospel and blues artists, brass bands and Mardi Gras Indians, Cajun performers, and other musicians, alongside local culinary delights and crafts, served a somewhat contradictory but ultimately synergistic function. The festival was designed to appeal to jazz aficionados and a cosmopolitan consuming public interested in broadening experience and working against aesthetic as well as social boundaries. However, its organizers were invested in presenting and preserving "authentic" local cultures in ways that mirrored various countercultural folk and youth pop festivals of the moment. Such festivals positioned "roots" (and ideally black roots) musical expressions as anodynes against commercialization, mass production, and other restrictive and alienating aspects of modernity.[15]

Jazz Fest principals and many fans believed it was precisely this fusion of genres, orientations, and goals that made the ongoing event successful. Many point to New Orleans–born gospel star Mahalia Jackson's impromptu 1970 performance of "Just a Closer Walk with Thee" on a Eureka Brass Band–led second line on the festival grounds, as embodying and initiating the event's dedication to spontaneity, collaboration, mixing of musical styles, celebration of place and history, and simultaneous commitments to "jazz and heritage."[16]

Wein, Miner, and others associated with the festival have claimed that the festival's emergence and its genre-blending ethos represented an active, albeit challenging, attempt to ameliorate racial divides. According to Miner's recollection of the first Jazz Fest, "It was just the beginning of an opportunity for people to party together, to hear each other. . . . So celebrating their culture with everyone there, black and white, became an opportunity for people to say 'Hey, this is spectacular! I've never heard anything like this because my parents didn't allow me to go out and hear it, but now I'm really gonna party, and I'm really gonna enjoy it, and I'm going to forget all of my prejudices from childhood and I'm gonna see things differently.'"[17]

Closely related to the perceived commitment to racial amelioration permeating the memories of Jazz Fest principals was the foundation's commitment (Miner is especially praised in this regard) to assisting local and "traditional" (and especially black local and black traditional) musicians, both financially and in terms of generating attention and respect for their work. Many claim that Jazz Fest has been critical to raising national and, indeed, global awareness of New Orleans music and culture. Some emphasize that Jazz Fest, which has featured brass bands and Mardi Gras Indian groups since the very beginning, has played a particularly important role in promoting these community-based cultural expressions, in effect rescuing them from obscurity. And while such claims by Jazz Fest insiders may be to a degree self-serving, prominent figures from the second line and Indian communities have made similar comments over the years.[18]

Of course the scale of these projects has changed over the decades of Jazz Fest's extraordinary growth, which has expanded the national and global market for New Orleans music and contributed significantly to the "branding" of New Orleans as a musical city. This growth has been accompanied by increasing and often controversial corporate sponsorship—though a certain level of that sponsorship was there from the beginning—that positions Jazz Fest firmly within a larger story of the expanding culture industry across the globe over the past several decades.[19] In-the-know music fans, the wealthier of whom have an increasing disposable income, consume a growing array of multicultural forms made available and knowable (even when deemed "traditional") by the speed of global markets and emergent communication technologies. Such experiences are made possible not only by the corporations that profit dramatically from the production of these cultural forms but also by increasingly powerful private businesses and foundations that sponsor culture to facilitate tax relief and name recognition.[20]

In addition to its growth in scale, Jazz Fest's imbrication in the global culture industry is symbolized by the increasing international flavor of the event, a trend that took off in the early 1990s with the introduction of the International Pavilion, designed to highlight each year the cultural expressions of a particular nation. Some have pointed to this internationalization not only as a reflection of an emergent global consciousness and a local cultural terrain that is increasingly cosmopolitan, but also as a marker of an increasingly sophisticated and well-traveled (read wealthy) festival audience.[21]

As it has grown over the decades, Jazz Fest has established itself as a powerful financial engine for the local economy. It has become integral to the local tourism industry, which has been a critical financial sector in the postindustrial period, by bringing large number of music fans to the city over two spring weekends and by helping to define New

Orleans more generally as a musical city, which encourages tourism at other times of the year. But with Jazz Fest's growth have come questions about and, at times, conflicts over who should and who has actually benefited from the festival's commitment to enhancing New Orleans's cultural life and giving back to the community.

During Jazz Fest's early years, a growing chorus of African American voices raised such questions. At a presentation on the roots of soul music at the first Jazz Fest, Reverend Fred Kirkpatrick shouted out "Where are the black people?"—probably referring to the relatively small percentage of African Americans in the audience at this event in what would become a black-majority city during the 1970s. But Kirkpatrick's comment would also have been accurate if he was referring to the relatively small percentage of black people among Jazz Fest's staff and producers, despite the presence of pianist and educator Ellis Marsalis as adviser.[22] In 1978 a group of black activists calling itself the Afrikan American Jazz Festival Coalition showed up at a foundation board meeting and called for a boycott and disruption of Jazz Fest if more was not done to give back to and include members of the African American community. Although the now profitable festival had recently developed a small grant program for community projects, with some money put aside for African American–initiated projects in particular, members of the coalition, whose prominent voices included Kalamu ya Salaam, Sekou Fela, Michael Williams, and Mohammad Yungai, argued that there was inadequate black representation on the board and Jazz Fest staff and among arts and crafts vendors. The activists also charged that the economic benefits from the festival were primarily flowing to white society.[23]

This activism caused no small amount of friction among Jazz Fest staff and board members, and some white members resigned. Wein and other principals responded quickly, even if some of their recollections of the conflict are a little defensive and self–serving—especially their claims that protesters could not quite grasp the organizers' commitment to the New Orleans black community.[24] Jazz Fest subsequently underwent significant changes in response to the activists' demands. Among the first was the creation in 1979 of the Koindu stage and crafts area for black artists, which, in Salaam's view, represented an emergent ethos of creating a stake in Jazz Fest for the black community and giving back to it financially. In 1988 Koindu was reinvented as "Congo Square" in an attempt to reflect some of cultural and spiritual "reality" created at that New Orleans site so many years ago.[25] The year 1979 also witnessed the naming of the first African American as foundation board president and invitations to other blacks to join the board. Eventually, the board became majority African American, with some presidents and executive directors also of African descent. Black representation on the Jazz Fest staff also grew.[26]

Many of these black members of Jazz Fest's board and staff expressed a commitment, as former president Dan Williams put it, to ensure "that the wishes and desires of the community are taken into consideration" and to make Jazz Fest a "365-day organization." Jazz Fest subsequently established a number of programs to increase African American involvement and "give back" to the community. A "community grants" program for artists and cultural workers was initiated in 1979. Other community-focused programs instituted over the next few decades include the distribution of low-cost Jazz Fest tickets to nonprofit and community groups, the creation of the Heritage School of Jazz Education, a community lecture series, off-festival music programming and neighborhood festivals, a newsletter, microlending programs for local small businesses, support for a local Musicians' Clinic that provides health care for low-income musicians, a home ownership program for musicians called "Raisin' the Roof," the purchase of the license and subsequent administration of radio station WWOZ, and various attempts via Jazz Fest programming to highlight African American contributions to New Orleans culture.[27]

Despite such efforts, however, the questions of whether Jazz Fest serves New Orleans's black community in a significant way and whether it might even help to reproduce racial inequality in the city have remained. Looking back on his tenure as executive director of the foundation from 1983 to 1987, Kalamu ya Salaam invokes the image of a slave who, after gaining access to the plantation house, "tries to slip as much food as he can back to the people in the field." Eventually he became frustrated in this position "because ultimately, the better I did my job, the more I built up the status quo."[28]

With this history in mind, the representations of democracy in action and African American distinction we witnessed at the 2006 Jazz Fest indeed present competing narratives, especially if one also considers the widely held perception that this particular iteration of the festival was a critical juncture in determining whether the future New Orleans cultural scene would be adequately responsible to local communities. One journalist said the 2006 festival "represent[ed] the two most crucial weekends in New Orleans' cultural history." Not only was there the question of whether the city's music scene would come back; also critical was the issue of whether it would be adequately rebuilt on the foundation of the "sounds of the streets."[29]

At the African American–oriented Congo Square we saw a shrine where one could honor both "the Ancestors of the Diaspora" and "those affected by our recent national tragedies."[30] And one could certainly read the brass bands and Mardi Gras Indian performances on the Jazz Heritage Stage, the second line processions winding their way through the fairgrounds, and the educational exhibits under the race course grandstand on Mardi Gras Indians and second lining as an explicit validation of unique, local musical cultures and also of the black working-class communities that have sustained them.

Second lining is a tradition that goes back to the nineteenth century. It involves public processions generally led by members of sponsoring organizations, brass bands, and dancers. These individuals constitute the "first" or "main" line of the parade. The term *second line* refers to members of the public who fall in behind them and join the parade. In New Orleans, one may see ersatz second lines at tourist-friendly or society events, but there is a much more communally focused tradition of second lining in black neighborhoods that is sponsored by social aid and pleasure clubs, some of which have also been around since the late nineteenth century. There are approximately forty active clubs at present, although many club members are still displaced by Hurricane Katrina and the policies that defined its aftermath. Each typically sponsors a yearly Sunday parade—some of which drew as many as five thousand people before the storm—but the clubs also hold dances and other functions and may parade for other reasons, such as jazz funerals.

These continually evolving, community-based second line events have long played important social roles in black New Orleans. Although diverse interests and orientations inform these participatory rituals, collectively they may be understood as facilitating a sense of connection to place, affirming members' neighborhoods and their histories, constituting alternative forms of community and civil society, reclaiming urban space for the community in the face of material and symbolic marginalization as well as police and drug trade violence, and engaging in implicit and occasionally explicit political protest against police brutality, gentrification, and other issues facing black working-class and poor people.[31]

As noted, second line clubs and Mardi Gras Indian performers have been featured onstage since the first Jazz Fest and continue to be central to its identity. They provide a kind of anchoring authenticity, as Helen Regis and Shanna Walton point out, that legitimizes the festival as remaining true to its roots and committed to its community, even with all the corporate sponsorship and big-name pop acts. Second line parades that snake across the Jazz Fest grounds create a sense of spontaneous community, again reproducing the aura of the early years and enabling fans to become performers in a sense. Mardi Gras Indian parades not only "infuse the atmosphere with the sacred mystery of their masquerade," but they also evoke a legacy of "maroonage," interracial (i.e., black/indigenous) collaboration, and diasporic cultural memory and pride.[32]

And given that at least some members of these social aid and pleasure clubs and Indian groups see it as their mission to share and generate respect for their musical traditions and their communities by making these rituals more public and by reaching out across racial and class lines, we may see in these Jazz Fest performances and exhibitions after the storm a kind of grassroots attempt, with official support, to cash in these cultural resources as a means of generating wider respect for and knowledge about New Orleans's working-class black communities that could go hand in hand with an equitable reconstruction of the city.[33]

Equitable reconstruction, of course, has not been the dominant trend since the storm. The suddenly apparent social conditions of poor (primarily black) people in New Orleans brought to light, for many, not only the white supremacist legacies of slavery and Jim Crow but also the continuing effects of a generation of deindustrialization, urban renewal projects, suburbanization, and neoliberal social and economic policies (cuts in education, health care, and welfare), often enacted against and justified through the lives of the black urban poor. So did the subsequent horrors many people experienced because of the government's slow and limited response to the crisis; officials' failure to improvise around bureaucratic roadblocks; the "passive indifference" and outright hostility toward poor black New Orleanians expressed by local, state, and federal officials; and the privileging of corporate profits rather than workers' or residents' rights through no-bid contracts, tax relief, and the relaxation of labor and environmental laws during the initial phases of rebuilding.[34]

Yet the fact that others read the government's failures as proof that the state should play a smaller role in society (outside of the military and criminal justice system, that is) illustrated the effectiveness of the power elite's cultural work around neoliberalism. Also serving the project of neoliberalism was the media hysteria surrounding black people's behavior during and after the event, which began with reports that they were irresponsibly slow to evacuate, continued through racially differentiated descriptions of removing food from shuttered grocery stores, and culminated with hysteria over a perceived return to savagery in the Superdome. Such media coverage played a functional role, justifying the state's neglect after the fact and reproducing the idea that black people represent a continuing threat to civil society.

In the wake of such devastation and representation, discussions about how New Orleans will be rebuilt and just who will populate the city in the future have been paramount. Local residents and activists across the country have argued eloquently for a right of return for all New Orleanians, regardless of race, class, or status as homeowners, as well as for their visions for the city to be realized when reconstructing the city. Yet, from the very beginning, the reconstruction of New Orleans, whether by design, indifference, or incompetence, has seemed geared toward excluding at least some of its lower-income population, especially poor black residents receiving some form of public assistance. Many New Orleanians are still displaced seven years after the storm. According to the 2010 census, the city's population is only 70 percent of its 2000 level. The number of displaced people, who are disproportionately black and poor, is no doubt greater than that represented by a 30 percent population loss, as there has also been an in-migration of Latino/a workers, young white professionals, and others. Mayor Ray Nagin's Bring New Orleans Back Commission (BNOB) defined the terms of reconstruction for the first several months after Katrina. While the commission included Wynton Marsalis—the trumpeter/composer and artistic director of Jazz at Lincoln Center, who was born and raised in New Orleans—and allies who publicly argued that all neighborhoods should be restored, others on the commission, primarily local business elites, voiced an exclusionist agenda. The BNOB report, released several months after the storm, suggested that it might not be economically or environmentally feasible to bring back certain neighborhoods, like the Lower Ninth Ward, giving validation instead to efforts to downsize the city, focusing redevelopment on its wealthier, higher grounded, and generally whiter areas, and making the city more amenable to corporate investment.

Nagin ultimately distanced himself from the plan when it became politically untenable and began promoting instead a "so-called market-focused recovery." Individuals seeking to return to New Orleans and rebuild would assess their own risk of future disasters and make their own decisions about how to proceed given available funds from government grants, insurance payouts, and loans. The city, in turn, would determine how much to invest in neighborhood infrastructure based on how many people decided to rebuild in the area. Although the ultimate outcome of such planning remains somewhat unclear, Lawrence Powell points out that there is "an unmistakable Darwinism to Nagin's market-driven recovery. . . . [O]nly the fittest seem likely to survive: those with resources and determination." Renters, especially the working poor, have very little influence under such a system and face high prices and limited supply in the rental market, contributing to high numbers of people who are either displaced or squatting or living with friends and relatives. The state's response to the rental crisis—providing tax credits to developers for building low-income housing—has generated cash flow to the small developers who sell these credits to corporations, who in turn use them to lower their tax bills, but who have, as of yet, provided little in the way of new low-income housing. Adding to the crisis is HUD's controversial decision to close down some of the city's still structurally sound public housing or to convert it to mixed-income units.[35]

The State of Louisiana's Road Home program, financed initially with a $7.5 billion federal block grant, finally began to provide funds for owners of damaged properties, but the program was rife with problems. Money was slow in coming, and it often did not provide sufficient funds to cover damages—a discrepancy that was more pronounced for working-class and African American households. The program offered homeowners grants based on whichever value was lower: the cost of rebuilding the home or its pre-Katrina value. In effect, this meant that residents of lower-income neighborhoods received less money. Moreover, the program offered homeowners a choice between obtaining a grant to assist with rebuilding or selling their damaged property back to the state, and the rate of people taking the buyouts was particularly high in New Orleans's black working-class neighborhoods with high rates of home ownership, such as the Lower Ninth Ward. The July 2011 settlement of a lawsuit charging that the valuation of homes under the Road Home program was discriminatory provided an additional $62 million for 1,400 homeowners who had not received adequate payments for rebuilding, but these benefits only reached a fraction of those shortchanged by the program. Given inadequate payments for rebuilding, the slow pace of and difficulties with the city's recovery in general, problems getting insurance payments or even proving title to their homes, and what many perceived as hostility to their return to the city, many simply gave up hope that their neighborhoods would be restored and decided that, rather than rebuilding, they would take the money and make a go of it in another city.[36]

In a local context where the connections between music and civic identity have been long established and a broader neoliberal context where "culture as resource" can be a "foundation for claims to recognition and resources," invoking music to respond to the exclusionary vision of the city's future has been appealing—especially given how audible the music has been in narratives across the planet about the city and its future. The state of the music has even been seen as a kind of "barometer" of the city's recovery. Locally, at least, the reopening of well-known nightclubs (for instance, the Maple Leaf on September 30, 2005) provided hope for the city's return.[37] The practice has continued over the years from within and without. A May 2007 NPR story about a Knowledge Is Power Program charter school, for example, used the somewhat dissonant sounds of the school band as a symbol that the public education system—albeit in a semiprivatized manner—was coming back.[38]

The argument has been made in various ways that New Orleans's musical legacy makes the city and its residents too valuable a cultural resource for the nation and the world to turn our backs on. Although New Orleans has a rich, multiethnic musical history and New Orleanians often speak of "the culture" in a general sense, much of New Orleans's national and international fame as a musical city revolves around black-created jazz, R&B, funk, hip-hop, blues, and musical expressions that defy genre and categorization. There has been much attention to unique forms of African American expression like Mardi Gras Indian groups and brass bands and second line parades. Arguments put forth by members of the second line community and like-minded people—that the project of preserving these local African American cultural forms can be marshaled to serve working-class and poor black people's specific interests and perhaps even provide a basis for a right of return for residents of the neighborhoods where much of this music originated—have had traction after the storm. And this is in no small part the result of the space opened up by the state's real and perceived failure to serve its citizenry.

In ways anticipated by the efforts of Jazz Fest's early organizers, who saw communion via black music as a form of activism, and in part as a result of the ways in which Jazz Fest has helped define New Orleans's identity as a musical city, music has indeed provided a vehicle for savvy, antiracist New Orleans activists of different backgrounds who cherish it, define their relationship to place through it, and draw sustenance for their political work from it. The music has clearly helped the broader population cope with destruction and displacement, has enabled cross-racial solidarity, and has engendered a commitment to the city and specific neighborhoods in the face of state and corporate indifference and hostility. Such local empowerment projects have also been directed outward, as artists, aid organizations, community groups, members of the business community, political leaders, and academics have mobilized around the idea that New Orleans's unique expressions form an important component of the national culture. Such contributions to the national project have been employed as a justification for rebuilding and repopulating the city. Because of the prominent role that African Americans in particular have played in building this culture, music has been a vehicle also for making said reconstruction more equitable across racial and class lines.

Music has also been deployed at a practical level to rebuild the city in ways that potentially counter probusiness and elite-serving visions for its future. And the civic engagement of the Jazz Fest community over the years likely helped to open up the political space for doing so. Musicians' Village, a Habitat for Humanity community being built in the Upper Ninth Ward, was originally conceived by New Orleans natives and musicians Harry Connick Jr. and Branford Marsalis. It was initially intended to provide homes for displaced musicians and places for them to perform, study, and record. But soon the project was expanded to offer housing to low-income people who are not musicians, and some has specifically been built for the elderly. As a description on its website puts it: "Musicians' Village has proven to be the leading example of how a meaningful vision and focused efforts can provide immediate relief as well as long-term hope for the survival of a great city and many of its most essential citizens."[39] There have been problems with this project, to be sure, as Bruce Boyd Raeburn points out. Some musicians have not had the credit history to qualify for units, and others do not want to be ghettoized in this community and would prefer to return to their old neighborhoods.[40] However, it is striking how much new construction has been undertaken in the area surrounding Musicians' Village, giving the appearance that this project has convinced other people in the neighborhood that it is worth their while to devote time and resources to rebuilding their homes.

Regardless of the antiracist aspirations of Jazz Fest organizers and music-loving community activists in the past and present, however, and despite the possibilities evident in the multiracial communion at Jazz Fest 2006, its theme of "Homecoming," and its dedication to local cultures, we should also pay attention to some of the disconcerting economic and social dynamics there. Such phenomena seemed less an antidote to than a reflection of the exclusionary aspects of the project of rebuilding New Orleans through music and otherwise. First, we must be clear that financial considerations often trump good deeds.[41] And we must come to terms with the ways the economic transformations that have facilitated Jazz Fest's growth have marginalized many black New Orleanians, even with the growth of black power within the political establishment and business community. While the emergent cultural economy has certainly provided the revenues that supported the Jazz and Heritage Foundation's community-focused projects, the balance sheet clearly favors businesses over community groups. In the early 2000s Jazz Fest organizers prided themselves on the fact that festival programs launched in response to the activism in the 1970s had redirected over one million dollars back to community organizations. Yet the Jazz and Heritage Foundation currently prides itself on the claim that Jazz Fest has surpassed Mardi Gras as the biggest tourist dollar engine in the city and pumps as much as $300 million a year into the local economy. While a significant portion of this money goes to city services in the form of tax revenue and into workers' paychecks, we must keep in mind that in the context of the neoliberal, postindustrial restructuring of New Orleans, the low-wage service sector jobs that many New Orleanians hold in the tourist economy provide substandard livelihoods, while sales taxes and hotel taxes (and in no small way civic corruption) still fail to provide adequate social services (and a social safety net) for less affluent residents.

One complaint voiced over the years has been that local (and especially black local) musicians, Mardi Gras Indians, and members of social aid and pleasure clubs at Jazz Fest are not given adequate respect, remuneration, facilities, or control of performance content, especially when compared with big-name acts from out of town.[42] There remains a significant racial and class hierarchy when it comes to who makes programming decisions, despite African American representation on the festival staff and board. Moreover, much of the programming is geared to appeal to a predominantly white and more affluent audience.[43] Such contradictions, of course, reflect a larger economic and political dynamic in a city with substantial black leadership.

Despite other programming designed to increase black participation at Jazz Fest, many within and outside of the Jazz Fest board and staff continue to comment that the black audience for the festival has remained relatively small. This low black participation may be partially attributed to rising ticket prices and the limited and, in recent years, declining numbers of free or discounted tickets available to low-income members of that community. Jazz Fest, like other financially driven entities, has scaled back its largesse during tougher economic times.[44] Yet some contend that black New Orleanians stay away from Jazz Fest not so much or only because of the costs, but because they see it as something for whites. Some even refer to the event as "white fest." And given the relatively high percentage of black people among the displaced population, it was not surprising that Jazz Fest was apparently even whiter after the storm than in previous years.[45]

Others we have spoken to described the city's Essence Music Festival, which was launched in 1995, as a more relevant event. Also produced by George Wein's organization and supported by corporate sponsor Coca Cola, this festival typically features big-name R&B and hip-hop artists, local acts, and inspirational speakers. The Essence gathering is targeted specifically to an African American audience (especially a female audience), and with annual attendance of approximately two hundred thousand, it plays a key role, along with the Bayou Classic football game between Grambling and Southern, in making New Orleans the top African American tourist destination in the United States. As a "party with a purpose," the festival has been not only a venue for individual self-improvement seminars but also a site for education and conversations about social justice and community empowerment.[46]

But perhaps more relevant to identifying the challenges of the cultural reconstruction of New Orleans than the shortage of black folk in the audience at the 2006 Jazz Fest was how that audience was differently integrated and defined by complex economies of interracial communion and social distance. It is important to note again that many performance spaces and practices in New Orleans defy simple analysis that links race, class, neighborhood, and musical taste in homologous fashion. Yet Helen Regis's work on pre-Katrina New Orleans is critically important for suggesting how local jazz performance trends embody and enact the exclusionary racial and class politics of the city in at least three intersecting ways, all of which were apparent at Jazz Fest. She shows how the geography of such performances reflects social hierarchies and social distance, how the tourist economy that supports a significant amount of jazz performance in the city is both a product of and engine of the neoliberal restructuring that has taken such a huge toll on black working-class New Orleans, and how the consumption of, and conversation about, this music produces a sense of connection across racial lines that obscures such social dynamics and produces an overly optimistic view of the state of the racial and classed social order.[47]

Not only are second line performances black cultural responses to a segregated city, but many, if not most, New Orleans whites have never been to a second line performance in a black neighborhood—in part because of the pervasive fear of black criminality—nor do they have much sense of their cultural significance. If they have been to one, chances are they merely watched (rather than participated in) a decontextualized, commercial version. Many middle-class African American New Orleanians themselves have ambivalent perspectives on second lining, often "view[ing] the tradition with a mixture of amusement, nostalgia, and embarrassment."[48] Meanwhile, as some locals point out, black New Orleanians of different classes simply do not frequent in large numbers jazz clubs in the French Quarter and along Frenchmen Street, which remain largely white spaces. Moreover, certain second line and Mardi Gras Indian gangs will not go into the French Quarter because of what they know about the exclusionary, racist history of the neighborhood and of the tourist economy that helps sustain it.[49]

I certainly witnessed at Jazz Fest some striking productions of social distinction through musical consumption that did not seem particularly troubling to those celebrating "the culture" and multicultural communion. As is often the case at jazz festivals, one trend in the audience demographic is that the "jazzier" the act, the whiter the audience. This was exemplified at various moments, perhaps most notably on Sunday afternoon, when black folks were out in force for the Doug E. Fresh, Slick Rick, and Big Daddy Kane performance on the Congo Square / Louisiana Rebirth Stage but appeared to make up only about 5 percent of the audience at the Ellis Marsalis post-bop jazz set happening in the Jazz Tent at the same time. Another multiracial yet differentially integrated space was the Economy Hall Tent, where I watched primarily white audience members, umbrellas in hand, doing a second line dance through the primarily white crowd.

Outside the fairgrounds, such dynamics were evident at the early evening jazz performance we attended at the Ogden Museum, adjacent to the old Confederate Museum. These "Ogden after Hours" shows returned to the museum only two months after Katrina and have been seen as symbolic of the music and arts communities' resolve in its aftermath.[50] And there is something compelling and potentially subversive about music with African American roots being celebrated within shouting distance of an institution once devoted to memorializing white supremacy and slave-ocracy. But perhaps not so much if one considers the primarily white, seemingly professional crowd at the Ogden, some of them there for the music, others to consume sophistication. I wondered about this too on Frenchmen Street while watching an excellent mixed "hot jazz" group—with folks in the audience sitting in—perform in another almost entirely white space, this one more bohemian and queer than the Ogden. There were only three black faces in the place. A fourth arrived in the form of "Uncle" Lionel Batiste of local brass band fame, who wandered in during a particularly hot number, danced seductively with several young women, and wandered out again to the cheers of the crowd.

The racial geography of musical taste coincides, of course, with the racial and class politics of the production of black music in New Orleans under neoliberalism. As the historian Thomas Holt argues, "Whereas under earlier regimes racialization was linked to the mobilization of blacks into productive relations, it is now marked by the exclusion of a significant plurality of black people from productive relations."[51] Anxieties about this phenomenon and the conditions it creates in urban centers across the country have figured prominently in conversations about an African American return to New Orleans. In the black community, the conversation about New Orleans becoming a white city takes many forms, focusing sometimes on political power, at other times on gentrification. On my visit to New Orleans shortly after Katrina, more than one black person told me that they believe many members of their community are no longer welcome because they are seen as unnecessary to its redevelopment. And nonblack and black people alike suggested to me that the city can no longer "afford" nonproductive members of the African American community, who, especially after the storm, would overtax the city's social services, health care, and criminal justice systems. Such sentiment has also made it into public political discourse in various ways, as in comments from 2006 mayoral candidate Peggy Wilson about the city's public housing developments supporting the drug trade, prostitution, and welfare fraud.[52]

Holt suggests that "black bodies—no longer a means of production—have become a means of consumption" in the postindustrial economy. He also encourages us to think about the racial "work" that the consumption of seemingly transcendent black images accomplishes, especially when we think about "whether and how the relatively benign images of the Michael Jordans and Colin Powells of the world articulate with—or perhaps are actually dependent on—those of ghetto youth and 'welfare queens.'"[53] In New Orleans, the exclusion of some blacks from productive relations and the consumption of transcendent black bodies have taken a particular form. Some black people have exercised significant political power in the city for decades, and others are necessary to the tourist economy as performers and as low-wage workers in the service and hospitality sectors. But this rather comfortable dependence on some measure of black power and a sufficient supply of black laboring bodies and consumable artists is fundamentally linked to anxiety about a black presence deemed dangerous and a financial drain on the city's resources. In other words, the low-income communities that produce the workers for the tourist industry and larger service sector of the economy, as well as many of the artists who create the distinctive cultural mosaic that makes the city appealing to locals and visitors alike, are also seen as sources of the crime and social unproductivity that threaten to undermine civil society and the economy.[54]

Thus we must keep in mind that there is a fundamental paradox when it comes to rebuilding New Orleans via culture because of the way the inherently unequal postindustrial tourist economy, based on a multiracial art form with African American roots, has developed hand in hand not only with increased social segregation but with an economy of fear and social distance. Black people as a group are necessary as the creators of the culture, have some role as individual workers (musicians, maids, and waiters) in the tourist industry, and can be beneficiaries as small business owners and municipal employees and leaders. However, as a group, they are also seen as a threat.

Such exclusions are not always apparent to and are often willfully ignored by those who desire this music and the culture that produces it. Lowe argues that one of the potentially regressive aspects of multicultural spectacle is the way it elides group histories when celebrating cultural achievements, thus making invisible material inequalities and social conflicts.[55] At Jazz Fest and other performance venues in New Orleans, inequalities and conflicts were obscured, it seems, through an emphasis on history and an erasure of the present. Regis discusses what she terms the "antiquification" of black cultural practices in photographic representations of the second line. She suggests that while such images may on the one hand challenge stereotypical images of black people as criminal, corrupt, or otherwise pathological, consigning these groups to the past not only makes invisible the dynamism of continually evolving second line practices, but may "provide [to those outside that community] illusionary access to a world they would never otherwise be able to enter. . . . It creates a virtual communion across boundaries of race, class, and culture."[56]

There is, of course, a long history of such "virtual communion" at jazz festivals in the United States. As Scott Saul notes in his account of the early years of Wein's Newport Jazz Festival, which served as a model for Jazz Fest, many jazz festivals have distanced the music from at least some of its urban African American associations, even as they have celebrated them. They have also been sites where a collective "white fascination with 'getting down' [has] coalesced with a rising sense of consumer entitlement," where under the guise of interracial solidarity emerged a "strange new form of white privilege—a way that [whites of different ethnicities] came together in the postwar period as a common group with a common investment in certain fictions of black life."[57]

At Jazz Fest, as Regis and Walton suggest, the production of whiteness in this liminal and temporary space over the years has been quite clear. For there, they argue, hip white consumers augment their whiteness, their hipness, and their privileged status as relatively affluent consumers by purchasing a blackened and unique cosmopolitan experience. They "participate in an imaginary leveling of difference," a particular kind of "virtual communion" with those often separated from them by race and class outside the fairground walls. They do this in a contained, safe environment—one that encourages the spontaneity that Mahalia Jackson brought to Jazz Fest in 1970, but which also manages it. And as they reenact the refusal of generic and racial categories emphasized by the folklore of Jazz Fest's history, they not only de-emphasize present-day social realities but construct identities that "often involve a claim to special status as dis-implicated in racist structures of domination and exploitation."[58]

We can ask, then, whether the embrace of jazz as black New Orleans's gift to the world, the championing of it as an expression of interracial communion, and its established function in the local tourist industry may actually help to further economic oppression in post-Katrina New Orleans and perhaps even antiblack attitudes and practices as well. At a basic level, a focus on culture may distract people from pressing socioeconomic problems. Some have pointed out that culture has been the cover for draconian, neoliberal planning. The BNOB Commission's final report, according to Darwin BondGraham, put forth a "vision for the future of New Orleans [that] promotes the city's 'culture' and music" but did so in such a way that a stated respect for and commitment to restoring the city's cultural landscape not only glossed over issues of race and economic justice but enabled the commission to put a benign face on not so subtly coded plans for "demolition and gentrification."[59]

But the bigger question may ultimately have to do with everyday acts of identification through the music outside the confined spaces of Jazz Fest. Can a commitment to the music sustain a political commitment to a population if affinities are inseparable from an economic regime that reproduces racial and class exclusions? And will such commitments, which in some cases go hand in hand with specific activist projects and deep human relationships but in other cases remain "virtual," be able to withstand the difficulties New Orleans faces as a city? John Valery White argues that "everyone wants to preserve the culture that underlies the food, the street musicians and second liners, the jazz, but no one wants the working poor who lived these 'quaint,' touristic lives."[60] I have heard some people talk about the necessity of the culture to rebuilding the city, and how important black musicians' homecoming is in particular, while simultaneously expressing anxieties about the black poor and black criminals returning to the city. It is important not to dismiss out of hand the very real cost (physical, economic, and psychological) that crime exacts from all members of urban communities. Nor should we merely write off as racist those who raise questions about the potential drain of "unproductive" people on the city's fragile infrastructure. But troubling still are observations that suggest there comes a moment for many in this difficult period when identifying with the music and musicians, who are venerated by tradition and a contemporary priority of culture, and who stand as a metonymic representation of a black New Orleans displaced by the storm and neoliberal policy, becomes a vehicle for people reaffirming their connections to the city after deciding that a more democratic reconstruction is not possible, feasible, or desirable.

Some of these paradoxes appear in quite interesting ways in the HBO series *Treme*, the second season of which ends with an episode featuring Jazz Fest. There, among other things, a new interracial relationship (Janette and Jacques) begins to blossom. To be sure, the first two seasons of the series address a variety of social inequalities in practice: the displacement of public housing residents, the inadequacies of the Road Home program, police violence, the criminal justice system's inability to keep low- and moderate-income people safe, the privatization of the public school system, and so on. The show also comments on the limits of multiracial communion, most notably through the character of Davis McAlary, the scion of a wealthy white New Orleans family, whose adventures include getting punched in the face in a Tremé bar after uttering the N-word and then claiming his right to use it because of his residency in the neighborhood and his affinity for blackness.

Yet Davis, who at first seems something of a buffoon, an extreme case of white privilege and naïveté, is redeemed over the course of *Treme*'s first two seasons as a generous soul, a kind of ethical compass, and the champion of an equitable and multiracial New Orleans. And ultimately, as cultural studies scholar Herman Gray argues, *Treme* backs away from a consistent critique of racism in post-Katrina New Orleans. What emerges instead is a longing for a multiracial, pre-Katrina cultural matrix, whose rebuilding must take precedence, perhaps even over the concerns of the city's neediest citizens. Moreover, not only is the paradoxical foundation of the cultural economy left largely unexplored (more attention is given to what is or is not "authentic"), but *Treme*'s celebration of the individual hard work and entrepreneurial spirit of New Orleans's cultural workers frames the challenge of reconstruction through a neoliberal lens—by venerating cultural workers who succeed by staying true to their art and becoming more effective market actors. Gray also suggests that, despite the well-publicized and no doubt well-intentioned efforts by the show's producers to hire local actors and cultural workers, contract with local businesses, and develop community partnerships, its relationship with New Orleans might exemplify "itinerant work and casual labor as the new normal for the city's black and poor citizens."[61] And all the while the show promotes a sense that the music will make it all better.

Ultimately, the politics of race, music, and reconstruction in New Orleans are tremendously complicated, and the story is still unfolding. However, given the place of the music in this city, the role given to culture in the neoliberal era, and the stakes for New Orleanians, it is surely a story that demands greater scrutiny. Among the important questions that must be explored further: To what extent will the consumption and celebration of "respectable," homegrown musical cultures affirm a connection to place, and to what extent will they symbolically obviate elements of the community from which the music comes? Will the focus on music enable healing and progressive politics, as it clearly has in some cases, and a challenge to racism? Or will it reproduce racism in familiar or unfamiliar ways? The existence of multiple interracial exchanges through black music, diverse in their significations, is not new, nor is the deployment of black political claims through music. Moreover, some of the on-the-ground political and social phenomena we observed in New Orleans are not limited to that city. The simultaneous embrace of black culture and anxiety about a black physical presence are long-standing national—and, indeed, global—phenomena. But there is something particularly compelling and illuminating when considering the role of music, and jazz in particular, in the reconstruction of New Orleans, given the meanings associated with the music's origins in the city and the way that this particular laboratory of postindustrial economics and neoliberal policy has been exposed for the world to see. So we should continue to think about how these interracial musical exchanges and collective consumptive acts might encourage reconstruction for all New Orleanians and make its black working-class and poor residents visible and audible in respectful, productive ways. But we should also think about how these exchanges have and may continue to facilitate collective claims on the city that rely on and reproduce social distance.

# HURRICANE KATRINA

PLATE 17. St. Claude Avenue, Ninth Ward, October 2005

PLATE 18. City Park, New Orleans, October 2005

PLATE 19. Bywater, October 2005

PLATE 20. Garden District, October 2005

PLATE 21. Baptism pool in gutted church, Lower Ninth Ward, 2006

PLATE 22. SPCA and FEMA markings, Lower Ninth Ward, October 2005

PLATE 23. Remains of dogs left during the storm, Lower Ninth Ward, 2006

PLATE 24. Lower Ninth Ward, October 2005

PLATE 25. FEMA markings, Lower Ninth Ward, October 2005

PLATE 26. Abandoned school with multiple watermarks, Central City, 2006

PLATE 27. Martin Luther King Library, Lower Ninth Ward, October 2005

PLATE 28. B. W. Cooper Apartments, October 2005

PLATE 29. B. W. Cooper Apartments, May 2006. Public housing was closed to prevent the return of residents.

PLATE 30. 1998

PLATE 31. October 2005

Fats Domino's house, Lower Ninth Ward, 1998–2006

PLATE 32. Graffiti after mistaken reports of his death, October 2005

PLATE 33. 2006

PLATE 34. By the remains of the house built by her father, Lower Ninth Ward, 2006

PLATE 35. Lower Ninth Ward, October 2005

PLATE 36. Lower Ninth Ward, 2006

PLATE 37.  Blackwater private security, Canal Street, October 2005

PLATE 38.  National Guard soldiers from Washington State by the levee, Lower Ninth Ward, October 2005

PLATE 39. New Orleans police officers, off St. Claude Street, October 2005

PLATE 40. Tremé, October 2005

PLATE 41. Robert Green by his FEMA trailer, Lower Ninth Ward, 2008

PLATE 42. Flooded band room, Martin Luther King Jr. Middle School, Lower Ninth Ward, 2006

PLATE 43. Martin Luther King Jr. school and library under construction, 2007

# FUNERALS AND SECOND LINES

PLATE 44. March against gentrification, Tremé, 2000

PLATE 45. Brass band at wake with Kermit Ruffins, Iberville Housing Projects, Tremé, 1994

PLATE 46. Wake, Iberville Housing Projects, 1994

PLATE 47.  Boy dancing at wake, Iberville Housing Projects, 1994

PLATE 48. Black Men of Labor Second Line Parade, 2011

PLATE 49. Tremé Brass Band at the dedication of a spirit house created by artists John Scott and Martin Payton, 2002

PLATE 50. "Uncle" Lionel Batiste, Tremé Brass Band, 2002

PLATE 51. Second line parade in Tremé, 2010

PLATE 52. Lundi Gras second line, St. Claude Avenue, 2008

PLATE 53. Lundi Gras second line, St. Claude Avenue, 2008

PLATE 54. Honor to the Lower Ninth Ward, Lundi Gras second line, Rampart Street, 2008

PLATE 55. Glen David Andrews, Tremé musician, 2008

PLATE 56. Brothers from a family of musicians, Tremé, 2008

PLATE 57.  Brass band under freeway after funeral, Tremé, 2008

PLATE 58. Gerald Emell, jazz funeral procession for Louis "Fritz" Nelson, Tremé, 2008

PLATE 59. Lous Andrews jumps on the casket, Tremé, 2008

PLATE 60. Funeral procession, Tremé, 2008

PLATE 61. Returning to the stables after a funeral procession, Tremé, 2010

PLATE 62. Grieving, Holt Cemetery, 2010

# MARDI GRAS

PLATE 63. "To the Ancestors," Guardians of the Flame Arts Society, Harrison family home, Upper Ninth Ward, Mardi Gras morning, 2007

PLATE 64. Mardi Gras day, Tremé, 2007

PLATE 65. Ronald Lewis, Backstreet Museum, Tremé, 2007

PLATE 66. Muses Parade, St. Charles Avenue, Uptown, 2008

PLATE 67. Flambeau, St. Charles Avenue, Uptown Parade, 2008

PLATE 68. Beginning of the Zulu Parade, 2007

PLATE 69. Zulu Parade, 2007

PLATE 70. Mardi Gras Indians, "Get the Hell out the Way," Yellow Pocahontas Tribe, Tremé, 2007

PLATE 71. Fi Yi Yi at the Backstreet Museum, Tremé, 2008

PLATE 72. Young Mardi Gras Indian brave, Algiers, 2010

PLATE 73. Asutua of the Yellow Pocahontas Tribe, Tremé, 2007

PLATE 74. Donald Harrison Jr., Big Chief of the Congo Nation, Tremé, 2007

PLATE 75. David Montana and his aunt, Yellow Pocahontas Tribe, Tremé, 2007

PLATE 76. Chanting at the Backstreet Museum, Tremé, Mardi Gras day, 2007

PLATE 77. Tremé, Mardi Gras day, 2007

PLATE 78. Joyce Taylor, Queen of the White Cloud Hunters, and Dr. John at the Backstreet Museum, Tremé, Mardi Gras day, 2008

PLATE 79. Tremé, Mardi Gras day, 2007

PLATE 80. Tremé, Mardi Gras day, 2007

# 3

# PARADING
# AGAINST
# VIOLENCE

On Lundi Gras (the Monday before Fat Tuesday) 2008, a second line parade began and ended at Louis Armstrong Park in the Faubourg Tremé, which by some accounts is the oldest African American neighborhood in the United States. The park and the Tremé sit just across Rampart Street from the tourist-friendly French Quarter. The New Orleans Social Aid and Pleasure Club Task Force (SAPCTF), an umbrella organization of social aid and pleasure clubs, organized the two-hour event.

The majority of community-based second line parades are sponsored by single clubs, but the Lundi Gras parade was the third post-Katrina event in which several clubs shared resources to sponsor a "unified" parade. It was also the first time the clubs were allowed to parade during Mardi Gras season. Although the parade traversed largely African American neighborhoods, its start and finish along the border of the Tremé and the French Quarter were strategic, designed to reclaim the tradition from the tourist industry, to deflect criticism that these parades have been magnets for violence, and to announce the community's resilience. As a spokesperson for the task force stated before the parade, "So many visitors are drawn to New Orleans by representations of second-lines. We want to show them the authentic parading tradition, and let everyone locally know that parading is about family and community. We want to show the city, and the world, that the SAPC community is back and stronger than ever."[1]

Building from my own experience of walking with this second line, this section examines some of the life- and community-affirming functions of parading in New Orleans, before and after Katrina. If the previous section tended toward pessimism,

I try here to be a bit more optimistic about the potential for reconstructing the city through culture and multiracial communion, even as I continue to keep an eye on some of the contradictions in such practices. I am particularly interested in how people have used African American–rooted parade traditions, improvised over time as life-affirming reactions to difficult conditions, to respond to what some have called the biopolitical exclusions evident in New Orleans before and after Katrina.

The 2008 SAPCTF parade can be read as a marker of the expanding array of parading practices that helped New Orleanians survive several years of post-Katrina chaos. Some parades have been organized by long-established clubs and other traditional African American community and family networks; some are the product of emergent cultural and political formations created by activists and cultural workers, whose networks may or may not be restricted to the Gulf Coast region; and some have been rather spontaneous affairs. I suggest here that such traditional and emergent practices may constitute "asset-based" models of civic engagement that continue to serve low-income New Orleans neighborhoods, not by "correcting [their] perceived deficits" but rather by building on community strengths and local knowledge. As such, they open up important political space for collaboration and reflection on key social justice issues.[2]

My analysis foregrounds activism around violence, an issue that has profoundly shaped the post-Katrina reconstruction of New Orleans. One component of this story consists of long-standing patterns of structural violence brought to bear on those at society's margins. We also saw after the storm the criminalization of black flood victims and their construction by the media and political demagogues as violent threats to the social order. But regardless of how street crime has been manipulated for political ends, it remains a real problem for New Orleanians, particularly poor and black New Orleanians. The city's residents have suffered immeasurably from extraordinary levels of violence both before and after the storm. The criminal justice and law enforcement systems have been unable to significantly decrease it, and at times they have perpetuated their own forms of violence. Our experiences in the city were shaped by interactions with people who feared going into (or leaving) certain neighborhoods after dark or who feared the police. Crime and inadequate prosecution of it have also contributed to an inequitable reconstruction. Marking certain communities as dangerous justifies neglect, while neglect and a high crime rate are among the reasons people continue to leave the city or delay their return.

I examine here how people of various inclinations and backgrounds have engaged in antiviolence work through parade practices, while simultaneously addressing larger questions regarding the right to residence in the city, the ownership of its culture, and the use of public space. I see these parade practices, as have others, as mobile public spheres, constituted in real time, but also as events that open up a broader, ongoing space for reflection on key issues pertaining to the future of New Orleans. This is in part possible because the state has failed so miserably in defining the future and because local musical cultures have been given such prominence in post-Katrina conversations about the future. Although many New Orleanians have long ignored traditional second lining practices, there is a growing recognition of their life- and place-affirming function post Katrina by a wide spectrum of the population and the media. Unfortunately, this visibility is also facilitated by high-profile conflicts between cultural workers and municipal officials. But out of such conflicts have come important referenda on the question of who bears responsibility for violence in post-Katrina New Orleans and much commentary on how it shapes the cultural and social landscape.

Some have pointed to the October 9, 2005, jazz funeral of Austin Leslie, a highly regarded Creole chef who died while evacuated in Atlanta, as a critical vehicle for restoring hope for the future among New Orleanians. Even though it was a relatively small event in comparison to past funereal practice for prominent local figures, the Hot 8 Brass Band–accompanied procession staked a claim to neighborhoods that were still largely abandoned. And as a small media event, it gave participants a chance to broadcast that optimism to the broader world. Hot 8 snare drummer Dinerral Shavers was quoted in an Associated Press story as saying, "It's going to get back to normal eventually. . . . We're going to bring the life back."[3]

The first few parades sponsored by social aid and pleasure clubs were also embraced as signs of the city's recovery. The Black Men of Labor SAPC paraded on November 26, 2005, and the Prince of Wales Social Aid and Pleasure Club followed on December 18. Speaking of the former event, Black Men of Labor member Sunpie Barnes indicated the group-specific meanings of such events. The parade was held, he argued, "to keep the culture alive. . . . FEMA and the Red Cross can't keep our traditions alive. . . . We have to take care of our own selves." And as jazz historian and Tulane professor Joel Dinerstein's recollection of the latter event indicates, such parades projected hope across social and cultural boundaries. "Because, post-Katrina, *I* needed it. Because my spirit was hurt. Because my city was in ruins. Because my future had become unstable. Because I needed pumping brass sounds and powerful rhythms to reboot my heart. Because I needed to know others shared my frustrations and grief, my hopes and fears. Because I needed to dance myself back to life."[4]

On January 15, 2006, four and a half months after the storm, the SAPCTF coordinated the efforts of members of twenty to thirty clubs to put on an "all-star" parade. Club members wore black T-shirts with "Re-New New Orleans" on the front and the club name on the back. The event drew eight thousand people, from across the socioeconomic spectrum—including more middle-class blacks and whites than usual—in part because, as the first big post-Katrina second line, it was embraced by a range of people seeking evidence that New Orleans's black cultural traditions and the city itself were coming back. It also drew large numbers of displaced people. One estimate is that half of the club members who attended were living elsewhere. Although many had to leave shortly after the parade, they were able to articulate publicly an intention, and perhaps a right, to return to the city. As SAPCTF head Tamara Jackson remembered, "It wasn't just about the parade; it was about unifying the city and unifying the spirits that was [sic] lost during Katrina."[5]

The SAPCTF was formed about three years before the storm, in part to intervene in tensions between the city and its culture bearers. It has continued this work into the post-storm period, while also struggling to rebuild the second line community following the displacement of many of its members and other residents of the neighborhoods in which they lived. Both the SAPCTF and individual second line organizations have been involved with disaster relief, raising funds for public schools, and other charitable projects.[6]

The 2006 event and the group's other projects speak not only to the prominent role of cultural activism in the neoliberal era but also to the claim some have made that even though the social aid and pleasure club community is smaller than before the storm, second lining now has a greater symbolic value to members of its community, and perhaps serves a more important networking function among a dispersed community than it did prior to the storm.[7]

The affirmative aspects of what we might call nontraditional acts of parading, or simply invocations of the second line, also figure prominently in recollections of and reportage about returns from displacement and the politics surrounding it. Writer Jason Berry recalls a November 2005 New Orleans Jazz Orchestra concert, held the night before Ray Nagin's BNOB Commission released its report, that featured dirges and parade anthems. "It was possible to believe," he writes, "at least for a night, that out of the flood wreckage a resurrected city might emerge in some possession of its soul."[8] Novelist Louis Edwards recalls witnessing a Halloween parade on the evening of his return to his French Quarter home and later listening to the Rebirth Brass Band at Jackson Square. "It was quite thrilling to stand there in front of St. Louis Cathedral and the Cabildo, in the heart of New Orleans, on the day that I returned and experience the best thing that there is here: the music. It's hard to believe, but that's exactly how I was welcomed back to this great city."[9] And some point to the symbolic importance of Sylvester Francis's return to New Orleans and the October 6 reopening of his tiny Backstreet Cultural Museum in the Tremé, with its important collection of Mardi Gras Indian suits and second line exhibits and its role as a gathering place for paraders.[10]

And this went on for months. Historian and photographer Keith Weldon Medley describes his participation in a 2006 Memorial Day event in the Lower Ninth Ward, a neighborhood where the porch stoops stood "like tombstones on a devastated landscape." Members of the Lower Ninth Ward Neighborhood Empowerment Network Association met at the site of the levee breach to recite the names of Katrina's victims. The Tremé Brass Band played a funeral dirge while people laid hands on the levee wall to keep the waters away during the upcoming hurricane season. Then "the band led us through a dev-astated Lower Ninth Ward in a defiant show of spirit and resolution. We walked through the worst parts, trying to revive a pulse to this community in pain."[11] A month earlier, a march across the Mississippi River Bridge organized by the Reverend Jesse Jackson and his Rainbow/PUSH Coalition had fused civil rights movement public protest with second line umbrellas and brass band music. The march brought attention to potential civil and human rights violations in the post-Katrina period. It simultaneously reminded people about the September 1, 2005, incident on the bridge—where members of the Gretna police turned back a large and primarily black group of pedestrians trying to flee the deteriorating conditions at the Ernest N. Morial Convention Center—and sought to ensure that displaced New Orleanians were able to vote in upcoming municipal elections. According to former mayor and National Urban League president Marc Morial, "This is the twenty-first century's ground zero in the fight to protect the Voting Rights Act."[12]

These life- and rights-affirming events speak to the continued importance in the post-Katrina period of practices established long ago. As Joseph Roach reminds us, parading and other musically enriched public rituals in New Orleans have long been sites where power and challenges to it are displayed in spectacular fashion. Through practices of what Roach calls "surrogation," members of communal performance networks have engaged in willful acts of remembering or forgetting, which are often related to the violence and displacement that have long defined the city.[13]

The transgressive but ultimately state-supported spectacle of late nineteenth-century Mardi Gras, for example, promoted and sustained a redemptive white supremacy through irreverent displays of white privilege, the denigration of Reconstruction, and erasure of the crimes of the South that occasioned federal intervention.[14] Meanwhile, contemporaneous working-class and black practices, such as jazz funerals, second lines, and Mardi Gras Indian parades, built upon West African and European rituals that bridged the sacred-secular divide, as well as connections between the living and the dead. As part of a longer history of creolized public displays of music and dancing in liminal New World spaces, such rituals were alternative vehicles for reclaiming bodies, souls, and memories in the face of the violence, spatial segregation, and white-supremacy-serving practices of public culture and memorialization in the postemancipation South. Death rituals like jazz funerals "offered this community an opportunity to affirm its semiautonomous but discretely submerged existence within or against the obligatory rituals of the better publicized fiction called the dominant culture." Brightly colored Mardi Gras Indians "danced to possess themselves again in the spirit of their ancestors, to possess again their memories, to possess again their communities. They danced to resist their reduction to the status of commodities. In other words, they danced—and they still dance—to possess again a heritage that some people would rather see buried alive."[15]

As discussed in the previous section, the social aid and pleasure clubs have, for over a century, provided aid and social services and alternative models for social organizing when such things were lacking. As Rebecca Solnit puts it, such organizations "provided tangible necessities (social aid) when things went wrong but intangible ones (social pleasure) when they went right."[16] Musician and educator Michael White argues that "these parades offered the black community a euphoric transformation into a temporary democratic world characterized by free, open participation and self-expression" while also gesturing "toward a more just restructuring of society, politics, and life in general."[17] And Ned Sublette describes second lines as "in effect a civil rights demonstration. Literally, demonstrating the civil right of the community to assemble in the street for peaceful purposes. Or, more simply, demonstrating the civil right of the community to exist."[18] However, understanding the full impact of the life- and rights-affirming impact of the expanding array of parading practices demands attention to a set of worsening conditions for many New Orleanians during the post–Civil Rights era, conditions that were simultaneously made visible and accelerated by Hurricane Katrina. And we are compelled to examine not simply the cultural events that respond to such conditions but the space for political reflection that these events open up.

The commentary of some local cultural workers has been instructive in this regard. Keith Medley argues that New Orleans cultural representations have been a means of transmitting the city's history "in the absence of monuments" relevant to all its residents. They also provide a "cultural safety net," particularly for young people. "So even though political and social forces may line up against black youth, the cultural expressions provide self-esteem and purpose beyond what could be found in mainstream society."[19] Drawing on the analysis of her mother, educator and cultural worker Herreast Harrison, Cherice Harrison-Nelson, Big Queen of the Guardians of the Flame, describes Mardi Gras Indians as "among the first organized civil rights workers because they knew, at one time, there was a distinct possibility that they would be arrested for freedom of expression."[20] She calls the Indians and social aid and pleasure clubs "spiritual first responders to predominantly African American neighborhoods" post Katrina, noting that they provided sustenance to those communities in the wake of profound state failure.[21]

I find it interesting that Medley and Harrison-Nelson use the regulatory language of the state, particularly that of emergency medicine and social service professionals, to describe the importance of traditional cultural forms during the city's recovery. This points to what some describe as the scene of "biopolitics" in New Orleans after the storm and, more specifically, to the ways in which post-Katrina planning has often seemed to be predicated on the belief that a significant percentage of the city's population is simply disposable.

Henry Giroux has argued that Hurricane Katrina and the slow and often punitive government response after the storm exposed the effects of a long history of race and class oppression, as well as a generation of deindustrialization, urban renewal projects, suburbanization, and neoliberal social and economic policies (especially cuts in education, health care, and welfare). It also brought to light what he calls a "new biopolitics of disposability: the poor, especially people of color, not only have to fend for themselves in the face of life's tragedies but are also supposed to do it without being seen by the dominant society. Excommunicated from the sphere of human concern, they have been rendered invisible, utterly disposable, and heir to that army of socially homeless that allegedly no longer existed in color-blind America."[22] Giroux, following the work of theorists Michel Foucault, Giorgio Agamben, Michael Hardt and Antonio Negri, and others, describes how the power to dispense fear and death has been replaced (or at least, in some cases, augmented) by the power to cultivate life or permit its antithesis (death). In the hands of the powerful, biopolitics is, as Mika Ojakangas puts it, the project of "distributing the living in the domain of value and utility. Its task is to take charge of life that needs a continuous regulatory and corrective mechanism."[23] Although biopolitical projects have long existed in the United States and have long been built upon race, gender, sexuality, class, and other exclusions, as well as state violence, Giroux contends that this new form is distinguished by diminishing state support for the needy and assumptions about the permanence of racial and class hierarchies. Not only do the state and other powerful entities enact violence by positioning certain human beings as disposable; they also legitimate themselves by marking those same populations as dangerous and unworthy of state protection.[24]

While it would be a mistake to suggest that all or even most black New Orleanians have been deemed disposable in this sense, some of the most abject among them have. Moreover, assumed and enacted disposability affects the quality of living for a much larger population. Many have commented on the ways that, as media representations of the immediate aftermath of the storm shifted focus from black suffering to black criminality, the critique of government neglect and hostility was replaced by their justification. Such representations also helped produce an official disregard for black people as victims or potential victims of crime. Feminist scholars and activists have pointed out that the reporting of sexual assaults, in particular, served that function. As Cheryl Harris and Devon Carbado argue, "The sexual assaults against women—the vast majority of them black—became markers of black disorder, chaos, and the 'animalistic' nature of New Orleans residents; but black women themselves could not occupy the position of victims worthy of rescue. Their injuries were only abstractions that were marshaled to make the larger point about the descent of New Orleans into a literal and figurative black hole."[25] As New Orleans activist Jordan Flaherty reminds us, "systematic violence against women," particularly displacement from public housing and homelessness, "was ignored, while Black communities continued to be criminalized."[26]

Addressing more broadly the relationship of criminality to the reconstruction of the city, John Valery White argues that "rumors of mayhem in New Orleans mark the beginning of the end of efforts to rebuild New Orleans."[27] The high murder rate has since served as justification for slow-paced and exclusionary reconstruction efforts and has contributed to the invisibility of the needs of low-income black communities, whose members are seen as the source of such violence. But the inability of the police department and the district attorney to successfully prosecute or even identify the perpetrators of many crimes is also a critical element in the story of disposability. As the usual victims of violent crimes, members of poor and working-class communities endure directly harmful acts: the effects of living in fear of murder, rape, and assault, and a more militarized brand of policing that further endangers them. And it continues to displace others, who stay away from their old neighborhoods because of the dangers there.

But Giroux is also attentive to the fact that "biopolitics . . . is also potentially about enhancing life by linking hope and a new vision to the struggle for reclaiming the social, providing a language capable of translating individual issues into public considerations, and recognizing that in the age of the new media the terrain of culture is one of the most important pedagogical spheres through which to challenge the most basic precepts of the new authoritarianism."[28] Indeed, in using regulatory terms, Harrison-Nelson and Medley speak not only of the language of the state but also to transformations in the life-enhancing functions of the venerable traditions of parading in New Orleans that have developed in the face of state and other violence.

So at this post-Katrina moment, when many members of second lining communities remain displaced, their return is important, as Rachel Breunlin and Helen Regis suggest, not only because it would be the right thing to support, but also because, with their long experience building community under conditions of deprivation, they can lend that set of skills to the reconstruction of the city and provide, in the words of AbdouMaliq Simone, a "platform for reproducing life in the city."[29] This project, however, remains precarious and ultimately demonstrates—especially as cultural workers and artists address issues of violence in the community—the complicated ways in which residual ideologies and disciplinary modalities remain embedded in such projects.

These public rituals have become vehicles for a broader dialogue about violence in the city and who bears responsibility for it. In other words, via sometimes regulated, sometimes not, official and unofficial public displays, we see the formation of a broader public sphere. This is apparent not only in the jazz funerals, second lines, and Mardi Gras Indian gatherings themselves, as they play out in real time, but also in the ways in which putting bodies on the line in the biopolitical present provide the occasions for a series of referenda that bear upon the future of the city. This happens in no small part because of the history of resistance and demands for visibility embedded in these embodied, improvised rituals, but also because the social order in New Orleans has long been reproduced by the state's regulation of rituals. And people are paying a lot more attention to them in the wake of Katrina.

Returning to the 2008 Lundi Gras second line organized by the SAPCTF, it is important to note that the parade almost did not happen. The task force had secured a permit in August 2007 and come to an agreement with the New Orleans Police Department about the date and route. As is customary, the NOPD agreed to provide security and traffic control in exchange for a fee. But on January 22, 2008, less than two weeks before the parade, after three bands had been hired and out-of-town guests invited, the police telephoned the head of the task force, Tamara Jackson, and asked her first to change the route of the parade, then to schedule it for another day. A follow-up letter, hand delivered to Jackson by police officers on the night of January 29, was more emphatic. It announced that the permit had been canceled because of public safety concerns regarding traffic and crowd control. Eventually, the American Civil Liberties Union intervened, and on Friday, February 1, a federal judge ruled in favor of the task force, allowing the parade to go on. Although many deemed the event a success, the experience beforehand was deeply frustrating to the organizers. As Jackson said, "I thought we were really making progress in forging a relationship with the NOPD . . . But sometimes it feels like they're just singling us out."[30]

Second line parades and Mardi Gras Indian gatherings have long been sources of conflict between the police and members of New Orleans's black community. Some explain police hostility toward such activities by the fact that the police realize they are not in control of the crowd, as order in the street is provided by the band and the clubs. Others assume that the police merely view a gathering of working-class people or African Americans as "inherently a problem" that needs to be dispersed. Both analyses make sense when we consider the complicated ways parading traditions have developed in relationship to the state and the needs of power in the city.

Roach argues that developing alongside the "transgressive" elements of carnival traditions in the city has been a tradition of "elaborated regulation of carnival activity to sustain at least the symbolic supremacy of the favored group." Looking at elite white Mardi Gras krewes in the nineteenth and early twentieth centuries, he points out that transgressive behavior (such as masking and orgiastic drunkenness) coincided with a symbolic presentation of white supremacy (lampooning blacks, immigrants, radicals, and women). Eventually, local ordinance and national precedence like *Plessey v. Ferguson* "adjusted the boundaries of transgression and immunity in the use of public accommodations." Laws that, for instance, protected parade routes from obstruction by vehicles or gave police power to clear streets "required practical civic assistance to the outlaw practices of the social elite, who could then merrily flaunt their transgressions, making a seasonal public spectacle of their eternally exceptional status." Mardi Gras krewes were also given exceptional status by a long-standing parish requirement for permits and expensive fees for public parades that exempted "bona fide organization[s]" celebrating Mardi Gras. And their protection by statute from lawsuits as a result of injuries that happen on parade defines their elevated public status by "extension of [the] legal doctrine of sovereign immunity."[31]

Although New Orleans's extraordinary Afro-diasporic culture has correctly been perceived as the product of an urban environment where certain transgressions were permitted, Roach reminds us that even liminal spaces such as Congo Square were regulated. The eighteenth-century French Code Noir and the Anglo-American Black Code of 1806 may have been permissive enough so that authorities would permit the drum circles and dances that were forbidden elsewhere in the South, but Congo Square still fit "a pattern of transgression indulged but also one of transgression carefully channeled into regulated conduits of time and space." So we should keep in mind that the carnivalesque revelry of the African American krewe Zulu is regulated, and by being regulated it has benefited from an exemption from parade fees for Mardi Gras organizations and the support of the municipal infrastructure. Second line organizations, by contrast, have not. And they have historically been unable to get permits to parade during Mardi Gras season.[32]

Mardi Gras Indian gatherings and spontaneous jazz funerals have usually been held without official sanction, but often with a tacit understanding from the police that they could go forward. But such agreements have been precarious, subject to the whims of individual members of law enforcement and the interpretations of city leaders about whether certain communities or their members currently represented a threat to the social order or otherwise needed to be kept in line. Regulation could then come down spontaneously, in seemingly arbitrary ways, and often in the form of a police officer's club. In early 2005 the NOPD broke up a second line parade, and then on March 19 of that year, they aggressively disrupted the St. Joseph Day gathering of Mardi Gras Indians, using the justification that a participant was reported to have a gun. Police harassed various gangs of Indians as they arrived at A. L. Davis Park. Indians were forced to remove their costumes in public, which many considered an indignity, and some were treated roughly and arrested. This harassment outraged the Indians, who took pride in policing themselves, sanctioning members who engaged in or advocated violence. In the controversy that followed, city officials justified their actions by arguing that the organizers had not obtained a permit for the event. But Indians and supporters pointed out that this long-standing event had never been subject to permits, thus demonstrating that a tacit agreement had been broken. At a subsequent city council discussion of the incident, Big Chief Allison "Tootie" Montana recounted a long history of police intimidation and broken agreements before he suffered a heart attack and collapsed at the end of his statement, dying shortly thereafter.[33]

A controversial and high-profile post-Katrina example of such tacit agreements breaking down occurred on October 1, 2007, when the police showed up at a spontaneous Monday night jazz funeral procession in the Tremé for New Birth Brass Band tuba player Kerwin James, who had died of complications from a stroke several days earlier. The procession was one of several planned for the week, culminating in a burial that Saturday. The police told the mourners to disperse as the musicians played the hymn "I'll Fly Away." When the musicians continued playing, the police waded into the crowd, physically quieting the musicians. But the mourners continued to sing, and officers ended up arresting drummer Derrick Tabb and his brother, trombonist Glen David Andrews, for disturbing the peace and parading without a permit. After negotiations between community organizations and the police, the procession continued the following night under permit.[34]

While one can be critical of the NOPD's harassment of such gatherings, it is, unfortunately, true that they have at times been sites of violent conflict. Three people were shot near the end of the January 2006 "all-star" parade discussed earlier. And a few months later, near a jazz funeral in Central City, a young evacuee who had returned from Dallas for the event was recognized and shot dead by an assailant who had tried to kill him two years earlier. Two weeks after the first shooting, NOPD superintendent Warren J. Riley had issued a memorandum announcing an increase in policing requirements for second lines and requiring that organizers be in compliance with bond requirements stipulated by Louisiana laws governing parades. The NOPD also increased the fee for second line parade permits from $1,200 to $4,445, based on the logic that additional police escorts were needed to contend with potential violence. After this, members of the SAPCTF met with NOPD representatives to work out a sliding scale, so that clubs that could not afford the new fees could continue to parade. But after the second shooting, the police rejected the sliding scale and set a standard fee for all second lines at $3,760.[35]

Eventually the American Civil Liberties Union filed a lawsuit on behalf of members of the second line community, on the grounds that these fees denied paraders the right to free expression under the First Amendment. The complaint alleged as well that Fourteenth Amendment protections had been compromised because the police escort and bonding requirements imposed on the clubs were unreasonable and excessive. It argued that these requirements threatened the very existence of the tradition. Ultimately, the ACLU was successful, and in late 2007 the NOPD settled, agreeing to return the fee level closer to the original and give the paraders an hour on the street after the parade to socialize and visit with friends and family.[36]

Debates and commentary about the fee increases provide a window onto conflicts and debates around rights to residency in the city, ownership of its culture, and use of public space in the post-Katrina period. Some have seen the increased fees as yet another hostile maneuver by municipal authorities, designed to discourage working-class or poor black residents from returning to the city and making them, in effect, disposable. As the ACLU stated in its complaint, "Many members of the clubs are working-class families. They are persons struggling to return to the city of New Orleans, dealing with the loss of family unity, the loss of homes and the loss of normalcy. The city of New Orleans, rather than encouraging their return, has instead created barriers to the resumption of an important means of expression for these returning New Orleanians." Others have made connections between the permit fees and the decision not to reopen public housing in New Orleans.[37]

The controversy over fee increases became a referendum on issues related to violence in the city and just who bears responsibility for it. The NOPD's argument in favor of the fee increases generally revolved around the assumption that the parades were lightning rods for violence and the clubs should bear the cost of increased policing. Second liners and activists, by contrast, while generally welcoming an increased police presence, claimed that the fee increase, as well as the criminalization of the community that justified the move, shifted responsibility away from the city. They argued that killings happened regularly in poor neighborhoods; violence on second lines was symptomatic of systemic problems that the police had failed to control. They pointed out that violence also happened regularly at post-Katrina Mardi Gras parades, which, though much larger, had lower fees that were protected by the city ordinance. As Tamara Jackson noted, "We cannot be responsible for what other people do. It's a hardship when you impose an astronomical fee on a self-sufficient culture. 'To protect and serve,' is the job of the police department for everybody. They're supposed to do the same job at $1,200 that they're going to do at $3,760. Violence is a citywide problem, and each club should not be responsible for problems that city has as a whole."[38]

The Kerwin James funeral incident provided the occasion for another referendum on violence and differential treatment of New Orleans populations, as well as related issues like gentrification and the city's support (or lack thereof) for neighborhood-based black cultures. Like the debate about the fee increases, such issues resonated in broader discussions about the city's future when the local and national press picked up the story and made it a hot topic in the blogosphere.

One prominent issue was the right of community members to control public space. There was disagreement among Tremé residents as to whether the mourners should have agreed to parade under permit the following night. Some argued that to do so was, in effect, giving up rights to both space and tradition. Others suggested that permitting was a means to legitimize a cultural practice and, more practically, obtain welcome protection from criminals who might show up. Beyond basic questions about residents' rights to public space and the NOPD's right to regulate it were those pertaining to whose interests were being protected when the NOPD decided to enforce or ignore official municipal regulations or unofficial implied contracts. In response to an NOPD statement that the protesters had broken the law and the city did not make exceptions to the ordinance that prohibited playing music on the street after 8 P.M., some commentators pointed out that exceptions to city ordinances were made all the time for Mardi Gras parades and other events in the tourist-friendly French Quarter. Others thought police intervention had come at the request of well-heeled new residents in the gentrifying neighborhood and noted at this post-Katrina moment, when both home prices and rental costs had risen, that newcomers' rights to lives defined on their terms were taking precedent over those of the long-time working- and lower middle-class residents of the neighborhood. This was, indeed, an ironic situation, given that the neighborhood culture, or at least a more regulated version of it, may have been part of the draw for some of the newer residents. As social aid and pleasure club official Ronald Lewis pointed out at a panel discussion three weeks later at Sound Café, "We have to contend with the invasion of the people coming into our community. . . . They say they love our culture, that's why they came here, but they lack education about it, and then they don't want it. They attack you, and then they justify it after the fact." He and Tamara Jackson also chided the police for their brutality, capriciousness, and ineffectiveness in addressing real criminal behavior.[39]

As a response to police violence and expectations of criminal violence on the second lines, the SAPCTF and some of the individual social aid and pleasure clubs now parade with an antiviolence message. By doing so, they articulate a sense that rebuilding black working-class and low-income New Orleans requires both a state commitment to reducing violence and the deflection of official rhetoric that would put responsibility solely on the community rather than on the state and broader social factors. Moreover, the prominence of Jackson and other women in the second line community, as well as their attention to domestic concerns in their social aid projects, may be seen as a gendered claim to space and rights in the face of an often unrecognized and unacknowledged form of post-Katrina violence—that is, the militarization of the city and mass displacements in the realm of public and private housing, education, and social services that have inordinately affected the lives of women as heads of household and mothers.[40]

However, this is complicated terrain for activist second liners. Prior to Katrina, the task force was known as the Second Line Cultural Tradition Task Force. After the storm, the group changed its name, according to Jackson, because "we wanted to separate from the term 'second line' because second lines have started to have a negative connotation. People when they heard 'second line' thought violence, and didn't see the true spirit of what we bring forth on a Sunday."[41] The task force's projects of cultural preservation and antiviolence, then, are enacted through distancing from a perceived community behavior, which is articulated with the kind of "politics of respectability" evident in the task force's mission statement: "Striving to raise the standards through examples: instilling dignity, respect, and reverence by way of socially acceptable presentations."

Such politics of respectability are, of course, often highly gendered. They speak of, and try to reassert, modes of masculine and feminine authority in a community seen by some as sorely in need of it. Tamara Jackson, who is also president of the VIP Ladies and Kids Social Aid and Pleasure Club, says her club looks for "family-oriented ladies" to become new members.[42] A similar approach is visible in the Black Men of Labor SAPC, which seeks to "honor the dignity of black working men" by bringing back a more traditional approach to second lining. A member of the Sudan Social Aid and Pleasure Club similarly emphasized to me that they perform only "traditional jazz" at their events. They might hire some younger brass bands, which often incorporate hip-hop and funk into their repertoire—the band at the funeral procession where our conversation took place, for example, riffed off of P-Funk's "Atomic Dog" (or perhaps it was Snoop Dogg's "Who Am I")—but they demand that the bands play a more respectable, traditional jazz at the events they sponsor.[43]

The determined activism of these second line organizations is nothing short of inspiring. They clearly counter efforts to mark their communities as disposable. Moreover, some second line organizations reject intracommunal distinction, for example, by honoring in memoriam, and sometimes even as parade kings, those who performed the "thug life" as entertainers or those who actually lived it. One such example is the Lady Buck Jumpers' honoring of slain hip-hop artist (and son of club president Linda Porter) Soulja Slim at its 2006 parade.[44] But one must still consider how some public presentations of respectable black working-class culture by second lines may enable a kind of "good Negro, bad Negro" discourse, as discussed in section 2, which allows New Orleanians of various hues to revere, develop an affinity for, and even claim a possessive investment in black musicians and black music as necessary to the city's reconstruction, but still permits an aversion to another mode of blackness (and a large, frequently displaced population) deemed transgressive, violent, parasitical, and a threat to the city's return. Although the ACLU's complaint rightly pointed out that the harassment of second line clubs may reflect a kind of official animus toward black working-class people in New Orleans, the second line clubs' responses may also contribute to a wider discourse in which the culture bearers are celebrated while other community members are made abject. Within this discourse, the musicians and social clubs are seen as necessary to the city's rebuilding. But as they seek to rebuild a working-class community, address a very real social problem (crime), engage in an important critique of the state's complicity in the rising crime rate, and at least implicitly put forth a vision of gender justice, activists must negotiate a disciplining biopolitical framework in which the second line is considered a better kind of black culture, authentically local and working class, a product of the community but not of the "ghetto."

What we see happening among members of the "traditional" second line community is both reflection and inspiration for an expanding set of intersecting, sometimes derivative cultural practices. Folklorist and journalist Nick Spitzer sees great possibility in the ways "the social aid and pleasure model has been replicated by other New Orleans institutions: Tipitina's long offered a place for old-school musicians to play, and now raises money for players in need; the Silence Is Violence campaign marches across the city to demand police and judicial attention in neighborhoods wracked by murder; 'voluntourism' groups encourage visitors to do home-building by day (social aid), and go to music clubs and restaurants by night (pleasure)."[45] As other individuals and organizations, such as SilenceIsViolence, build on the "social aid and pleasure model," they often contribute to the conversations regarding public space, violence, and social responsibility, while doing what they can to provide a life-affirming response to the biopolitical regime in post-Katrina New Orleans.

Hot 8 drummer Dinerral Shavers had certainly been doing his part to "bring the life back" to New Orleans in the year after the storm. In addition to the concerts, the second lines, the jazz funerals, and all the rest, he was raising his children and teaching music in the public schools. But his life was taken on December 28, 2006, when a teenage assailant, presumably gunning for Shavers's teenage stepson, who had called him to be picked up from a home in a hostile neighborhood, shot into the car full of family members that he was driving. According to some accounts, the conflict was at least in part a result of the stepson's recent transfer to a school in an unfamiliar neighborhood—a common occurrence for students in the fragile public education infrastructure of the post-Katrina city.

Shavers's murder provoked outrage across the city, in part because of his prominent position as a brass band member and teacher. Over a thousand mourners attended his Central City jazz funeral. But there was already anxiety about a rising homicide rate after several months of respite following the storm. As before the storm, such crimes disproportionately targeted black men under thirty. Among the factors affecting a rising crime rate in the wake of Katrina was a lack of any comprehensive strategy for assisting at-risk youth or engaging in antiviolence work. The Recovery School District was doing a reasonable job serving higher-performing students in charter schools, but more marginal students were falling through the cracks. Moreover, as may have been a factor in the Shavers killing, the practice of busing students across town because of damaged schools or the new charter status of neighborhood schools was exacerbating gang rivalries and less codified interneighborhood animus. Meanwhile, the NOPD was doing a particularly poor job of preparing solid crime reports, and the district attorney's office was having great difficulty securing indictments for these killings. According to one statistic, the office returned only about fifteen indictments for every hundred killings. Concern and outrage increased after the January 4, 2007, murder of popular filmmaker Helen Hill in an early morning attack in her Marigny home. Hill's husband, physician Paul Gailiunas, was shot three times while he cradled their toddler.[46]

SilenceIsViolence emerged in the wake of the Shavers and Hill killings, formed from a network of family members, cultural workers who knew the victims, and other concerned New Orleanians. A few days after the Hill murder, musicologist and bookstore and café owner Baty Landis, writer Ken Foster, and cellist Helen Gillet organized a community meeting at Landis's Sound Café. The site was appropriate: Hill had visited Landis's adjoining bookstore with her toddler, the Hot 8 Brass Band played at the Sound Café on Wednesday nights, and members of the group frequented the space at other times. Moreover, the space served as a generative site for brass band music. Dr. Michael White had worked there with younger musicians, and trombonist Glen David Andrews led brass band jam sessions in the space. Although there was disagreement at the meeting about whether adding more police was the solution to the crisis, there was a significant sense among participants that the city's leadership—Mayor Nagin, district attorney Eddie Jordan, and NOPD superintendent Warren Riley—had failed. A march on City Hall, led by members of the Hot 8 Brass Band, was called for January 11. Similar themes were voiced at this successful protest. When Nagin showed his face, the crowd called for his resignation. With as many as five thousand people in attendance, some called it the largest protest in the city since the civil rights movement. While the crowd at the Sound Café community meeting was largely white, the march drew widely across racial lines, in part because of the overtures organizers made to African American ministers. And music as a life-generating force in the community figured prominently in the framing of the event. In addition to the musical accompaniment to the march, there were calls for music education. And in an emotional address to the crowd, Andrews criticized thugs who brought guns to second lines as well as the police who harassed musicians. He called out Mayor Nagin for not doing more to stem the violence and positioned young people in brass bands as survivors who provided a necessary service to the city.[47]

Drawing from the sense of possibility occasioned by the event, Landis, Gillet, and Foster organized SilenceIsViolence as an ongoing campaign against violence in the city. The ranks of the organizers were augmented by Nakita Shavers, sister of the slain drummer, who also runs the Dinerral Shavers Educational Fund, founded in memory of her brother. SilenceIsViolence's mission statement, at the time of this writing, was "to call upon both citizens and public officials to achieve a safe New Orleans across all communities. We engage youth in positive expressions and actions to counter the culture of violence. We demand respect for every life, and justice for every citizen in our city."[48] Although the mass outrage that was channeled into political expression at the January 8, 2007, march and protest at City Hall has not been sustained, the group has continued to organize January events to memorialize the victims of violent crime and has been vocal in its criticisms of city officials for not doing more to address crime, all the while creating an expanding web of grassroots activities aimed at making New Orleans a safer place.[49]

Many of SilenceIsViolence's ongoing projects focus on young people and seek, through arts education in particular, to keep them out of trouble while simultaneously fostering in them a commitment to their city and to social justice (in particular, antiviolence) work. The group has established antiviolence forums in schools, called "peace clubs," in which students participate in arts workshops and antiviolence discussions. Although led by established local artists, student knowledge and analysis and peer education is also stressed. SilenceIsViolence also sponsors after-school "youth empowerment programs in the arts." Clinics in writing and visual arts encourage students to express their ideas and sentiments about violence and other issues facing their communities. The longest-running program is the weekly music clinic held at or near Sound Café, which is subsidized by some of the organizations that have emerged (or continued to work) following Katrina to support musicians and traditional local musical cultures. In these clinics, local professional musicians provide instruction in basic technique and lecture on musical traditions in New Orleans and business aspects of music. The clinics are open to young musicians of all abilities and are intended in part as an opportunity for students to decide whether to pursue more serious studies. Such pursuits are encouraged via opportunities to participate in jam sessions with professional musicians and some subsidies underwriting private lessons for those who participate regularly in the weekly clinics.[50]

The organization has also worked on an ad hoc basis with student organizations involved in their own antiviolence efforts. For example, the group lent their name and support to a March 2008 antiviolence march organized by the City Heroes student service club, which ended with a rally at City Hall, where activists made a particular effort to educate people about domestic violence and its persistence because of the unwillingness of the criminal justice system to prosecute offenders and, more generally, society's unwillingness to take it seriously.[51]

SilenceIsViolence has also made efforts to improve relations between community members and the district attorney's office and NOPD, while holding these and other agencies' feet to the fire to do more about crime in the city. The Victim Allies Project pairs victims and their families with volunteers who help them navigate the criminal justice and law enforcement bureaucracies and ensure that their cases do not fall through the cracks. At one point the organization even paid for an administrative assistant in the district attorney's office unit handling homicide cases. Evening peace walks through crime-impacted neighborhoods "are intended to nurture connections among neighborhoods, to establish a positive, anti-violence presence on our streets." When members of the NOPD join them, there is hope that trust between police officers and members of different communities can be reestablished. The group has also been among the various antiviolence organizations and bloggers seeking to get the NOPD to be more forthcoming with crime statistics and specific information about violence in different neighborhoods.[52]

SilenceIsViolence's emphasis on communal regeneration via arts education—and especially, music education—and neighborhood parading in the face of structural violence and street crime can be seen as attempts to tap into and build upon self-help and public performance traditions long established in African American neighborhoods as a means of ameliorating biopolitical exclusion. And given the enhanced knowledge about these traditions post Katrina, their invocation provides the basis for a public dialogue about the issue of violence that addresses the stakes for working-class and poor black communities rather than simply positioning them as the source of the problem.

The group has specifically joined forces with members of the second line community in promoting its message and programs. These collaborations have emphasized the role that the second line community can play in ameliorating violence. Two months after the Lundi Gras parade, the SAPCTF and SilenceIsViolence organized a second line in the Tremé, intended in part to bring people together to talk about how to address violence in the neighborhood, the challenges of rebuilding it, and the importance of maintaining cultural traditions. Like the march two months earlier, organizers hoped to dispel the idea that second lining somehow promoted violence. As Tamara Jackson put it, "in those few cases" where parades witnessed violence, "it's youngsters who are bringing their problems to our gatherings. . . . It's not the groups. We want to take this city back and protect our culture."[53] Shortly after six bystanders were shot on a Garden District street on Fat Tuesday 2009, Jackson organized in that neighborhood the first of a series of peace walks in collaboration with SilenceIsViolence. And in May 2010, in an event tragically reminiscent of the one that led to the group's formation, SilenceIsViolence teamed with the SAPCTF for a peace walk to honor twenty-two-year old brass band musician and music teacher Brandon Franklin, who was murdered in a dispute at a friend's home. The march was led by members of Jackson's VIP Ladies and Kids and New Orleans Bayou Steppers social aid and pleasure clubs along with Franklin's band members, family, and students. Members of the second and third districts of the NOPD also joined the march. The organizers "hope[d] that Brandon's violent death [would] summon the attention of our new city leaders [i.e., the Landrieu administration, which replaced Nagin's earlier in the month] to the cultural impact of the violence in our city—and the potential for culture-based responses and creative solutions."[54]

As the Franklin killing makes clear, SilenceIsViolence and the SAPCTF are fighting an uphill battle. The murder rate has remained high. Hill's murder was never solved. Shavers's alleged killer was acquitted of the crime, after a key (and young) witness was first prevented by her mother from testifying in open court and then could not identify the shooter at the subsequent retrial. The defendant was later sent to jail for a non-fatal shooting he committed just twenty-four days after being released following his acquittal in the Shavers homicide. And while antiviolence groups' dissatisfaction with district attorney Eddie Jordan may have been one factor that led to his 2007 resignation, Nagin gave the appearance of being relatively unconcerned with the issue through the remainder of his term. Meanwhile, plans for community policing and other programs designed to make officers more responsive to the concerns of particular neighborhoods have been slow to develop. And frustration with and distrust of the criminal justice and law enforcement systems remain high.

Moreover, the high crime rate continues to prevent the return of some cultural workers whose life-affirming projects might help even more in ameliorating this state of affairs. The blind New Orleans pianist Henry Butler was quoted in 2008 as saying that crime was one significant reason why he had not returned to the city: "You got to understand: I'm a blind person who if I was in the wrong area and somebody wanted to get me, it would be pretty easy for them to do it." Butler also expressed suspicion about the city's commitment to addressing crime adequately: "I don't think they're interested in controlling the crime right now. They say they are, but they're not doing much about it. That's been the case for a long time. . . . You would think if you really put a full effort into something, you could do it."[55]

We must also contend with the ways in which the goals of such grassroots organizing and the modes of mobilization can lend themselves to the biopolitical project of marking certain populations as disposable. As noted earlier, there is a way in which the privileging of culture bearers as healers and agents of reform can lead to the abjection of other members of working-class and poor black neighborhoods, given the complicated and often contradictory investments that people have in "the culture." Moreover, the focus on more effective criminal justice and law enforcement is a double-edged sword, given that the increasing militarization of policing in lower-income black communities has been incredibly disruptive and has marked its members as simultaneously invisible and threatening.

Residents of working-class and low-income African American neighborhoods have been distrustful of the NOPD because of long-standing patterns of abuse, corruption, and aggressive policing of minor offenses. Relentlessly arresting and prosecuting minor offenders in the hope that more serious crimes will be prevented is one factor in Louisiana's dubious distinction of having the highest incarceration rate in the United States. Although African Americans constitute about a third of the state's population, they make up almost three quarters of the state's prison population. High rates of incarceration have created in New Orleans a local version of a national spiral of social disruption—punishing the innocent, exposing imprisoned nonviolent participants in illicit economies to truly dangerous people, breaking apart families and communal networks, and marking people as unemployable. As Jordan Flaherty puts it, "Prison makes us all less free—by breaking up families and communities, by dehumanizing the imprisoned both during and after their sentences, by perpetuating a cycle of poverty, and by making all citizens complicit in the incarceration of their fellow human beings."[56] And at a larger structural level, in Ruth Wilson Gillmore's words, we are seeing how a "new kind of state—an antistate state—is being built on prison foundations. The antistate state depends on ideological and rhetorical dismissal of any agency or capacity that 'government' might use to guarantee social well-being."[57]

While many involved in antiviolence activism agree that a fairer and more competent system is needed, there have been disagreements among activists about whether or not the city needs an expanded police presence. Some antiviolence organizations, including some that have worked with SilenceIsViolence on issues such as developing greater citizen oversight of the NOPD and participated in its marches, have focused on prisoners' rights and developed somewhat different strategies for addressing violence within communities. Safe Streets / Strong Communities, for example, developed out of the People's Hurricane Relief Fund as an organization devoted to reconciling the agendas of groups that advocate for prisoners and those that advocate for victims. The group's original emphasis was on helping the innocent and minor offenders who were lost in the prison system during and after Katrina. They were also successful in pressuring the city to reform its public defender system—rather than its prosecutor's office—moving from one based on private contracts with freelance attorneys to one run out of an independent office with dedicated attorneys.[58]

The approaches of SilenceIsViolence and Safe Streets / Strong Communities have been contrasted as representing those of the "middle classes" and the "lower classes" respectively. One point of contention seems to have been whether the key to a safer city lies in more effective policing or in a radical reshaping of the NOPD's culture to eliminate their recent destructive presence in certain neighborhoods and the cycle of fear it perpetuates.[59] The "Community Voice" section on SilenceIsViolence's website, where users post comments, often about unsolved crimes committed against loved ones, has also been used to comment on police brutality, evidence tampering, and unfair prosecutions—all of which could be triggered by activist demands for more effective police investigations and prosecutions. And some have raised questions about the prominent representation of whites or perceived white interest in this organization, despite SilenceIsViolence's dedication to creating a multiracial movement that represents all neighborhoods in the city and emphasizes the rights of black crime victims and their families. Such a critique makes sense given that mobilization around crime and speaking out from the position of victim in many cities has been a catalyst for punitive policing and judicial projects directed toward communities of color across time and space in the United States.[60]

But whatever the problems, there still seems to be great potential here—one embedded in the life and communal affirmations of parading cultures that have been forged as ritualistic and visible responses to violence in New Orleans over the decades. Even if the contemporary focus on these practices plays into a fetishization of the culture, it also makes visible those communities deemed disposable. It defines them not as sources of crime but as human beings whose lives have become precarious not only because of poverty, joblessness, and police brutality, but because the criminal justice and law enforcement systems cannot control violent crime in their neighborhoods.

Moreover, making crime visible in these communities, rather than making criminals visible, challenges the ways in which community needs have been subordinated to those of the tourist industry, whose fundamentally unfair system of distributing resources is augmented by the practice of downplaying crime statistics to keep the tourists coming. Whatever racial inequities or power imbalances more generally may persist in the frameworks by which violence as a problem is voiced, there also seems to be potential in the sometimes messy, interracial, interclass, intergeneration, and cross-neighborhood collaborations and dialogues occurring among brass band musicians and within the mobilizations for which they provide the first line.[61] And the potential grows when such movements get covered in the press and the blogosphere, and subsequently are discussed on front porches, across dinner tables, and in barbershops. As longtime social aid and pleasure club activist Ronald Lewis put it at the January 2007 community meeting at Sound Café, remarking that an issue of long concern in New Orleans black communities was finally getting wider attention: "Everybody done woke up."[62]

Struggles over music and public space will apparently continue. Musicians, including Glen David Andrews, took to the streets in June 2010 to protest the sudden enforcement (under the new Landrieu administration this time) of the noise ordinance prohibiting music on the streets after 8 P.M., after harassment this time directed at musicians performing in Jackson Square and other tourist areas.[63] Consistent with his comments at the 2007 rally following Shavers's death, Andrews has recently linked the struggle for musicians' rights to antiviolence work via an organization called Trumpets Not Guns, whose mission is to "preserve the culture of traditional jazz and to enrich the lives of children through music, not violence, by providing musical instruments to the youth of the City of New Orleans."[64]

Leaders of the Mardi Gras Indian community called a meeting with police and city officials after police broke up a meeting of the Red Hawk Hunters and 9th Ward Hunters on Mardi Gras Day 2011. Indian representative Bernard Butler referred to the meeting as a "continuation" of the conversation at the 2005 city council where Chief Tootie Montana passed away.[65] At the time of this writing, a task force led by Councilwoman Kristin Gisleson Palmer had proposed a revision to the ordinance limiting music on the street that a member of the mayor's staff described as "more enforceable for police, and more respectful to musicians." Tensions between Mardi Gras Indians and city officials also seemed to have lessened.[66] But if history and post-Katrina demographic changes are any indication, these relationships will continue to be complicated.

Still, the public African American cultures of New Orleans, under siege as they have been by flooding, displacement, and being ripped from their neighborhood contexts, continue to aid activists in their struggle against a wide range of biopolitical projects impacting the lives of New Orleanians. A March 2009 second line organized by the Fyre Youth Squad and other local activists protested the "cradle-to-prison pipeline" in the city.[67] Tamara Jackson was one of the main organizers of a September 2009 protest (which included two brass bands) outside the Hale Boggs Federal Building that was intended to let Senator Mary Landrieu know that her constituents supported a public option in the health care legislation then being discussed by Congress. Jackson said she was inspired by the fact that many black New Orleanians—social aid and pleasure club members and local musicians, in particular—lacked access to care and were "suffering." She called particular attention to the crisis caused by the post-Katrina closing of area hospitals, including the controversial shuttering, right after the storm, of Charity Hospital, which provided two-thirds of the care for the uninsured in New Orleans, and more recently, New Orleans Adolescent Hospital, which had taken on much of the burden of mental health care following Charity's closure. Jackson also noted that residents in largely African American neighborhoods on the city's east side lacked a local hospital. Making community voices heard on this issue, she argued, followed directly from the social aid and pleasure clubs' histories as benevolent societies that assisted the sick while they simultaneously pushed for an equitable reconstruction of the city and regeneration of its cultures.[68]

Second line protests held during 2010 included a jazz funeral protesting budget cuts at the University of New Orleans, a funeral parade led by the Krewe of Dead Pelicans to benefit the Gulf Coast following the Deepwater Horizon oil spill, and two second lines on a Friday afternoon in April—the first marking an Amnesty International conference in the city and the release of their report *UN-Natural Disaster: Human Rights on the Gulf Coast*, and the second protesting the Southern Republican Leadership Conference happening the same weekend and calling for renewed support for education and health care in the face of the Republican budget-cutting and privatization agenda that has hit the city and its poorest residents so hard both before and after Katrina.[69]

Brass bands accompanied a May 1, 2011, march for workers' rights that was put together by local organizations that have been attentive to the struggles of immigrant guest workers and other laborers and have worked to build cross-racial coalitions among low-income workers, especially Latina/os and African Americans.[70] A June 17, 2011, second line and community forum led by Women with a Vision, a local grassroots African American collective working on health and social justice issues for marginalized women and their communities, marked the fortieth anniversary of Nixon's declaration of a "war on drugs," sought to raise awareness about the failures of subsequent government policies to stem drug use and their devastating effects on low-income communities, and symbolically called for an end to the war by marking its death with a jazz funeral.[71]

Again, one can argue that expansion of the use of parading in New Orleans after the storm contributes to the dissolution of traditional second line musical and dance practices and to the diffusion of the African American community's control of such practices.[72] One might even suggest this could lead to obviation of long-standing second line activists themselves by rendering their activities unnecessary as other constituencies find their voices. But these nontraditional second line events are also clearly spaces of improvised collaboration, as musicians, activists of various inclinations, and those who spontaneously join the second line join forces to share ideas and sentiments. And as public interventions, they open up space for communal and sometimes national reflection, through which the issue of biopolitical exclusion and possible resolutions of the problem are thought about seriously. In other words, they create venues where what Dinneral Shavers described as the mission to "bring the life back" to the city can be embraced.

SILENCEISVIOLENCE MUSIC CLINIC, MARIGNY, 2010

AIR GUITAR OUTSIDE BLUES CLUB, FRENCH QUARTER, 1994

# 4

# RECONSTRUCTION'S SOUNDTRACK

We memorialize disaster quickly, if not always deeply, in our mass-mediated world. And in the years after Irish rocker Bob Geldof and the supergroup Band Aid's 1984 Ethiopian famine relief single, "Do They Know It's Christmas?," our expectations of musicians to raise awareness of and help the victims of catastrophe have been high. There is, of course, a centuries-old history of folk music and more formal musical expressions commenting on the injustices of the world and longing for a better one. Moreover, musicians have successfully fused protest and popularity throughout the twentieth century. There are early antecedents like Joe Hill's "The Preacher and the Slave," Lead Belly's "The Bourgeois Blues," Billie Holiday's rendition of Abel Meeropol's "Strange Fruit," and Woody Guthrie's "This Land Is Your Land." Benefits and protest songs in jazz, rock, soul, reggae, and other genres increased in frequency and impact with the social movements of the second half of the twentieth century. Yet Geldof's project ushered in a particularly collaborative and commercially successful form of "charity" records and performances, as well as cultivating a market and an audience that expected musicians to respond to all manner of crises.[1]

Band Aid's single was followed in 1985 by the American famine relief single "We Are the World," performed by another collaborative supergroup, USA for Africa; the simultaneous Live Aid concerts in London and Philadelphia, which were broadcast globally; and the first of the still ongoing Farm Aid concerts, designed to raise money for and bring awareness to the plight of small family farmers in the United States. More radical statements included the "Sun City" concert and album, and Nelson Mandela tribute concerts challenging South African apartheid. More recently we have witnessed benefit concerts in the wake of the Asian tsunami of 2004 ("Tsunami Aid: A Concert for Hope") and the 2010 Haitian earthquake ("Hope for Haiti Now") as well as a host of CD and music releases and music downloads that sought to raise funds for the victims of these tragedies.

Many of these concerts and benefit recordings were, as Susan Fast suggests, "staged as an intervention, in response to government doing little or nothing about humanitarian or political crises." Yet tributes and benefits have also served to consolidate rather than challenge power. Such was the case with post-9/11 events such as "America: A Tribute to Heroes" and the "Concert for New York," which served an important healing function at a moment of profound tragedy but also helped to legitimize a sense of American righteousness (and Anglo-American righteousness, given the proliferation of British acts at the latter) and perhaps even "compassionate" imperial power in the run-up to the retributive wars that followed.[2]

With marketability and popularity have come questions of efficacy and audience. Artists producing and participating in mega events have been accused of simplifying or even depoliticizing issues—not to mention making bad music—in their efforts to appeal to the compassion of a large audience of potential donors.[3] Yet we can also acknowledge—particularly when politically savvy musicians supplement what they sing or play on record with comments in interviews, stage performances, lectures, and liner notes—a powerful pedagogical and political function in tributes and benefits, particularly when they come out of collaborations among artists. And sometimes good music is part of the package.[4]

The array of recorded and live post-Katrina benefits, tributes, and incantations has been vast, in terms of quantity and content. And the recordings, at least, keep coming. Some of the music is not very good, but some of it is breathtaking. Either way, there is great value in taking the time to listen to it. Building on the work of people who have characterized musical performance in Katrina's aftermath as a kind of "soundtrack" of disaster and displacement, I suggest in this section that the complex, multifaceted array of poststorm performances has addressed and made audible the initial experiences of Katrina victims, while putting them into broader historical and spatial frames.[5] I also point to ways in which these recordings have mapped the regeneration of the city, demographically, culturally, and politically, over the past several years, for better and for worse. I explore as well how such recordings, as part of broader economy of charity music, have intervened in national conversations about New Orleans's plight. The soundtrack has accompanied, fundamentally comprised, and sometimes opposed narratives about the city that emerged post Katrina. With displaced and eventually returned musicians playing key roles in shaping the soundtrack, these recordings made audible and sometimes helped constitute local and national communities bound by affinities to New Orleans. While some of this attraction has been predicated on a rather simplistic politics of outrage or an elitist noblesse oblige, we can also hear in these recordings more radical horizons of political and social possibilities forged out of collaboration.[6]

I begin by surveying the terrain of post-Katrina tributes, benefits, and incantations, building on work that has characterized some of them as responses to the positioning of Katrina victims as refugees. I next look at some of the early collaborative musical responses by local musicians and outsiders, showcasing the possibilities of symbolically forging a renewed community and nation via post-Katrina recordings. I focus first on the New Orleans Social Club's *Sing Me Back Home* and the Dirty Dozen Brass Band's remake of Marvin Gaye's *What's Going On*. After a brief look at underground hip-hop videos produced by the local collective 2-Cent, I conclude by looking at the Preservation Hall Jazz Band's 2010 album *Preservation* and its collaboration that same year with rapper Mos Def and other musicians on the single "It Ain't My Fault," which drew attention to the effects of the Deepwater Horizon oil spill that spring and raised money to help in the cleanup. I argue that these 2010 performances map the reconstruction of the city five years after the storm while offering valuable portrayals of New Orleans's worldliness post Katrina, its place in people's imaginations as a site of possibility.

With its prominence as a musical city, and with musicians and their neighborhoods visibly among the victims of the storm and levee breaks, musical invocations of New Orleans and benefits for its residents proliferated quickly. First were the high-profile televised benefits held outside of the city which featured international music stars and prominent New Orleanians. These included "A Concert for Hurricane Relief" on September 2, "Shelter from the Storm: A Concert for the Gulf Coast" on September 9, and Lincoln Center's September 17 "Higher Ground Hurricane Relief Benefit Concert." Each of these events raised money in real time and via subsequent CD or DVD releases. These concert reproductions were quickly followed by a plethora of singles and albums seeking to raise money for Katrina victims, commenting on the tragedy in humanitarian or political terms, or both. Some releases were recorded by individual musicians or groups, either from New Orleans or elsewhere. Others were compilations that brought together outsiders or local musicians, or both together. Some artists framed individual albums entirely or almost entirely as tributes to New Orleans or benefits for the city, while other efforts contained just a song or two that spoke of the disaster. Some post-Katrina music was actually recorded prior to August 29, 2005, but took on new meaning in the postdiluvian period, while other expressions were intended as responses to Katrina from the moment they were imagined, composed, or selected for recording.

Artists across genres—R&B, jazz, indie rock, country, classical, hip-hop, folk, pop, electronica, punk, gospel, you name it—created this music, including the famous and not-so-famous. Equally diverse were the organizations for which funds were raised: these organizations addressed everything from immediate shelter for victims to the restoration of the wetlands to the rebuilding of housing to human rights issues. An extraordinary number raised money for organizations—such as the Tipitina's Foundation, Musicians' Village, Music Rising, the Grammy Foundation's MusiCares initiative, the New Orleans Musicians' Clinic, and Sweet Home New Orleans—dedicated to assisting New Orleans musicians who lost instruments, gigs, and homes, or who were otherwise affected by the storm.

Musician-centered musical charity work followed the assumption that sustaining and reviving the local music scene would assist in the reconstruction of the city. Outside interest in a culture that Katrina made visible was one factor, but more important was local knowledge of the life-affirming function of New Orleans' various musical practices. After collectively witnessing the tragedy and injustice of Katrina, people across communities looked to musicians for redemption. Ultimately, concern for the city and its future was displaced onto musicians as victims and saviors, which in turn created demand and enthusiasm for New Orleans music. It is no small irony that Katrina opened up space for collaborations and a growing worldliness and sense of possibility among local players, helping to energize careers that had been relatively moribund.[7] And some local musicians were inspired—Dr. John's 2008 album, *City That Care Forgot,* is one example—to bring a previously submerged political edge to their music.

Recordings by outsiders and local musicians that commented on, rather than simply raising money for, Katrina-related issues voiced a diverse range of concerns. Some artists addressed the human tragedy of the event or the resilience of the people of the city. Others expressed solidarity with the people of New Orleans. Some spoke directly about the injustices of Katrina, while others situated that event within longer histories of racism, poverty, government neglect and incompetence, militarization, environmental degradation, and the oil extraction economy. And in a post-Katrina context in which some human beings were deemed disposable, even music without explicit social or political commentary but which conveyed a life-affirming message may be read as radical.

Although placing this music in its post-2005 context is critical for understanding its meaning, we should be attentive to the ways meanings from the past have been embedded in some of these recent recordings. This is perhaps most obvious in covers and in the sampling of older recordings. In such cases, meaning is informed by the identities of the songwriters and others who have recorded them, the genres out of which they came or to which they were transported, and the historical moments and geographical spaces in which they are seen to have originated. The past is also invoked in the lyrics' descriptions of historical events and in the sounds of instrumentation, musicianship, recording technology, and genre. In other words, we hear in post-Katrina recordings the civil rights movement, the anti-Vietnam War movement, and the Popular Front as moments of political possibility; Congo Square, Detroit, and Nashville as sites of cultural generation; and the utopian aspirations of artists such as Woody Guthrie, Bob Marley, and Curtis Mayfield. Although sonic repetition can produce a rather apathetic nostalgia, it can also politicize by invoking shared experience. And sometimes the two can coexist.[8]

Many early examples of Katrina-responsive music raised questions about the displacement and citizenship status of New Orleanians. Some have argued that post-Katrina musical statements responded directly to the often heated national and international discourse around the supposed "refugee status" of displaced New Orleanians.

Like refugees fleeing disasters or wars elsewhere, many victims of the levee breaks left their homes with little, if anything, more than the clothes on their backs. And government inaction during the crisis did, in a sense, render them at least temporarily stateless, like refugees in other parts of the world. As media commentators used the term *refugee* (and pondered whether or not it was useful) when describing displaced New Orleanians, a debate ensued about its appropriateness. Many displaced residents thought it was disrespectful and served to strip them, at least symbolically, of their rights and status as U.S. citizens. Some argued then and later that describing displaced Katrina survivors as "refugees" put into a natural order of things the social inequalities exposed by the storm, defining poor (and particularly poor black) New Orleanians as an economic drain on society. Others maintained that positioning New Orleanians as refugees made the event "exceptional," an aberration, which in turn helped absolve the powerful of responsibility for conditions they had helped to create. Such implications were framed by a national media that assumed a generally white and middle-class viewing and listening public and that positioned as outside that public the very visible poor black victims in this story. Some of this was done via the hysteria around black criminality discussed in previous sections, but even sympathetic representations of suffering and neglect often depicted the population as voiceless victims, beyond the pale of participatory citizenship. It also seemed to make their displacement permanent, which was not surprising given the explicitly stated desire of politicians, members of the business elite, and everyday citizens to make New Orleans after the storm smaller, wealthier, and whiter.[9]

Consequently, as Adeline Masquelier argues, rejecting the term *refugee* was a means of "reclaiming one's rightful place in the national order of things" by asserting a connection to and history in New Orleans or the Gulf Coast and a broader claim to U.S. citizenship. But Masquelier still suggests there is some critical potential in embracing the persona of the "refugee," even though it appears that most black New Orleanians rejected that label, as a means of calling out the failures and misdeeds of the powerful. She quotes Melaku Kifle of the All-African Council of Churches, who asserted, "It is the refugee . . . who reveals to us the defective society in which we live. He is a kind of mirror through whose suffering we can see the injustice, the oppression and maltreatment of the powerless by the powerful."[10]

Some scholars have pointed out that early post-Katrina musical performances helped turn a depoliticized and carefully managed scene of mourning into a crucial lesson on history and politics. Such performances redefined Katrina victims (albeit often implicitly) as wronged citizens and actors within a diasporic experience rather than positioning them simply as suffering refugees.

Paige McGinley, for example, sees an "alternative soundtrack" composed of sources as disparate as local folklorist and NPR personality Nick Spitzer's repeated playing of

Randy Newman's "Louisiana 1927" on his *American Routes* radio show and rapper/producer Kanye West's performance of "Jesus Walks" at the "Shelter from the Storm" concert, held a week after he made his controversial remark about George W. Bush not "car[ing] about black people" during "A Concert for Hurricane Relief." Rather than simply mourning the disappearance of the city and its residents in a way that emphasized "moving on" from a "natural" disaster, such musical texts focused on the more active process of displacement. Although West withheld further comment on the Bush administration in his second concert appearance, he still managed to voice a critique, as he transformed lyrics originally criticizing representations of race and sex in hip-hop so that the song (and the video images of Katrina victims and black soldiers projected behind him) spoke to militarism's high cost for people of color. Meanwhile, Spitzer's repeated programming of Newman's song about a previous series of levee breaks that decimated poor communities in Louisiana and Mississippi put the present tragedy in a historical continuum of government neglect, thus refusing interpretations of Katrina as exceptional.[11]

Daphne Brooks, meanwhile, reads Mary J. Blige's partially out-of-tune duet with Bono and U2 on their hit song "One" at the "Shelter from the Storm" benefit concert as a kind of irruptive performance that provided an affirmative statement of black female presence in the face of a web of media representations that focused on black female suffering post Katrina but marked that presence as shameful and strangely silent. In the context of the benefit concert, this song became a "soundtrack" for Gulf Coast black women, enabling them to have some say, even if by proxy, in the web of post-Katrina representation. And this worked not only because of Blige's dissonant/dissident voice, but because her well-established image as a "survivor" shaped the rearticulation of "One" in performance. Blige "channels" that persona, Brooks argues, "into an interventionist anthem that champions the preservation of difference and specificity as a fecund site for coalition building: 'We're one but we're not the same / We get to carry each other / Carry each other.' Blige here rejects 'crawling' in the temple of love, the temple of democracy, demanding instead recognition of her worth as a citizen in this 'contract with America.'"[12]

Zenia Kish's analysis of local hip-hop artists' responses to Katrina takes things a step further by demonstrating the specific challenges artists offered up in the face of the "refugee" discourse and by suggesting that certain musicians even took on the refugee persona as a critical positionality. Local bounce artists Mia X, in her song "My FEMA People," and 5th Ward Weebie, in "Fuck Katrina (The Katrina Song)," described a decimated city from the position of the displaced, linking previous "socioeconomic disasters" with that wrought by Katrina. Mia X described the city as a war zone like "Beirut [and] Iraq," and both artists commented on the profound failure of government and aid organizations in responding to the needs of the black and the poor in the city. Recordings like these, sometimes improvised in front of audiences full of fellow displaced New Orleanians, affirmed the city as a culturally important node in a new diaspora experience that was part of a longer one. Meanwhile, Master P and the 504 Boyz' benefit compilation CD, *Hurricane Katrina: We Gon' Bounce Back,* marked a hopeful collective commitment to the renewal of the city, in which hip-hop and their communities would take part.[13]

Kish also examines how national figures brought the refugee critique into the larger media frame and came at it from differing perspectives. Papoose's "Mother Nature" directly refutes the "refugee label" by pointing out that many of the displaced were home-owning citizens and not the unproductive members of society described by some in the media. K-Otix's online release "George Bush Doesn't Care about Black People," which remixed Kanye West's "Gold Digger" and referenced his controversial statement, implicitly imbued the refugee with critical potential in speaking from the persona of the displaced and directly about government neglect. Mos Def's "Dollar Day (Katrina Klap)" and Chuck D's "Hell No (We Ain't Alright)" compared New Orleanians to "refugees" from other places by situating them in a global system of poverty that breaks down along racial lines and noting the misplaced priorities of a government devoting resources to fight foreign wars instead of using them to ensure the safety of its own people. Kish also notes that this work called for the return of New Orleans residents and renewal of the city's political system.[14]

Building from such accounts, I am interested in exploring the forging of renewed community and nation via post-Katrina recorded collaborations among New Orleans musicians and between them and outsiders. Many of these were recorded in part or in whole while participants were displaced from their homes. They may be seen, like some of the singles discussed above, as attempts to narrate the experience of exile and displacement in ways that intervene in the refugee discourse. They also speak forcefully of a future homecoming to and renewal of New Orleans. Yet, as collaborative ventures, they do something more. By means of personnel, instrumentation, and musical content, they explore the challenges facing New Orleans in relation to previous struggles. They also begin to map emergent networks of artists from inside and outside the city, which themselves symbolize broader patterns of social and political communion.

One early example is *Sing Me Back Home,* a project recorded over the course of a week in Austin, Texas, in early October 2005, at the instigation of producer Leo Sacks. Billing themselves as the New Orleans Social Club, a core group of displaced New Orleans musicians—Henry Butler, Cyril Neville, Leo Nocentelli, George Porter Jr., and Raymond Weber—living in exile in Austin and elsewhere chose and arranged most of the material and brought in other prominent New Orleans musicians to join them on individual tracks.

Like some of the songs mentioned above, *Sing Me Back Home* is a performance of being displaced as well as a refusal of the refugee discourse in the immediate aftermath of the storm and levee breaks. This is accomplished directly by the album's title, which refuses the idea that there is not a home to go back to, and by several songs that speak directly or implicitly of a return to New Orleans and a renewal of the city. These include

Dr. John's version of Dave Bartholomew's "Walking to New Orleans," Troy (Trombone Shorty) Andrews's "Hey Troy, Your Mama's Calling You," Henry Butler's version of Stephen Sondheim and Leonard Bernstein's "Somewhere," and the group's version of the Meters' "Loving You Is on My Mind," in which the city replaces the human object of affection.

The album also lingers on band members' status as displaced persons, defining that positionality as critical. The name of the group—the New Orleans Social Club—connects them to the history of social aid and pleasure clubs from the city, which for over a century have addressed the needs of working-class communities. Sacks insists that the musicians are "musical healers, and from this diaspora of musical genius they came together to heal themselves."[15] Their name also situates their experience—via an implied connection to the Cuban group, the Buena Vista Social Club—as broadly diasporic, albeit with the previous site of displacement now serving as the symbolic site of return.

The performance of displacement also challenges refugee discourse in explicitly political terms. Cyril Neville's remake of Curtis Mayfield's 1968 recording "This Is My Country" claims a right to black citizenship grounded in a history of labor expended (especially under slavery) and rights-oriented protest that forced the nation to (at least partially) live up to its principles. The message is brought home both by the lyrics, which quote the U.S. Constitution, and through the iterative process of covering an original produced during the black freedom movement. In an interview, Leo Nocentelli states that this song was intended to counter the way "some people say we don't have the right to say it's my country" and to mark their agenda as one of civil rights, because "most of the people who got hurt down there were people of color."[16] Neville explicitly raises the question of economic rights in the post-Katrina context: "Those words from Curtis could have been written yesterday. . . . Maybe now we can start a dialogue on the imbalance of economic power in this country."[17]

Big Chief Joseph (Monk) Boudreaux's original "Chase," meanwhile, comments specifically on the displacement and gentrification that many in New Orleans's black community anticipated would define the rebuilding of the city. His lyrics make an argument similar to Mayfield's, defining citizenship status through contribution and transforming the larger frame of civil rights to one of a "right to the city" as he laments being chased away from his "old home town" that his father "helped to build."[18] And with its reggae beat and arrangement, "Chase" further situates black New Orleanians' experiences within a larger New World diaspora.

Some of the love songs from the 1960s on *Sing Me Back Home* evoke diaspora in a somewhat different way, as they carry the listener back temporally to a more mundane soundscape of the black freedom struggle. These include Irma Thomas and Marcia Ball's version of "Look Up" by Allen Toussaint (under the pseudonym Naomi Neville); the subdudes' version of Earl King's "Make a Better World"; and Willie Tee's version of his own "First Taste of Hurt." Such songs, recorded in a new context, express the wide range of sentiments—despair, longing, injury, hope, loneliness, perseverance, and solidarity—experienced by displaced New Orleanians. They also speak of the emotional experience of migration and displacement and about the work intangible affects like hope and self-possession accomplish historically as a means of survival.[19] Tapping into a previous generation's soundtrack provides, to evoke Albert Murray, "esthetic equipment for living" in the present.[20]

Another important first-year release was the Dirty Dozen Brass Band's remake of Marvin Gaye's 1971 politically conscious soul suite, *What's Going On*. Formed in the late 1970s, with roots in Danny Barker's Fairview Baptist Church Marching Band, the Dirty Dozen has been one of New Orleans's most prominent brass bands and a key player in the genre's post-1980 revival. The band has defined itself through its fusion of traditional brass band music and other jazz and nonjazz styles, having recorded and toured with artists such as Dizzy Gillespie, Norah Jones, Elvis Costello, David Bowie, the Black Crowes, and Modest Mouse.

Gaye's wide-ranging repertoire, his exploration of moods, and the complexity of his music had long appealed to Dirty Dozen members, especially trumpeter and flügel-hornist Efrem Towns, who had referenced him in rehearsals for decades. The band had tentative plans to remake Gaye's album before the storm. The experience of being exiled and witnessing the devastation and neglect in New Orleans—several band members lost homes—inspired the group to finalize their arrangements of *What's Going On* and record it in Los Angeles and Austin. The album was released on Katrina's one-year anniversary. It was, as noted in the liner notes, a "tribute to the people and the city of New Orleans, Louisiana; may our spirit survive through our irreplaceable culture." The group hoped to rebuild that culture by donating part of the proceeds to Tipitina's Foundation, which has worked before and after Katrina to support musicians and music education in Louisiana.[21]

The album was also, per the liner notes, "a plea for common sense, decency and cooperation." Gaye's album certainly provided an appropriate vehicle for invoking such themes. Composed over several years, the songs on *What's Going On* marked a critical moment in Gaye's personal and professional life. Gaye had been depressed following the illness and eventual death of collaborator and friend Tami Terrell, as well as the dissolution of his marriage. He had also been questioning his own status as a pop icon churning out hits for Berry Gordy's Motown assembly line. Like many of his contemporaries, he was searching for social relevance. He was inspired by the social movements of the era and the free-thinking and antiestablishment attitudes of members of the counterculture. As Gaye put it, "In 1969 or 1970, I began to re-evaluate my whole concept of what I wanted my music to say. I was very much affected by letters my brother was sending me from Vietnam, as well as the social situation here at home. I realized that I had to put my own fantasies behind me if I wanted to write songs that would reach the souls of people. I wanted them to take a look at what was happening in the world." So Gaye took time out from performing, shed his clean-cut image by growing a beard, and put together an extraordinary album.[22]

*What's Going On* has been called the first soul concept album, both in terms of lyrical content and the sound of the music itself. Gaye insisted on breaking from Motown's typical division of labor among songwriter, arranger, producer, and singer. Although he wrote only one track alone—"Mercy Mercy Me"—the album's overall concept was his, and he had a hand in composing or producing all its songs. *What's Going On* is both a deeply personal examination of Gaye's own spirituality and a powerful commentary on a range of issues facing black urbanites and the broader sweep of humanity. With Gaye's brother Frankie as the "main character," it addresses the human and other costs of foreign wars, drug abuse, poverty and joblessness, political corruption, environmental destruction, and the possibility of nuclear war—in other words, issues that defined the politics of the moment and which continue to haunt us. Yet *What's Going On* also leaves the listener with hope that such problems may be overcome through the work of the heart and the spirit of cooperation among human beings. Helping define the album's cohesiveness is a distinctive sound enabled by arrangements that fuse elements of funk, soul, gospel, jazz, and classical, with thick orchestrations balanced with elements of instrumental and vocal improvisation. The transitions between songs are also fairly seamless.[23]

Also relevant to the album's continued resonance as one of the key musical statements of the black freedom movement era is the way it opened up the possibility of more politically relevant roles for established black musicians. It also showed a broader public that soul music could provide a vehicle for articulating the shared aspirations of community activists. As Suzanne Smith notes, despite Gordy's initial discomfort with Gaye's content, the album showed Motown that politically oriented music by big stars could sell and encouraged the company to support artists moving into politically active roles. For example, Gladys Knight and the Pips, the Temptations, and Gaye were among the Motown recording stars who participated in Jesse Jackson's first Operation PUSH (People United to Save Humanity) Expo in 1972, which used as its theme the title of the song "Save the Children" from *What's Going On*.[24]

With this history as a backdrop, the Dirty Dozen Brass Band reinterprets and transforms the album while retaining aspects of its original message. As band member Keith Harris puts it, "Our interpretation was different from Marvin's, but the feeling is still there. The concept is still there. The message."[25] Continuity and transformation are created by adhering to Gaye's (and the band's) ethos of blending musical styles but adding new elements to the mix through the band's arrangements and guest musicians from different genres. They use Gaye's lyrics but also transform them, adding new sung and spoken elements. And at times the band replaces lyrics with its own horn arrangements. Through such practices, the Dirty Dozen's *What's Going On* invokes a history of displacement, representing problems from the past that remain with us in a shifting present. Their album also speaks of a political possibility rooted in the black freedom movement of the sixties and seventies, when Gaye's album was produced, and in Gaye's own social commitment and spiritual purpose.

The band recruits hip-hop artists to perform on the title track, "Mercy Mercy Me," and "Inner City Blues," the three most politically explicit songs from the original, which were also successful singles. This move helps situate Gaye's album as a political statement that is both timeless, through its incorporation into a brass band tradition, and relevant to the present, through rap performance. The title track begins with a sample of Mayor Ray Nagin's expletive-filled plea to the federal government to show leadership and devote resources to the post-storm crisis, thus framing "what's going on" in New Orleans as not simply the result of national disaster but part of a larger crisis of misplaced government priorities. Gaye's vocal lines on the piece are performed by the horns, but Public Enemy's Chuck D provides rhymes that build from his own "Hell No (We Ain't Alright)." He characterizes the crisis that followed the levee break as a result of global militarism, while identifying the critical potential of an informed citizenry once it recognizes the government's hypocritical perpetuation of inequality in the aftermath of Katrina. But he also chastises a political community that limits itself through its parochialism and self-destructive actions. Chuck D laments racism in the media, Americans' parochial understandings of the world, and members of poor communities buying into a "no-snitch" ethos that mobilizes community solidarity but ultimately serves the interests of predatory criminal enterprises in their neighborhoods. Being better educated is the way forward. The song's refrain makes explicit the implied question as answer in the song title: "What's going on, and that's going on."

G Love raps the lyrics of "Mercy Mercy Me" more or less as written, situating Katrina as an environmental disaster and anticipating the broader context of critique and analysis that would incorporate the Deepwater Horizon oil spill. Guru's rhymed lyrics for "Inner City Blues" transform Gaye's description of a righteous urban dweller struggling against crime, police brutality, and economic deprivation into a description of someone who admittedly lived the hustler life and is now searching for balance and self-respect. While this could be read as a conservative (or neoliberal) embrace of personal responsibility as the solution to difficult social problems, in the context of the album and its political critique, this song provides an important and explicitly articulated distillation of the personal political commitment that Gaye brought to *What's Going On*. It puts responsibility and power to define New Orleans's future, "the moment when the tables will turn," in the hands of its residents, whatever their faults have been.

For "What's Happening Brother," the Dirty Dozen add veteran vocalist Bettye LaVette, a Michigan native raised in Detroit, who was a teenage sensation in the sixties and had an off-and-on-again career in the decades that followed before hitting it big again in the twenty-first century. This song tells the first-person story of Gaye's brother Frankie's homecoming from Vietnam in 1966. Frankie declares, "War is hell" and longs for its end and the moment when "people start getting together again," before narrating a difficult transition reentering society and finding a job in a tight economy.[26] But beyond prosaic financial concerns, there is a deeper sense of uncertainty about the direction in which culture and society are moving "across this land."

As a post-Katrina performance with backing from a New Orleans brass band, "What's Happening Brother" shifts the temporal and spatial context. This is no longer a story about an already realized return from fighting a war but rather an only partially realized return from a displacement caused, in part, by a government that has prioritized foreign wars over domestic infrastructure (among other things) and is unable or unwilling to mobilize people and equipment committed elsewhere to serve people on the Gulf Coast. The uncertainty is partly about the future of New Orleans but also about the society that allowed Katrina to happen.

As a female singer, LaVette asks us to consider the effects of militarization on both men and women. Today, women increasingly participate in the military as noncombat personnel and as soldiers too, as jobs and forms of public assistance disappear. Women—especially women of color—bear the costs of an increasingly militarized society in the twenty-first century: expectations of more restrictive, patriotic gender roles, increased surveillance and incarceration, racial and gender inequalities in employment, and cuts to social spending that make providing and caring for children more difficult. As she repeats the title phrase, "What's happening brother," through the song, while never uttering Gaye's perhaps more gender-exclusive line "What's happening, my man," she speaks of a shared, if not synonymous, experience between men and women under twenty-first-century conditions of militarized deprivation and uncertainty. As the feminist organization INCITE! has argued, the "militarized response [to Katrina] is another piece of a racist pattern of dehumanizing poor people of color," with particular costs for women.[27]

Yet the meaning here still depends on the context of the original. LaVette, a veteran soul singer, invokes the black urban North of the 1960s. One of the interesting moves LaVette makes in her interpretation is to change the question posed by the original lyric about the chances of the local "ball club win[ning] the pennant" to specifically reference the Detroit Tigers' chances of doing so. By explicitly invoking the place of her upbringing, LaVette points to the ways that being positioned by an unequal, militarized economy today is part of a longer history that played out differently in other times and spaces. Ditto for the uncertainty about the future of society. Yet there is hope, too, in this song as performed post Katrina. Detroit circa 1970 was experiencing profound social costs related to the militarization, poverty, suburbanization, and deindustrialization that continue to define it, but one can also look back to that time and place as being defined by the possibilities in activism—in music, in the labor movement, and in ethnic mobilizations. Again, performing Gaye's music thirty-five years later connects New Orleanians to a history of urban displacement and to a diaspora of hope forged in the struggle to rebuild at this moment, energized by the knowledge of previous struggles.[28]

It is "Wholly Holy," rearranged as an instrumental number, that speaks most directly of a future-oriented hope grounded in New Orleans cultural practice. Gaye's original is a slow piece, dominated by lush string textures, above which he centers Jesus Christ and the Bible as the connective tissue that allows a community bound by spirit to "conquer hate" and "holler love across the nation." The Dirty Dozen Brass Band performs the song as a funeral march, and they do it without lyrics. Even though the tempo remains slow throughout—there is no up-tempo release at the end—the feeling is joyous. Like the traditional jazz funeral, the band bridges the worlds of living and dead, carrying the spirits of Katrina's victims into a plan for the city's future. More so than in Gaye's original, forging a national feeling of community is both a sacred and a secular project. It suggests that a commitment to New Orleans, at least as much as to the Bible, is the mechanism for forging a broad, humanistic vision.

Although more recent collaborative ventures continue to voice perspective on such political issues as gentrification, militarization, and government neglect, some also energize political and creative community by musically invoking generative possibilities across time and space. They speak of New Orleans as an emergent site of cultural, social, and political possibility not simply for itself but for the nation and the constituents of the various diasporas of which it is increasingly a part. They also begin to map the city's piecemeal and contradictory recovery.

One of the important collective arts organizations active during the post-Katrina period has been 2-Cent, a collective of twenty-something New Orleanians who came together in 2004 and have since tried to position themselves as a group "that truly speaks for the young generation by educating and entertaining at the same time." Producing a web-based television program and music videos and engaging in community work such as digital media workshops and self-empowerment programs in public schools, the group has attempted to "look at the issues Katrina exposed." Their videos have both mapped the recovery over the past several years and provided critical commentary on it. Their "Freedom Land Project," a song and video bringing together a number of conscious hip-hop artists from the city, speaks of issues including police brutality and militarization, government neglect on fronts like public education, and unemployment. Referencing a history of African American struggle through a sample of the freedom song "Ain't Gonna Let Nobody Turn Me 'Round," archival video clips, and rhymed references to Malcolm, Martin, and the Black Panther Party, it imagines a new future for the city defined through a resurgent black freedom struggle and participation in the electoral process. Their short video, "New Orleans for Sale," comments on disaster tourism, noting the irony that money is being spent on witnessing devastation rather than rebuilding the city. "Project NO," with rapper Dee-1, describes the slow pace of recovery three years after the storm while arguing that the "new optimism" of young artists and their fans can sustain reconstruction.[29]

An above-ground performance of recovery is the Preservation Hall Jazz Band's 2010 album *Preservation,* designed as a celebration of New Orleans music and a benefit for Preservation Hall and its outreach and education programs. The band performs with nineteen different vocalists associated with folk, rock, country, pop, Afropop, and various hybrid idioms, one gospel vocal group (Blind Boys of Alabama), and one decades-old recording of a jazz vocalist (Louis Armstrong singing "Rockin' Chair"). In addition to representing a diversity of styles, the guest artists display a range of generations—from indie folk rockers in their twenties to ninety-year-old Pete Seeger—and include many known primarily for their songwriting or vocal chops and others—Seeger, his grandson Tao Rodriguez Seeger, Ani DiFranco, Richie Havens, Steve Earle, Angelique Kidjo, and Tom Waits—whose artistic reputations are inextricable from their social activism. Although publicity for the project defines the performed songs as part of a "classic New Orleans repertoire," it may also be read as a kind of survey of the American songbook. We hear two Mardi Gras Indian songs—"Tootie Ma Is a Big Fine Thing" and "Corinne Died on the Battlefield"[30]—but also heavy representation of blues and Tin Pan Alley songs from decades from 1910 to 1940 that have been seamlessly incorporated into traditional jazz and brass band repertoires. We also hear several religious, torch, and folk songs, including the civil rights anthem, "We Shall Overcome," which Seeger helped popularize.[31]

Preservation Hall and its musical band were established in 1961 by Allan and Sandra Jaffe, "as a sanctuary, to protect and honor New Orleans Jazz which had lost much of its popularity to modern jazz and rock n roll."[32] Preservation Hall played a critical role in the resurgence of traditional jazz in New Orleans in the 1960s. Although the band's recordings have been sporadic, it has toured extensively, recorded on others' releases, and performed regularly at the hall—which is a key node in the New Orleans musical tourist economy. Although the emphasis has remained on "tradition" and "authenticity," the band's vision has become more eclectic, cross-generational, and multigeneric over the past two decades under creative director Ben Jaffe (Allan and Sandra's son), a tuba player trained at the Oberlin Conservatory of Music, who took over the institution in 1993 and incorporated rock-and-roll tunes into a repertoire defined by standards such as "I'll Fly Away" and "When the Saints Go Marching In." Tradition became something to honor but also to complicate, as well as a means of surviving financially, culturally, and spiritually. As Jaffe put it, "Protecting one's heritage is a risky and challenging task. How does one breathe new life into a 100 plus year old musical tradition? Is the music we create today relevant? How does one perpetuate a tradition? Allow it to blossom? Maintain the integrity of the past?"[33]

Although the concept for *Preservation* originated with Preservation Hall's record distributor, Jaffe took over its development. On one level, the album continued the band's practice of participating in benefit recordings and concerts for the rebuilding of New Orleans and the protection and preservation of its culture, which began immediately after Katrina. Yet Jaffe sought to define it as something other than "a Katrina project." "I really felt that it was time for us to address something that is fragile and intangible and undocumented and that's a lot of our musical traditions, and parade traditions, and dancing traditions." So Jaffe came up with a wish list of musicians who would come to New Orleans to perform with the Preservation Hall Jazz Band and received an overwhelming response from those concerned about the future of the city and its cultural resources. Participants were educated about local history (including that of Preservation

Hall) and recent transformations. Recordings were done at Preservation Hall, some-times using historically important equipment and instruments, such as the megaphone and amplifier used by Yim Yames on "Louisiana Fairytale" and "St. James Infirmary."[34]

One could certainly raise the issue of whether this shift away from directly address-ing Katrina and toward a postcrisis orientation might represent, at least symbolically, a lack of concern for some of New Orleans's neediest, who were still engaged in day-to-day struggles to survive Katrina as a biopolitical project or who simply couldn't get back to town. We could read it as reproducing Preservation Hall's own privileged and rather quaint status as a French Quarter tourist site, legitimating an exploitative tourist economy.

Such analysis would certainly be consistent with the concerns raised here earlier about how honoring and preserving New Orleans music can obscure important polit-ical-economic issues, serve as cover for draconian political acts and social policies, or become part of an economy of cross-racial and cross-class desire that affirms the pres-ence and contributions of cultural workers but enables apathy or even hostility toward the needs of members of poor or colored communities who are not engaged in such pro-duction. And there is always a danger—with art or policy-oriented activist projects—in outsiders taking control of and reaping the benefits of representations of New Orleans.

As many have discussed, huge problems in the recovery emerged when outsiders—whether members of traditional aid agencies like the Red Cross, radical grassroots organizations like the Common Ground Relief Collective, neighborhood associations, or simply the wave of YURPs (young urban rebuilding professionals) in fields like edu-cation, health care, and urban planning—brought to New Orleans, along with their love for the city and extraordinarily hard and effective reconstruction work, paternalism, tokenistic approaches to incorporating local activists and competiveness with them, fleeting commitments, a lack of accountability, self-righteousness, and sometimes, good old-fashioned racism and sexism (though more often cluelessness about these issues). And even though the artists and art professionals, including many art activists, who flooded the city after the storm have helped reestablish New Orleans as a site of inno-vative artistic production, certain largely outsider-run events, like the massive 2008 biennial exhibit *Prospect.1,* came with charges of elitism and marginalization of local artists.[35]

Yet there also seems to be something richly, if contradictorily, symbolic in this recording several years after Katrina—the songs on *Preservation* were recorded in 2008 and 2009—that is very much the product of a New Orleans that is making it through the aftermath of the storm and defining a future at least in part on its residents' own terms. In other words, *Preservation* seems to symbolize New Orleans's collective regen-eration. We see this in the ways the project seeks to build community across time and space via the songs and musical personae represented on the album. As Jaffe put it, "We now have a New Orleans family that extends way beyond the Orleans Parish line. All the way back to the protest songs of the 1950's, Woodstock, New Orleans in the 1920's, Nashville, VH1, overseas and beyond."[36]

Tapping into a shared history of activism and a shared musical history, *Preservation* represents, and makes visible on the national and international stages, a dedication by committed artists and activists from outside to a city and populace still facing profound difficulties but having on some level made it through the disaster of Katrina. And, as with some of the most effective and democratic (if somewhat short-lived) political organizations that were supported by outsiders in the wake of Katrina—including the People's Hurricane Relief Fund, INCITE!'s Women's Health and Justice Initiative and New Orleans Women's Health Clinic, and the New Orleans Center for Workers' Justice—the people of the city largely defined the terms.[37] *Preservation* is not another example of musical noblesse oblige but rather one of outsiders being incorporated into a community of musicians whose members were either born in the city or have strong roots there.

Some of the guest musicians went to New Orleans primarily to record, but others have been regular visitors and have participated in specific cases of musical activism, such as the artist activism retreats sponsored by the Air Traffic Control and Future of Music Coalition, which have brought outside musicians together with local community leaders and tradition bearers in New Orleans since 2006.[38] Regardless of individual musicians' levels of service, we can read *Preservation* as performing political community dedicated to transforming society in a more equitable way, whose commitments build from the knowledge of New Orleans's worldliness following Katrina and the city's growing importance in insiders' and outsiders' imaginations as a site of social and political possibility. Even if the urgency of commitments to the city has waned, we can see the stabilization of an important economy of care and analytical interest. This economy, granted, is defined by its contradictions, but it also signals what might be accomplished, in the city and at a national level—in a political moment shaped increasingly by fear, greed, and exhaustion—by reasonable, caring, informed civic engagement forged out of communion across social boundaries. The album implicitly theorizes a way of representing and performing New Orleans as a zone of radical possibility defined by the often mundane, sometimes heroic relationships of its citizens and sustained through alliances from outsiders.

Music also shows us that New Orleans is a city with a political culture and a cultural politics that continue to be transformed. As the levee breaks recede into the past, the critique thereof is informed by other major events, like the Deepwater Horizon oil spill. And all the while the city undergoes an artistic and civic renaissance. Three months after the release of *Preservation*, the group collaborated with hip-hop artist Mos Def on a remake of drummer Smokey Johnson's 1964 rhythm and blues hit "It Ain't My Fault," with actor Tim Robbins providing backing vocals and rock guitarist and vocalist Lenny Kravitz and Trombone Shorty also performing. Written by New Orleans arranger Wardell Quezergue, the song has a prominent place in New Orleans music history, as it has since become a Mardi Gras and brass band standard and was remade by New Orleans rappers Silkk the Shocker and Mystikal in the late 1990s.

The idea for this recording came first to Jaffe, as he and the other musicians were preparing to perform at the Gulf Aid benefit concert on May 16, 2010, which was held to raise funds for Gulf Coast environmental protection, local fisherfolk, and the seafood industry. Over the course of a hectic twenty-four hours, Mos Def wrote lyrics, the band rehearsed and recorded the performance, and the engineers mixed it. The resulting iTunes mp3 and video were released the following month as a benefit for the nonprofit Gulf Relief Foundation.[39]

Like the Preservation Hall recordings discussed above, this performance preserves and pays tribute to New Orleans's musical traditions. It also takes the Preservation Hall Jazz Band back into the mode of post-Katrina critique while expanding its frame into the arena of environmental justice. By doing so, the recording builds upon an established musician-generated critique of the oil industry and its impact on the local ecosystem and economy. The Voice of the Wetlands All-Stars, a local group of prominent musicians led by Tab Benoit and Cyril Neville, gathered shortly before the storm to make a recording that would educate people about dangers to the region (including the possibility of catastrophic flooding) following the erosion of local wetlands. Although the resulting album, *Voice of the Wetlands,* received little attention amid the avalanche of recordings focusing on the city and its inhabitants, John Swenson suggests that these musicians and their recording presciently linked environmental and social concerns. Subsequently, Dr. John addressed oil company malfeasance and environmental destruction in his 2008 recording *City That Care Forgot.* Later he was forced to issue an apology after criticizing Jazz Fest sponsor Shell Oil for contributing to the deterioration of the Louisiana coastline and wetlands and, consequently, to the flooding of New Orleans.[40]

In "It Ain't My Fault," Mos Def's lyrics explicitly link the Deepwater Horizon disaster with Katrina, describing the deterioration of the Gulf Coast wetlands as both unnecessary damage to the natural world and a threat to the human built and inhabited world because of the way the wetlands provide a buffer against hurricanes. The refrain—"Aww, it ain't my fault"—blames both disasters on governmental and corporate incompetence and refusal of responsibility.[41] "It Ain't My Fault" also performs a politicized musical community coming into its own and broadening its horizons. Says Jaffe: "That's what's blowing my mind about this. We haven't seen how big our voice is yet."[42] At the time of the recording, Mos Def had recently moved to New Orleans from Brooklyn and Kravitz had made New Orleans his primary U.S. residence. The presence of these big-name migrants on the album speaks of the artistic renaissance in New Orleans, which has drawn a diverse group of young (and not so young) musicians, visual artists, dancers, art entrepreneurs, and others to the city for temporary and permanent stays. It is a phenomenon that extends on the ground and in the national and transnational imagination the radical critique being generated in the city. It is a cultural remapping that has displaced local artists—we cannot lose sight of that—but it also can result in productive insider-outsider collaborations.

As a way of concluding this section, I would like to suggest that these Dirty Dozen Brass Band and Preservation Hall Jazz Band recordings may help us rethink the meaning of New Orleans jazz in its twenty-first-century national context and as part of a broader jazz culture that is very much defined by invocations of tradition in performance and on record, as well as via marketing campaigns. In their recent jazz history survey, musicologist Scott DeVeaux and journalist Gary Giddins use the term *historicist* to characterize the last three or four decades in the music. This is a trend they are somewhat ambivalent about. While they look more favorably at eclectic invocations of the past that blur generic boundaries or bring unexpected material into the jazz repertoire—the work of Anthony Braxton, for example—they worry that other performances of tradition are something of an artistic dead end and ideologically problematic. They situate Jazz at Lincoln Center's neoclassicist vision of the 1980s and 1990s as a product of Reagan-era nostalgia, a cautious movement designed to secure arts funding in a conservative climate. "[Wynton] Marsalis," they argue, "was the ultimate Reagan-era jazz musician."[43]

Some of Giddins and DeVeaux's disdain for Marsalis is no doubt fallout from the jazz canon wars of the 1980s and 1990s, in which Marsalis was a vocal participant and quick to condemn musicians who strayed from a mainstream tradition. But I do not think he can be easily characterized as a Reagan-era conservative. His celebration of a jazz tradition emblematic of American values and carried forward by black achievement is part of a long genealogy in which celebrating African American musical contributions has also served as an argument for black humanity and citizenship rights. And we also should keep in mind that Marsalis's African American exceptionalist vision, his positioning of black folk as embodying democratic ideals by creating a national art form, was in part a response to the pernicious antiblack discourse that accompanied cuts to social programs under Reagan and Bush.[44]

Marsalis's activism around the fate of New Orleans—his efforts to use cultural resources and ideas about the importance of New Orleans's musical traditions to rebuild the city—clearly continues the struggle against such denigration. In the months after Katrina, Jazz at Lincoln Center (of which Marsalis is artistic director) raised and distributed over three million dollars to musicians, "music industry related enterprises," and others in the New Orleans area through its Higher Ground Relief Fund. Marsalis and the Lincoln Center Jazz Orchestra conducted a weeklong residency in New Orleans, where they premiered the composition "Congo Square," cowritten by Marsalis and Yacub Addy.[45]

Marsalis has spoken publicly on a number of occasions about how culture can help bring back New Orleans, both by mobilizing resources and by reminding people of the value of this city and its inhabitants. In "Saving America's Soul Kitchen," a September 2005 article in *Time* magazine, Marsalis described the city as a particular variant (a "musky gumbo") of the "American melting pot." The tragedy of Katrina provided the nation with an opportunity to reflect upon its capacity for caring, as witnessed by the thousands who came to the aid of its victims, but also on the unresolved racial and class inequalities that still demand our attention. Katrina and New Orleans also provided an opportunity for "reacquainting" the nation with the great art form (jazz) that expresses the multicultural soul of the nation and performs its democratic future.[46]

As appealing as such calls may be, however, we should remain aware of the political stakes of exceptionalist narratives vis-à-vis New Orleans. Historically, figurations of New Orleans as an exceptional space have helped define the norms—political, racial, and sexual—that putatively stand at the center of the United States. And in response to that project, as Lisa Ze Winters's analysis of the work of nineteenth-century black female travel writer Eliza Potter tells us, we should "expose the normalcy of the city within a national landscape" defined in part by its social hierarchies and exclusions.[47] The challenge, of course, is to do so while also paying close attention to the political and social possibilities embedded in New Orleans's unique musical expressions.

Narratives that define New Orleans's unique culture as distinctly American can also elide those hierarchies and exclusions by perpetuating self-aggrandizing nationalist myths that gloss over pressing social problems and the need to address them. It is worth remembering how New Orleans often figures into the "jazz as quintessentially American" mythology. One prominent example is Ken Burns's 2001 documentary *Jazz*, shaped significantly by Marsalis as consultant and talking head, which begins with a consideration of nineteenth-century New Orleans as the symbol of a cosmopolitan, multicultural, and potentially integrated America and ends with the sense that American society has somehow become postracial. Hurricane Katrina and its aftermath, of course, provided an effective rejoinder to such narratives, but they only increased the sense that New Orleans music—and jazz, in particular—somehow mattered when talking about the future of the city and the nation.

So one does well to consider Salim Washington's rejoinder to Marsalis's *Time* article. Washington suggests that the invocation of New Orleans as incubator of America's soul "continues a long tradition of comfort with creating myths that hide much more than they reveal about our national culture." Namely, they elide "systemic racism and class-based oppression; fiscal and managerial mishaps over the institutional ravages insured by modern day capitalism; the laudatory tweakings of a bourgeois, liberal democracy over the imperialistic domination its affluent lifestyle is based upon; and evidence of a fictive melting pot culture over the widening alienation and vicious behavior between various 'Americas.'"[48]

Although the embrace of jazz traditionalism remains a precarious enterprise, recordings such as *What's Going On* and *Preservation* remind us that there still remains great creative and critical possibility in reimagining a jazz tradition. These projects suggest that the jazz historicist project is not a dead end. Rather than reproducing a sense of uncritical American or African American exceptionalism, these recordings stand as performances of New Orleans that resituate the city in the jazz historical imagination—

not as the exceptional site that generates and roots a national art form but as a site of new forms of creolized creativity. It's not just their eclecticism, their stretching of the boundaries of tradition that make these recordings interesting—although I think that is important—but also the ways in which they participate in, interrogate, and dare I say resituate New Orleans as a symbol of the possibilities of multiracial democracy in practice.

MUSICA LATINA, MAGAZINE STREET, 2010

ROSE TAVERN, CENTRAL CITY, OCTOBER 2005

UPTOWN, CARROLLTON NEIGHBORHOOD, 2011

# 5

## TO REINVENT
## LIFE

Terence Blanchard's 2007 album *A Tale of God's Will* is the musical response to Katrina I have listened to the most. In addition to enjoying its haunting textures, plaintive solos, and affirming modulations, I like it because it helps me think about New Orleans as an intersection of diasporas. Opening with "Ghosts of Congo Square," the album situates Katrina and post-storm cultural production in a long history of displacements and related cultural fusions. The piece begins with polyrhythmic bass and drum lines, replicating a Congo Square drumming and dancing circle. When the musicians chant, "This is a tale of God's will," in dialogue with Blanchard's trumpet, they put a Christian god into dialogue with an African spirit world. Blanchard and Lolis Elie's liner notes interrogate the myth of Congo Square as the origin of jazz, that famously creolized North American art form, acknowledging an important site of cultural regeneration that is also defined by histories of almost unimaginable horrors. Congo Square was also a place, they tell us, "where they displayed the severed heads of men who revolted against slavery." These souls of Congo Square, then, "saw much and I have a feeling that they understand more deeply how this current, devastating, heartbreaking pain fits into the larger saga of God's will. They saw the worst before we did. Perhaps they understand better than we do how a story such as this one unfolds in the end."[1] Putting Katrina into such an epic continuum of spiritual reckoning is aided by the invocation, on "Ghost of 1927" and "Ghost of Betsy," of the souls lost in other floods that disproportionately affected poor people. Such pieces, of course, also situate New Orleans in the natural world on which it rests and connect it to a patchwork of geographical networks.

The opening of the track "Levees," gesturing toward the calm before the storm, bespeaks the "laid back pace" of life in New Orleans, which is at once a creolized response to life's difficulties and a cause of collective complacency toward the deplorable conditions some residents have faced. "Wading Through," "The Water," and "Funeral Dirge" depict the tragic circumstances that followed the breaking of the levees. Blanchard composed these four pieces for Spike Lee's award-winning 2006 documentary *When the Levees Broke,* and they provide much of the film's soundtrack. With Lee's visual analogue in mind, Blanchard's music enhances our understanding of the tragedy of Katrina, as it invokes memories of those who died during and immediately after the storm, the harrowing experiences of survivors, the long-term health problems, and the social costs. The diasporic experience thus continues into a new moment of exodus.

But *A Tale of God's Will* also speaks of reconstruction and survival. Indeed, with elements of it also contributing to the soundtrack of Lee's more affirmative 2010 film *If God Is Willing and da Creek Don't Rise,* the compositions by Blanchard and his band members convey a shared commitment to reinventing the city and the lives that produced it. We see this most poignantly in "Dear Mom," which narrates Blanchard's mother's on-camera return to her devastated home in the first Lee film. In the liner notes, Blanchard speaks of his mother's strength and bravery and her insistence that this moment needs "to be seen by those people around the world who don't know what has happened here. What is happening here." Witnessing this return is also important for "New Orleanians exiled in Houston and Portland and Kalamazoo who will one day return and see their own homes and cry their own tears, just as we have seen and cried ours." As heard in the second Lee film, which shows Blanchard's mother now situated in a new home, this music signals a return and remaking of the city. But it is an incomplete reconstruction, as shown in the film's subsequent treatment of continued African American displacement from New Orleans because of the high costs and bureaucratic roadblocks preventing homeowners from rebuilding, skyrocketing rents, the demolition of public housing and conversion of some of it to mixed-income housing, and criminal violence.

Like recordings discussed in the previous section, Blanchard's is one of several post-Katrina performances that have helped me consider the past, present, and future of New Orleans as a diaspora city. These recordings demand that post-Katrina analyses of New Orleans be attentive to questions of survival, renewal, and regeneration; to multiple experiences in and commitments to the city; and to the ways in which a long history of creolization in southern Louisiana is entering a new phase as members of established and emergent diasporas collide in rapidly transforming urban spaces, highly mediated arenas of cultural exchange, and the political interstices conditioned by neoliberalism. As a way of concluding this book, which considers what New Orleans and its people offer us as we stand at a crossroads seven years after Katrina, I suggest here a frame for further narrating the contradictions and the possibilities that emerge as New Orleanians, in the city and elsewhere, whether long-standing residents or new arrivals, "reinvent life."

As I hope the preceding sections made clear, writing about New Orleans and its music post Katrina—and by writing I mean engaging in a project of representation with political and humanitarian stakes rather than simply conveying information—requires engaging with the city's multifaceted history and the complicated ways in which it gets invoked in cultural practices and the work of the imagination. New Orleans is, and has long been, a node in overlapping empires, economic networks, cultural matrices, and human diasporas. The city sits at the southern edge of what is now the United States. But it is also on the northern edge of the Gulf of Mexico, a body of water ringed by the southern United States, Mexico, and Cuba, connected to much of North America by the rivers that empty into it, and also, via the Yucatán Channel and Straits of Florida, to the Caribbean and the mainlands and islands that define its borders. As such a node, it has been connected to similar nodes in the form of the port cities (Havana, Vera Cruz) and river cities (St. Louis, Memphis) within nautical proximity, by railway and highway to nodal points along those lines, and more recently, to other cities via airports and flight paths.[2]

New Orleans before it was New Orleans was a crossroads for Native American people. The French founded the city in 1718. It was subsequently Spanish, then French again briefly, before becoming part of the United States in 1803 as a result of the Louisiana Purchase. Consequently, those who have lived on or passed through this site include indigenous peoples like the Chitimacha, the Houma, and the Tangipahoa as well as those who migrated by choice or against their will from France, Spain, and elsewhere in western Europe; from Senegambia, the Kongo, and elsewhere in western Africa; from Cuba, Saint-Domingue, and Haiti, and elsewhere in the Caribbean and Latin America; from British North America, French Arcadia, and the United States; and more recently, from Sicily, Croatia, Cape Verde, Honduras, Vietnam, Mexico, all those lands that sent previous waves of migrants, and many more places.

And with these people came intertwined histories of, among other things, conquest, militarism, empire building, enslavement and slave trading, revolution, institutional-ized religion, the rise and fall of King Cotton, urbanization, war, racial terrorism, Jim Crow, industrialization, deindustrialization, political corruption, the development of the Keynesian state in its abridged southern form, unemployment, urban blight, white (and black) flight, urban "renewal" and post–Jim Crow urban segregation, criminal and state violence, neoliberal social and economic policies (cuts in education, health care, and welfare), and levee breaks. But also histories of rebellion, emancipation, syncretic religious practices, labor and union activism, mass civil rights movements, grassroots activism, community building, and thousands upon thousands of unrecorded but no less important instances of small individual and collective struggles for dignity and happiness. And with these histories came a profoundly complicated mix of cultural expressions that have spoken, first, to the ways in which a lot of different people with roots in many different places have influenced one another in these multiple contexts of power and, second, to the ways in which those who produce culture have done so with an eye to individual and collective struggles for dignity and happiness.

We often talk about the creoleness (or *créolité*) of New Orleans and about the ways its striking cultural past, present, and future may be seen as a result of historical processes of creolization. With etymological roots in Portuguese, Spanish, and French, *Creole* and its variations were used early on, perhaps first in reference to Cape Verde and then regarding the Americas, to refer to members of colonial or settler societies who were born in the new land and likely had a different bearing or culture because of it. The terms subsequently came to signify the mixing that resulted from contact among indigenous, African, and European peoples in the "New World" in the realms of language, cuisine, material culture, music, and human bodies. Indeed, the term *Creole* is often used, in Louisiana and various parts of the Caribbean, to refer to a person of mixed race. *Creolization,* then, refers in a variety of ways to the process of transformation and fusion that happens when distinct groups of people come into contact and they and their cultures change over time. It describes not a linear process of assimilation or the stasis of cultural retention, but a dynamic and interactive project, which involves a collision of complicated cultural and social systems that transforms all participants, both those with power and those without.[3]

There are ongoing debates among scholars about the use of the terms *creole* and *creolization.* Some question whether it is appropriate to use the terms outside a specifically Caribbean colonial and postcolonial context, while others suggest that it may not be an accurate descriptor of cultural phenomena other than language. But I am convinced by those who suggest that *creolization* is a useful term for understanding both a particular, early phase of cultural interaction that was specific to conquest, slavery, and trade in and around the Caribbean *and* a more recent, more widespread phenomenon that can be connected to the development of global capitalism, the speedup of communication and travel, and other transformations of the late twentieth and twenty-first centuries.

If we are to use *creolization* in this broader sense, we must keep in mind that creolizations are products of time and place, with differences in what the resulting mixtures look like and what they mean, while also being aware that manifestations of creolization from the past may persist. We should thus keep in mind the long-established function of creole cultures as bulwarks against horrific modes of physical, psychic, and economic violence in the Caribbean—what Sidney Mintz called "embattled creativity"—and at least put on the table the question of whether more recent forms might play a similar role. We must simultaneously acknowledge a history of *Creole* as a marker of privilege, a means of distinguishing mixed-race people in the Caribbean from those deemed blacker or more African, and therefore be reminded to keep an eye out for hierarchies and internal contradictions in creative expressions in the present.[4] And we must recognize creolization's contradictory claims. Recent meditations on créolité stemming from the Caribbean emphasize the contemporary value of affirming creole multiplicity in the face of racial essentialisms and exclusionary universalisms, even as others note that other manifestations of creolization stake claims to cultural purity.[5]

As mentioned, people use the terms *creole* and *creolization* to refer to Louisiana, New Orleans, and their residents. The terms are used to refer specifically to a mixed-race population (descended from African slaves and freed people; Spanish, French, and Anglo-American planters; poor whites; indigenous peoples; and colored refugees from the Haitian Revolution, directly and by way of Cuba) that formed a caste between black and white (although such distinctions have lessened somewhat) and that often maintained a distinctive French-influenced language and culture. Yet the terms are also used to describe more generally Afro-Euro-indigenous practices that define the city, the southern part of the state, and other parts of the Gulf Coast region.

It is through the lens of creolization—whether theorized explicitly in academese or gestured toward through more vernacular terms like *mixing*—that we have often understood New Orleans musical phenomena, including the eighteenth- and nineteenth-century drumming and dancing circles at Congo Square, the emergence of jazz in the early twentieth century, the city's vibrant R&B scene, zydeco, bounce, and other hip-hop scenes, and long-standing, unique forms of black expression discussed earlier, such as Mardi Gras Indians, brass bands, and second line parades.

Some of the most compelling writing on the city and the region and its people that was produced soon after Katrina identified and made an argument for saving a valuable, cosmopolitan creole culture that connected southern Louisiana to the Caribbean and, by extension, Africa, the indigenous Americas, and Europe. I am thinking here about Roger Abrahams's (with Spitzer, Szwed, and Thompson) *Blues for New Orleans* and Ned Sublette's *The World That Made New Orleans*. In these books New Orleans's créolité connects it to the Caribbean, thus marking its worldliness, but it is also foundational to the development of U.S. culture and society. The city and its people thus deserve a fair and equitable reconstruction that preserves their cultural richness for the rest of us. Like others who praise the creoleness of New World societies, Sublette and the *Blues for New Orleans* coauthors document the central role of West African peoples (and their descendants and cultural practices) in the making of New Orleans—thus arguing for a black right of return. And beyond merely stating the importance of protecting New Orleans's creole culture, these authors suggest, following the logic of creolization theorists Bernabé, Chamoiseau, and Confiant's "In Praise of Créolité," that the functional affirmation of cultural mixing itself, most notably in Mardi Gras, provides a resource from which New Orleanians of all colors might rebuild the city on their own terms.[6] Abrahams, Spitzer, Szwed, and Thompson conclude their book by stating, "The future of an authentic Land of Dreams is in the hopes and will of the people who have always made it the Creole heart of America's soul."[7]

As compelling as such arguments are, however, I think they served the devastated city and place-affirming needs of its residents better in the immediate post-Katrina environment than they do several years after the storm. Though they are attentive to historical and geographical contingencies in the creolization process, these narratives focus on the survival of a creole past in the present and make an argument for the preservation of an important cultural and social matrix based on the existence of this foundational cosmopolitanism.[8]

But I want to argue here for a somewhat different approach to writing about New Orleans, one that is more focused on the emergent "messy encounters," layered over the established forms, that are remaking the urban landscape as Katrina becomes history. This approach must be foundationally invested in investigating different frames of diasporic history and its cultural confluences. Several years after the storm, we are very much aware of emergent diasporas, which are related to but not adequately defined by the conceptual frameworks explaining the messy encounters of the colonial and immediate postcolonial period. As we move down this path, we must be attentive to how power is expressed via "culture as resource" and also to the democratic potential in cultural acts. We must contend as well with an array of cultural and media "noise" surrounding New Orleans and its future.

The word *diaspora* has long been used to describe displaced and relocated populations and the individual and collective sensibilities members may have about their bearing in the world as a result of that displacement. Diasporas are defined both by the nodal points that define their scope and by homelands, both real and imagined. Cultural critic Juan Flores emphasizes the multiplicity of diasporas as they develop over time and under changing conditions. Although *diaspora* most commonly refers to subordinated populations (e.g., Jews and West Africans) who were forced to leave home, geographic displacements may also stem from a group's relative power and prestige (e.g., British settlers in East Africa, wealthy Taiwanese immigrants in Southern California). The fact that diasporas follow different kinds of power relationships—colonialism, imperialism, the free market, genocide, sexism, persecution based on sexual orientation—results in different contours. Regardless of structuring principles, diasporas are also internally complicated, as Brent Hayes Edwards points out. Diasporic communities are not monolithic; they may be riven by political, ethnic, class, and regional hierarchies. A person may be a member of several diasporas simultaneously and therefore have connections to nodes in multiple geographic networks, more than one of which may signify home or the site of displacement.[9]

Thinking about New Orleans as a site of diaspora in these terms helps us keep in mind that the city and its culture have been shaped by waves upon waves of humans who have inhabited its spaces but who remain part of larger human networks with connections to other places. We can understand New Orleans as a product of histories of human geographies that have sometimes but not always been synonymous with the physical and commerce-bound geographies I sketched above. And we can think about the city as a place where these multiple movements of human beings are closely linked to multiple regimes of power, which secondarily are expressed in and through the cultural lives of the people who inhabit the city.

Flores also stresses the temporality of diasporas and of their imaginative aspects. Diaspora experience begins not when people arrive somewhere, "but only when the group has begun to develop a disposition toward its place of origin, as well as some relation to other sites within the full diasporic formation." And as historically contingent and shifting constructs of the imagination and products of physical circumstance, "the cultural experience of diasporas is shaped by the dialectic of community and change, tradition and disjuncture, the extension and prolongation of inherited cultural backgrounds on the one hand, and ruptures and innovations stemming from life in the new setting on the other."[10] But the layering becomes even more complex when we consider that such paradoxical states of diasporic being, which emerge at particular moments, become part of the cultural background—the tradition, if you will—that is invoked, challenged, rejected, and embraced at moments of rupture and innovation. Diasporas in the present are also defined by a greater proximity occasioned by the forces of globalization—a process that Flores describes as the "merging of homeland and host land into a single arena of social action and determination."[11]

Following Flores, future writing about culture (and music in particular) in New Orleans may do well to foreground diaspora as an ongoing and evolving process. While recognizing the importance of narratives of creolization that link New Orleans to a colonial and postcolonial Caribbean, we can also see that creolization in the post-Katrina era is a multilayered process, constituted by many kinds of displacements and rebuilt human networks of both long and short duration. Flores uses the phrase "créolité in the hood," which is an apt descriptor of New Orleans as a present-day diaspora city. "The 'hood,' in a word, is the site of new creolizations, the meeting point of multiple diasporas and the crossings and intersections of diasporas. In [Édouard] Glissant's term, it is the ultimate, modern-day 'point of entanglement.'"[12] Thinking about New Orleans as a diaspora city, then, requires that we consider twenty-first-century processes through which New Orleanians have engaged in the time-honored process of what Bernabé, Chamoiseau, and Confiant describe as "reinvent[ing] life" under changing conditions of displacement and hardship.[13] This is the story that is coming into focus several years out, as New Orleanians seem to be spending less time making pleas for their city's survival than they are staking claims for how best to save it.

When we look at present-day Mardi Gras Indians, traditional New Orleans jazz, second line parading, gumbo, and architecture, we see embedded in them the legacies of the cultural practices of people who came from Senegambia, and France, and Haiti, and Cuba, and Virginia, and other places. We also see how they comment—whether explicitly and consciously or implicitly and unconsciously—on connections to and distance from West Africa, and Europe, and the Caribbean, and the southern United States, and what it means to be in New Orleans or in a particular neighborhood in the city. Such cultural forms also reflect upon power in its various manifestations, and they often reproduce power given the internal dynamics and intersecting nature of diasporas.

In the wake of Katrina, these cultural forms have changed under new and radically accelerated conditions of displacement, as New Orleans residents were forced from the city and a few weeks later began a slow process of return or movement between home and site of exile. New Orleans, then, as a historically important node in a series of "overlapping diasporas," to use Earl Lewis's phrase, has now, in the postdiluvian present, become "home" for a new diaspora of displaced people.[14] In other words, the site of displacement and rupture is again the object of longing, the place of tradition. I say "again" because this has happened before, as during the Great Migration, with profound implications for the cultural history of the world. Think of Louis Armstrong, Kid Ory, Jelly Roll Morton, King Oliver, and the rest.

New Orleans as diaspora city also changed as others came to the city, through processes that augmented historical formations already in place (as with Honduran and Mexican immigrants) or as the city became an emergent node in a diasporic experience (as with twenty-first-century West African immigration) that had previously been primarily focused elsewhere. New Orleans, then, in the post-Katrina moment, is a product of many diasporas, with their own dynamic orientations toward tradition and change. The city has been reproduced through the work of the imagination in cobbling together such experiences into an understanding of what culture means and how it functions.

The widely viewed photographs by Air Force personnel Aaron Pultz and Neil Senkowski, of primarily African American Katrina evacuees sprawled through the fuselage of a C-17 Globemaster III military transport plane, bring to mind those horrific drawings of African slaves being transported prone in the holds of ships, through the middle passage. While the situation was very, very different—especially in terms of the status of the displaced and the chances of surviving the journey—the recent image was a stark reminder that African-descended Katrina victims were part of a long history of displacement going back to the slave trade.

This history of displacement is of course intimately related to the needs and distribution of capital. The slave trade across the Atlantic certainly was, and so was that which brought slaves to the New Orleans market from across the Caribbean and down the Mississippi River. And that which brought free black people to the city in the nineteenth and twentieth centuries for work in industry, petroleum production, construction, government, and more recently, the service economy. And in the post-Katrina moment, we see the continued displacement of people of African descent caused in part by a neoliberal restructuring that, among other things, diminishes government aid for disaster victims, raises rents, and privatizes public housing, as well as by a labor market that looks for lower-wage, civil-rights-deficient, undocumented or H-2B visa workers from Mexico, Central America, or Asia.[15] Census data from 2010 suggests that there are 118,000 fewer African Americans in the city than there were in 2000, mostly the result of displacement by Katrina and the shape of the reconstruction efforts that followed. Census data also suggests that displacement, patterns of return, housing politics and prices, and other factors have made some primarily African American neighborhoods, such as Gentilly and parts of East New Orleans, blacker than before the storm, while parts of what Tulane geographer Richard Campanella calls the "white teapot," which stretches from Carrollton and the Tulane area, along St. Charles Ave. and Magazine Street, into the French Quarter, Marigny, and Bywater, have become whiter than before.[16]

People have remarked on the creative regeneration of Afro-diasporic cultural forms in the post-Katrina moment. As noted in the previous section, compelling, political hip-hop songs like Mia X's "My FEMA People" were forged in a context of displacement, in front of audiences that included other evacuees, and energized by the idea of home. We saw something similar with the New Orleans Social Club's album *Sing Me Back Home*. The activities of Finding Our Folk provide another important example of performing diaspora. Created by Omo Moses, the son of black freedom struggle veteran Robert Moses, this project began with a January–February 2006 tour of cities in Louisiana, Texas, Alabama, Mississippi, and Georgia by the Hot 8 Brass Band and other performers—including actor Danny Glover, Palestinian American poet Suheir Hammad, and members of the Black Men of Labor Social Aid and Pleasure Club—in an effort to reach out to Katrina survivors across this new diaspora while simultaneously educating locals. As the organization put it,

> Finding Our Folk tells the story of young people, who after the destruction caused by Hurricane Katrina organized themselves, other students, artists and community members from around the country to document and share the stories of Katrina survivors, to connect these stories with the narratives of individuals in marginalized communities across the country, to share the cultural spirit and heritage of the people of New Orleans and offer the work that they and Gulf Coast residents must do to rebuild their communities and lives as an indicator of the work that needs to take place across this country to shift social, political and economic arrangements.

Or, as Hot 8 leader and tuba player Bennie Pete put it, it was an opportunity to "reunite New Orleanians, just to really heal and bring some life back to people." Subsequent tours over the next few years, with the Hot 8 band an anchoring participant, developed an expanding range of performances, exhibits, workshops and clinics, community forums, and other activities, in venues ranging from community centers and public schools to universities and established cultural institutions to the 2007 U.S. Social Forum, which brought together radical grassroots activists in Atlanta. As the story of New Orleans after Katrina unfolded, the group tried "to build awareness that New Orleans is serving as a litmus test for the future of America with regard to housing, education, economics, environmental health and justice and racial justice and to help draw connections between what happened and is happening in the Gulf Coast, their communities and the country."[17]

Another trajectory of Afro-diasporic expression is being produced by New Orleans cultural workers who have relocated to other cities. For example, pianist, vocalist, photographer, and *Sing Me Back Home* contributor Henry Butler left New Orleans after

Katrina, moving first to Colorado and finally setting in New York as of 2009. As a blind person, he found negotiating the city, its disrepair and its crime, just too difficult. Being in New York has afforded him possibilities for branching out musically, including reconstituting musical connections between Cuba and New Orleans. In June 2010 Butler played a New York concert with Cuban pianist Osmany Paredes, featuring compositions from the nineteenth and early twentieth centuries that gave evidence of the circulation of musical ideas around the Caribbean.[18]

We also see new cultural emergences occurring when people return to the city and seek to remake their lives there. People have written about the Mardi Gras Indian tradition as an outgrowth of Afro-French-indigenous contacts, as an aspect of the carnival tradition that developed across the Gulf region and Caribbean, and as a necessary cultural affirmation in the face of Jim Crow in the U.S. Gulf Coast. And members of these groups have themselves emphasized their commitment to long-standing historical traditions when describing their value to the community and when engaging in activist educational programs in schools and elsewhere. All true, but it is also interesting to consider the ways in which what has been defined as traditional is self-consciously imagined and contested in the present, in the context of emergent, diasporic relationships.

Cherice Harrison-Nelson, Big Queen of the Guardians of the Flame, notes that her group started putting beaded Sankofa figures (Akan symbols signifying the need to remember the past as you move into the future) on the children's Mardi Gras suits in 2007, with adults wearing them in 2008. The group has also had women and girls carry African fertility symbols in the post-Katrina context because they are "fertile and pregnant" with "hope for the future," on the way to giving birth, as cultural workers, to "something beautiful, . . . something we can't even imagine." Following the late Big Chief Donald Harrison's opposition to hatchets and other symbols of violence, they have used these alternative symbols to cultivate communal resilience.[19] So rather than simply (and anachronistically) reading these practices as part of a centuries-old story of Akan influences in the New World, as one might be inclined to do, we need to understand them instead as imaginative acts of seizing the past to redefine life in the present and future—as examples of, as Flores puts it, "the extension and prolongation of inherited cultural backgrounds on the one hand, and ruptures and innovations stemming from life in the new setting on the other."[20]

Harrison-Nelson's interest in the Sankofa figure stemmed in part from her studies in Ghana and Senegal on a Fulbright scholarship in the 1990s and the profound experience she had visiting the "House of Slaves" on Gorée Island in Senegal. In other words, it is an outgrowth of a familiar experience of people "returning" to the "imagined home" in self-conscious acts of cultural regeneration. In the post-Katrina context, the Sankofa figure as emergent Africanism is a product of a new diasporic experience emanating from New Orleans and the return home. Harrison-Nelson sews beaded Sankofa patches on suits at a moment when cultural production serves to fill a political void, when Mardi Gras Indians are invested in increasing their visibility in an attempt to build communal affirmation and stake out a right of return. The figure has become increasingly important to Harrison-Nelson as an tool for educating young people about Mardi Gras Indian culture and about the Afro-diasporic aspects of the culture. It is pedagogical in the sense that it provides young people with cultural affirmation in the face of a failing education system and rising crime in their neighborhoods; it is a means for addressing the posttraumatic effects of the storm that Harrison-Nelson saw manifesting in hostile behavior between children. And, like other diasporic cultural forms, it is contested. Some Mardi Gras Indian gangs are highly invested in exploring African roots. Others remain focused on Louisiana and the United States as the geographical source of inspiration.[21]

Watts's photo of Harrison-Nelson is from a blessing ceremony at her family's house on Mardi Gras Day 2007. Several months later Harrison-Nelson held a blessing ceremony at her home in Musicians' Village. Presiding over the West African–influenced ritual while bringing his Christian faith to the ceremony was Shola Falodun, an Anglican priest from Nigeria who had arrived in the city in 2002 to minister to a growing population of Nigerian Anglican immigrants and led the Church of All Souls in the Ninth Ward for some time following Katrina.[22] So again we have an African American spiritual and cultural practice drawing on reconstructed African traditions and forged as a response to the displacement caused by Katrina, but which also reflects the growth of a somewhat different African presence in and around New Orleans. This emergent African diaspora in the United States, as a general rule, occurred in the wake of a history of war, neocolonialism, and structural adjustment across the African continent in the late twentieth and early twenty-first centuries.[23] The remaking of New Orleans via waves of diaspora was brought home to me in a quite symbolic way at (Robert E.) Lee Circle one afternoon in April 2010, when I saw sitting on the base of the general's statue a group of African immigrant men in animated conversation and a group of African American boys and girls singing retro soul songs—all of them thus talking back in different ways to the Confederate hero.

Such regeneration extends beyond African diasporas. Much has been made of the influx of documented and undocumented Mexican and Central American workers into New Orleans to assist in the reconstruction of the city, of the resultant conflicts with low-wage white and especially African American workers who saw themselves displaced by this immigrant labor. Some have analyzed the exploitation of this new labor source by employers who reneged on contractual commitments, withheld pay, and exposed them to unsafe conditions. One commentator went so far as to observe that Katrina marked the end of "the century of black labor" and ushered in "the new century of brown slavery."[24] And of course, a concomitant anxiety about the Latino/aization of New Orleans— signified by the undocumented, unskilled laborer and the taco truck—has been voiced by politicians, media commentators, and ordinary people. Hostility toward Latino/a workers is often connected to worries about their role in the displacement of African American residents and workers—a discourse that was exacerbated by controversial comments by Mayor Ray Nagin and others about the city being "overrun by Mexican workers." Yet, several years later, the climate for Latino/a immigrants has improved—thanks in part to the New Orleans Workers' Center for Racial Justice and other organizations that have struggled for immigrant rights and sought to alleviate interracial tensions—and public officials have been speaking out in support of fair treatment.[25]

New Orleans and Louisiana more generally were until recently among the least Latino/a of places in the United States, with the "Hispanic" population in 2000 amounting to only about 3 percent in the city of New Orleans and 4.4 percent in the greater metropolitan area. There has been much debate over population growth since then, with Catholic Charities estimating that the Latino/a population in the region grew soon after Katrina to upwards of 150,000 people, making up perhaps 20 percent of its post-storm population. That number was almost certainly too high, and many who entered the city in the storm's aftermath left within a matter of months. Estimates of the metropolitan region's Hispanic population five years after the storm ranged from 6.6 percent (5.2 percent in the city and 12.4 percent in Jefferson Parish), based on 2010 census data, to community groups' figure of 10 percent, which takes into account estimates of the numbers of undocumented workers who were likely missed by census takers.[26]

Lost in many discussions about the Latino/aization of New Orleans but thankfully clear in others are the ways that Caribbean, Mexican, and Central American diasporas are also being rearticulated in New Orleans post Katrina. Emerging studies of the cultural side of these demographic transformations make it clear that Katrina has enabled a simultaneous continuation and transformation of existing diasporic relationships and created a context for reimagining them. We are not simply witnessing an influx of documented and undocumented workers new to the area, who will either move on or settle down to form an eventually Americanized Latino/a population in the city. Many new arrivals already had friends or family members in the city or perhaps had connections to the city via family members who had lived in the city previously.

For example, the largest Latino/a group in the New Orleans area over the past several decades has been Hondurans. Many early immigrants from Honduras came to New Orleans as employees of United Fruit or as service workers for the company's executives. Others were children of United Fruit employees who came to the United States on educational visas. With an established Honduran community in place, other immigrants came to the city in the wake of the devastation caused by Hurricane Mitch in 1998. Subsequently, they were connected to their homeland through visits and by varying degrees of migration back and forth between the two nations. Honduran entrepreneurs in construction and other businesses who recruited their compatriots as workers have served as a major impetus for such migrations over the past several decades. This pattern has continued post Katrina, with new arrivals motivated both by opportunities for employment and by cultural and family connections long established in New Orleans.

Other groups' immigration and migration patterns have been somewhat different, but they likewise indicate an ongoing process of diaspora. Mexicans, of course, have had a significant presence in the city going back to the nineteenth century, even if they have been less visible than Hondurans in recent decades. The current Mexican presence in the city must also be understood as part of larger circuits that help define the more recently arrived Mexican labor force in the United States. This circuit often involves travel back and forth between the United States and Mexico and movement among various sites across the United States to follow seasonal work patterns and ebbs and flows in the economy. As mentioned, many Mexican workers left the city once the initial wave of construction projects ended. New Orleans also has functioned differently as a node in the Mexican diaspora than it did for the Honduran diaspora. Although the Mexican population in Louisiana is now probably bigger than that of other Latino/a groups, Mexicans are not as focused in the New Orleans metropolitan area as Hondurans are. Mexicans are distributed across the state, with a particularly vibrant community emerging in Baton Rouge. In fact, as of a few years ago, the one working Latino band in that city, Mestizo, performed a combination of musical styles from across Mexico to appeal to the city's diverse and growing Mexican immigrant population.[27]

Cuban Americans in New Orleans have a different story, with a long history of cultural exchange and movement between Havana and New Orleans undergirding contemporary cultural developments. We often talk about how travel between Cuba and New Orleans in the eighteenth and nineteenth centuries was important to the creation of its creole mix. More recently, New Orleans has been shaped by multiple phases of Cuban migration to southern Louisiana since the 1959 revolution. South Louisiana's Cuban population today is primarily composed of members and descendants of the primarily white and generally more affluent Cubans who fled the revolution in the 1960s, the mostly Afro-Cuban population who came to the United States during the Mariel boatlift of 1980, and the Balseros (or rafters) who fled Cuba in 1994.[28]

For many years, diasporic experiences and encounters in New Orleans have produced a Latin music scene that is at once ethnically specific and hybridly pan-Latino/a. For example, a visible, specifically Cuban cultural base in the city has been sustained through emergent and continuing organizations such as the Club Cubano de Profesionales, which operated primarily from the 1960s through the 1990s; Comité Organizador del Festival Latinoamericano (COFLA), which was founded in 1973 and ran for about ten years; La Tienda Música Latina, a Latin music store run by COFLA producer Juan Suarez and his wife, Honduras-born Yolanda Estrada, who also hosts a Latin music show on WWOZ; the Latin music festival Carnival Latino, which Romualdo "Romi" Gonzalez and Carlos Gonzalez produced in the 1980s and 1990s and brought back in 2007; and more recently, the CubaNola Arts Collective, dedicated to addressing historical and present-day connections between Cuba and New Orleans. Cuban musicians, producers, and patrons were also key players in the vibrant "Latin" club scene in the city of the 1970s and 1980s, which revolved most significantly around Magazine Street establishments.[29]

The simultaneous production of ethnically specific and pan-Latino/a orientations in New Orleans stems in part from ethnically specific cultural organizations laboring within sociological conditions—like the lack of large, geographically bounded ethnic Latino/a enclaves and a history of integration into European American or African American neighborhoods—that tend to produce undifferentiated Latino/a cultures. But we can also point to general patterns in Latina/o cultural production and the marketing of Latinidad throughout the United States during the twentieth and early twenty-first centuries, which has enhanced simultaneously the ethnically specific and the multiethnic. Cultural production has been shaped by non-Latino/as' desire for "Latin flavor," which is in turn connected to the presence of Latino/as as workers. Alicia Schmidt Camacho describes "the national desire for the racialized migrant, both as a pliable source of labor and as a cultural resource in the economy of consumption."[30] New Orleans Latina/o culture in the post-Katrina period has thus built upon earlier infrastructural and cultural foundations while being enhanced by new diasporic formations. In turn, the dynamic mix of the ethnically specific and the pan-Latino is enabled by market expectations that New Orleans is becoming a more Latino/a city because of the influx of workers.

The influx of Mexican and Central American immigrants after Katrina at least temporarily created an audience for an increasing number of Norteño and Banda shows at dance clubs like the Copacabana in Metairie. At least one of the local Spanish-language radio stations increased its Mexican music programming while decreasing the Caribbean music it played. Immigrants also helped to energize a resurgent pan-Latino salsa scene that has been consistently vibrant since 2005.[31] On a much smaller scale, post-Katrina Garifuna immigrants have also helped push things in these two directions. Drummer Efrain Amaya came to New Orleans after the storm to do reconstruction work and ended up playing in a New Orleans East Garifuna band named Legacy. Another Garifuna drummer, Jose Dolmo, also went to New Orleans to do reconstruction work, but his musical contribution has been to a pan-Latino band called Ecos Latinos.[32]

Evacuation from New Orleans following Katrina and subsequent immigration to the city have combined to move other Honduran New Orleanian cultural workers in both ethnically specific and pan-Latino directions. Members of the New Orleans Hispano American Dance Group, for example, have been trying to preserve and resurrect traditional Honduran music and dance. They see themselves as serving a function in the post-Katrina city, for established residents and new arrivals alike, because people have needed something to "enjoy." They seek to counter a long-standing assimilationist orientation among Hondurans, manifest in an embrace of Americaness or Latinoness or both. And they are inspired by new arrivals, not necessarily Honduran, who have made local Latina/o culture more visible. But of course, the energizing effect of recent immigration to the city also helps reproduce a multiethnic Latinidad in which Hondurans also participate and out of which new, hybrid forms are emerging. Group members Ronald Avila and Belinda Avila have expressed the desire to create a New Orleans brass band that would blend traditional Honduran music with local brass band culture—a motivation that they suggest stems both from a push for things Latino/a in the context of post-Katrina immigration and the influence on young people in their community of an established, though increasingly visible and fetishized, local musical culture. The dance group's activities also indicate a perceived need to address the negative side of the current attention to things Latino/a in New Orleans: the fear of Latino/a criminality, competition as a marginalized labor force, and general foreignness. Ronald Avila argues that such activities are in part designed to show outsiders that Hondurans "have a wider culture and provide talent to the community. It is a way to show people that we are more than workers or criminals."[33]

Resurgent Latinidad on the cultural front, whether pan-Latino or ethnic-specific, does not stem only from the influence of Latino/a populations that have grown post Katrina. Although Cubans have not been a significant part of the wave of post-Katrina immigration to the city, the band AshéSon formed in 2006 in the context of growing interest in things Latino/a and hit the club scene with a primarily Cuban repertoire. The group features Cuban immigrant Geovanis "Dongo" Palacios and Houston-born Javier Olondo, who as a child moved with his family back to Cuba, where he studied music before returning to the United States and settling in New Orleans as an adult.[34] Of course, this promotion of New Orleans as an emergent Latino/a cultural space is not driven solely by Latino/a artists and audiences. Fredy Omar leads a popular Latin band that has long had a large non-Latino/a following, while Ovi G and Las Ranitas is a Guatemalan band that has played mostly for Latino/a audiences but is starting to have crossover appeal in the post-Katrina period.[35] Los Po-Boy-Citos is a group of non-Latinos who came together after the storm to perform classical Latin dance tunes and Latini-fied New Orleans classics like "Big Chief." A local writer's review of their 2008 album *New Orleans Latin Soul* demonstrates the expectation that a cultural transformation is under way, a lack of familiarity with what some Latino/a artists are already doing to reshape the city, and an inability to quite grasp that diasporic cultural regeneration and expectation are already beginning to reshape the "mainstream" of New Orleans music: "We've waited for the post-Katrina influx of Latinos to be felt in New Orleans music, and despite the album title, we're still waiting. These are a bunch of white guys and likely crate diggers."[36]

We also see established and emergent cultural institutions promoting Latin music for a city increasingly aware of its Latino/aness. In 2007, Carnival Latino's organizers brought the festival back as a celebration of pan-Latino crafts, food, and music. At the 2008 festival, which drew as many as a hundred thousand people, the musical styles showcased included Tejano, Norteño, Afro-Cuban, merengue, mariachi, and samba. As organizer Romi Gonzalez argued, "Our State and the Gulf Coast were rescued from the devastation after Hurricanes Katrina and Rita in 2005 largely by immigrant labor and continues [sic] to recover on the backs of the new arrivals. . . . It is opportune that on this 'Dia de la Raza' weekend we welcome and thank this new, growing sector of our community by holding a first-class event featuring their rich cultural heritage." The event also celebrated the "first local Hispanic owned TV station," a Telemundo affiliate.[37]

The fact that the event was held at Mardi Gras World and featured a parade through the French Quarter indicates the growing integration of Latina/o culture into the New Orleans cultural apparatus. Lt. Governor Mitch Landrieu spoke of the event as benefiting the entire community rather than simply Latino/as. That year Carnival Latino was a showcased city event held around the time of Landrieu's World Cultural Economic Forum at the Morial Convention Center. Modeled on the World Economic Forum in Switzerland, the local event was designed to put New Orleans cultural workers and producers in dialogue with those from other countries and to determine how to best use such means as outreach and foreign investment "to add value to raw [cultural] materials and teach people how to use culture to build the economy."[38] This is a cultural economy, as we have seen, that is often fundamentally unequal. Indeed, Latina/o workers in the tourist industry have been exploited since Katrina, as evidenced by the lawsuit brought by H-2B guest workers against the Louisiana hotel chain Decatur Hotels LLC.[39] But, as we have also seen, the city's cultural apparatus also provides avenues for political and cultural regeneration at the neoliberal moment.

When Jazz Fest announced its signing of Dominican merengue superstar Juan Luis Guerra for its 2010 lineup, the festival organizers suggested that they recognized the importance of a growing, post-Katrina, multiethnic Latino/a population as an emergent market. At a press conference, the organizers admitted that signing Guerra represented a shift from earlier programming decisions, which brought in Latina/o artists (including Tito Puente and Celia Cruz) associated with Latin jazz and its constituent salsa, as well as earlier histories of immigration, but who drew disappointingly small audiences. Now the organizers were moving more self-consciously into Latin American pop in response to the presence and musical tastes of recent immigrants, who were exerting their power to reshape how New Orleans understands itself culturally and represents itself culturally to the world.[40]

These last few examples of how emergent (yet repeated) diasporic cultural expressions figure into an economy of "culture as resource" show the importance to this story of the "noise" surrounding them. As noted throughout this book, the media has made New Orleans's complicated cultural matrix simultaneously more accessible and distorted. Also making noise in New Orleans are the participants of still more diasporas: those who have descended upon the city to study it, help with it, profit from it, and experience it. They have embraced the unique cultural aspects of the city where they landed, made it precious and consumable, and defined their righteousness through it. And the city itself and the land on which it sits help this noise resonate in ways that are both particular and universal. So let me conclude by thinking through noise via a listening, so to speak, of yet another post-Katrina benefit album: *Proud to Swim Home*. The point is not that this noise is the definitive part of the story. I hope that Lewis's photographs and my writing make clear our preferred focus on everyday human beings' and artists' struggles to reconstruct New Orleans. But the point is that despite all that is inherent in image and deed, addressing the city's cultural scene seven years out also requires attention to this noise.

*Proud to Swim Home* is a 2006 compilation released by Backporch Revolution, a New Orleans–based, primarily Euro-American artists' collective and record label dedicated to experimental music "encompassing many genres including electronic, noise, drone, [and] dub." The artists represented on the album had been established in New Orleans before Katrina, were then exiled, and for the most part had returned. The collective itself established its commitment to the reconstruction of the city—"a call to arms," they called it—by producing in the immediate aftermath of the storm "New Orleans: Proud to Swim Home" bumper stickers (a variant of the "Proud to Call It Home" sticker) that found their way onto "tens of thousands to cars of returning residents." Proceeds from the bumper stickers went to Habitat for Humanity and the Humane Society. The motivation was in part the "unparalleled incompetence of government agencies," which is reflected on the compilation by King Ghidorah's "Bring Me the Head of Michael Brown" and by the unnamed, unattributed eight-and-a-half-minute bonus track consisting of a looped and increasingly distorted recording of George W. Bush lending support to his soon-to-be-disgraced FEMA chief—"And Brownie, you're doing a heck of a job." Yet the compilation is also an affirmation, "a tribute to everyone who has committed to return to their City to rebuild—as well as to all the rescuers, volunteers, and others who have given and continue to try to save New Orleans."[41]

This tribute to volunteers in particular speaks to the important role that the young, the white, and the not-from-New-Orleans have played in rebuilding the city and assisting some of its most dispossessed and disenfranchised residents. Yet these volunteers—these participants in a diaspora of care and activism—have been reshaping the city and its cultural landscape through their attempts to protect, serve, and consume what they and others might deem local or authentic culture. And this is an important part of the story of the cultural regeneration of New Orleans, for better and for worse.

One interesting track on *Proud to Swim Home* is "Bayou Teche" by the Uptown Cajun All-Stars. This noise recording was originally part of an album called *The Uptown Cajun All-Stars Present an Old Tyme Cajun Fais Do Do!*, which was "packaged-up as a long-lost Cajun recording." Named after a waterway running through what is known as "Cajun country," "Bayou Teche" comments on and seeks to undermine the fetishization of folk authenticity in New Orleans cultural discourse.[42] The grinding noise of the recording also reminds us that such an embrace of the folk can contest and reproduce power. Similarly, Harrison-Nelson discusses how visual artists, filmmakers, and journalists from all over the world celebrate Mardi Gras Indian culture and other traditional cultural expressions, weaving images of suits and snippets of interviews into a web of often digitized representations of the culture. It is a visibility, she believes, that does some good things, like facilitating donations of books for the education program she runs, but it also furthers what she sees as a discourse of exoticization, where familiarity with "authentic" New Orleans culture— one's ability to claim some sort of insider knowledge by virtue of one's relationships (even casual ones) with prominent cultural workers—becomes a means of accruing power and prestige. Although this is not a new phenomenon, it is one she believes is on the increase because of the post-Katrina attention to New Orleans culture, the privileged role of this culture in redistributive relationships after the storm, and the large numbers of cultural workers and those just invested in culture who have come to New Orleans to make lives for themselves over the past several years.[43]

Of course much of this fetishization of culture is produced in local, national, global, and virtual media, as disseminated through various formats. The HBO series *Treme,* as noted earlier, certainly has not done anything to lessen this effect.[44] *Proud to Swim Home* reminds us of this, given Backporch Revolution's practice of releasing music in multiple formats. And the distortion on such recordings speaks to the way in which the narration of New Orleans as diaspora city will always, well, distort. This is not to say that the distortion prevents the experience from being narrated further; one just needs to be aware of these distortions and those we necessarily bring to the story. It is a realization that points to the need for care and accuracy, but which also permits some freedom to recognize and embrace one's own investments—one's own, in our case, outsiders' perspectives.

Finally, several pieces on *Proud to Swim Home* situate these diasporic cultural experiences in a complex ecology of the city that also exceeds the city. The acoustic drone group Murmur's "Secondary Fermentation," recorded in a fermentation tank in the dilapidated Dixie Brewery, situates the cultural scene in New Orleans's postindustrial environment and an ongoing transformation of urban space and economy. The pulsating rhythm of B. Killingsworth's "Downed Powerline Blues," recorded on the shores of Lake Pontchartrain, situates cultural production at the rhythmic nexus of the electrical grid and the earth itself and brings home the fact that the meaning-making sonic force of New Orleans music is part of a broader regional array of place-defining sounds created by "natural" phenomena (crickets, rain, the river) and an array of human activities.[45] So does Archipelago's "The Earth Moves Five Ways," which blends folk, world, noise, electronics, and drone while deploying manipulated human voice, percussion, electronic and acoustic instruments, and sound effects to link human activity, natural landscape, and the machine world. Haunting tenor saxophone lines are almost drowned out by the rest of the mix, but we can still hear the jazz resonance. The saxophone speaks of how generations of local musicians—outsiders like Ellington and ordinary participants in multiple diasporas, the most central of which is the one that connects New Orleans to the Caribbean and Africa—continue to perform the life of the city, to reinvent it in the face of, despite, or as part of the noise.

# NOTES

**PREFACE**

1. James Lincoln Collier's take on Ellington's late suites is one with which we take issue. See Collier, *Duke Ellington,* 288.
2. Lambert, *Duke Ellington,* 295.
3. Ellington and Dance, *Duke Ellington in Person,* 158.
4. We are not the first to invoke Ellington's composition when writing about New Orleans post Katrina. Roger Abrahams's (with John Szwed, Robert Ferris Thompson, and Nick Spitzer) *Blues for New Orleans* (2006) uses the title of the album's lead track in its elegiac account of the city, its creole culture, and its hope for the future. But by using the title of the larger work we hope to convey a somewhat broader, more contradictory story.
5. Willis, *Reflections in Black,* xv, 4.
6. Work by many of the photographers listed is collected in Willis, *Reflections in Black.*
7. Robin Kelley, "Foreword," in Willis, *Reflections in Black,* x.
8. Faulkner, *Requiem for a Nun,* 73.
9. For an important recent survey of such meanings see Raeburn, *New Orleans Style and the Writing of American Jazz History.*

**SECTION 1**

1. These are the closing stanzas of Williams's untitled poem, reprinted in the liner notes to *Dear New Orleans.* The notes indicate that Williams presented this piece at a May 22, 2009, artist activism retreat, as described below.

2. *Dear New Orleans* liner notes; press release, "*Dear New Orleans:* A Digital Benefit Compilation Dedicated to the City of Music Five Years after the Levees Broke," August 18, 2010.

3. Ibid.

4. Chris Rose, "Dear America," *New Orleans Times-Picayune,* September 6, 2005; America, "Dear New Orleans." Both reprinted in liner notes, *Dear New Orleans.*

5. Solnit, *A Paradise Built in Hell,* 234–46.

6. See Klein, *The Shock Doctrine.*

7. Solnit, *A Paradise Built in Hell,* 9.

8. Amnesty International, *Un-Natural Disaster.*

9. Jonathan Dee, "New Orleans's Gender-Bending Rap" *New York Times,* July 25, 2010, Sunday Magazine, MM22.

10. Dyson, *Come Hell or High* Water, 14.

11. Mudimbe, *The Invention of Africa,* ix.

12. Quoted in Alex Williams, "Into Africa: For a Continent Célèbre, Blockbuster Interest," *New York Times,* August 13, 2006, sec. 9, 1, 8.

13. John Harwood, "A Special Weekly Report from the Wall Street Journal's Capital Bureau," *Wall Street Journal,* September 9, 2005, eastern edition, A4.

14. Kelley, "Foreword," in Willis, *Reflections in Black.*

15. One fine example of an early post-Katrina book that argues for the city's survival is Tom Piazza's *Why New Orleans Matters.* Piazza argues that part of his book's project is to get people "to think hard about what is worth fighting to save" (p. xxii) and to ask the question, "What is the meaning of a place like that, and what is lost if it is lost?" (p. 9). At the end of the book, he argues quite eloquently for an equitable reconstruction of the city (see pp. 154–62). A recent example of a book that emphasizes resiliency and survival in the work of political and cultural activists is Jordan Flaherty's *Floodlines.*

16. See, for example, Gray, "Recovered, Reinvented, Reimagined."

17. Piazza, *Why New Orleans Matters,* 55; Sothern, *Down in New Orleans,* 208.

18. Woods, "Katrina's World."

19. Salvaggio, "Forgetting New Orleans," 306.

## SECTION 2

1. See, for example, Radano, *Lying Up a Nation;* Cruz, *Culture on the Margins.*

2. For an earlier version of this analysis, see my "Jazz and Revival." Regis and Walton raise a similar set of issues: "After looking at the social structure of the production of the New Orleans Jazz and Heritage Festival, the events and crises that came in the wake of Hurricane Katrina seem inevitable and sadly predictable." "Producing the Folk," 429.

3. In the words of Matt Sakakeeny, "Place has anchored culture and culture has anchored place in New Orleans, creating a dialogic relationship whereby culture is constituted in place and constitutive of place." "Resounding Silence in a Musical City," 43.

4. "Homecoming," in *New Orleans Jazz and Heritage Festival 2006: Official Collectors' Guide,* 17.

5. Jan Ramsey, "Love Is Not Enough," *OffBeat Magazine's JazzFest Bible 2006,* 14.

6. Harvey, *A Brief History of Neoliberalism*, 2.

7. Yudice, *The Expediency of Culture*, 1, 9–11. Yudice writes that culture "is the lynchpin of a new epistemic framework in which ideology and much of what [philosopher Michel] Foucault called disciplinary society . . . are absorbed into an economic or ecological rationality, such that management, conservation, access, distribution, and investment—in 'culture' and the outcomes thereof—take priority."

8. "Art and Death in New Orleans," *NPR: News and Notes*, January 9, 2007, www.npr.org/templates/story/story.php?storyId = 6761681&sc = emaf (accessed February 15, 2008).

9. Yudice, *The Expediency of Culture*, 20, 34, 56.

10. Lowe, *Immigrant Acts*, 85–91.

11. The literature voicing such perspectives is vast and impossible to survey adequately here. For an introduction to how such issues have been addressed in jazz historiography, see DeVeaux, "Constructing the Jazz Tradition." Two key books in African American letters that have significantly shaped aspects of this conversation over the past several decades are Jones, *Blues People*; and Murray, *Stomping the Blues*. An important treatment of how such narratives are put to different political uses in the present is Lipsitz, "Songs of the Unsung." For an account of how such issues have been articulated by African American musicians over the years, see my *What Is This Thing Called Jazz?* And for a survey of the ways New Orleans jazz and its practitioners have been represented in jazz criticism and jazz historiography, see Raeburn, *New Orleans Style and the Writing of American Jazz History*.

12. Gotham, "Theorizing Urban Spectacles," 228–29, 240–43.

13. Wein, *Myself among Others*, 352–58; Souther, *New Orleans on Parade*, 119–21; Clifford and Smith, *Incomplete History*, 2–3.

14. Clifford and Smith, *Incomplete History*, 19, 349–50.

15. Regis and Walton "Producing the Folk," 407–11; Jazzfest website, www.nojazzfest.com/ (accessed July 2, 2010); Wein, *Myself among Others*, 359–60; Clifford and Smith, *Incomplete History*, 349.

16. Jazzfest website, www.nojazzfest.com/ (accessed July 2, 2010); Clifford and Smith, *Incomplete History*, 10; Michael Smith, *New Orleans Jazz Fest*, 10; Federico, *Our Heritage in the Making*, 46, 48. For a different take on Jackson's symbolic legacy, see Jabir, "On Conjuring Mahalia," esp. 649, 654–55. Although Jabir does not address Jackson's 1970 performance, he argues that, in a post-Katrina context, listening to Jackson's recordings "conjur[es] into existence a [specifically African American] communal hope that critiques the politics, representation, and rememory of Katrina." We can also hear an interrogation of the reduction of "a New Orleans musical sensibility" to a tourist-friendly, symbolically hedonistic "jazz."

17. Wein, *Myself among Others*, 359; Miner, quoted in Clifford and Smith, *Incomplete History*, 347; Smith and Miner, *Jazz Fest Memories*, 18–19; Michael Smith, *New Orleans Jazz Fest*, 12.

18. Smith and Miner, *Jazz Fest Memories*, 9–11, 19–21; Clifford and Smith, *Incomplete History*, 16–17, 237, 354; Michael Smith, *New Orleans Jazz Fest*, 139, 200.

19. For brief accounts of the increasing corporate sponsorship of Jazz Fest that begins with

the first festival, as well as controversies surrounding it, see Federico, *Our Heritage in the Making*, timeline, n.p.; Clifford and Smith, *Incomplete History*, 6, 264–65, 280–81.

20. Regis and Walton, "Producing the Folk," 401.

21. Michael Smith, *New Orleans Jazz Fest*, 9; Jazz Fest website, www.nojazzfest.com/ (accessed July 2, 2010); Clifford and Smith, *Incomplete History*, 241–42, 342. The first "culture" recognized was Haiti, which was indeed a particularly relevant choice given the Haitian influence on New Orleans's cultural scene after the Haitian Revolution.

22. Clifford and Smith, *Incomplete History*, 10–11.

23. Ibid, 20, 70–72; Michael Smith, *New Orleans Jazz Fest*, 73–74; Wein, *Myself among Others*, 370–71.

24. Wein, *Myself among Others*, 372–75; Michael Smith, *New Orleans Jazz Fest*, 15, 73–74; Clifford and Smith, *Incomplete History*, 20.

25. Clifford and Smith, *Incomplete History*, 160. The authors note that the greater visibility of Cajun and Native culture at Jazz Fest from the 1970s forward was also a result of cultural activism. See pp. 352–53.

26. Ibid., 80–81; Wein, *Myself among Others*, 372; Michael Smith, *New Orleans Jazz Fest*, 11–12, 132.

27. Jazzfest 1992 program book, 5–7; Michael Smith, *New Orleans Jazz Fest*, 11–12; Clifford and Smith, *Incomplete History*, 20–21, 155, 161. One significant example of emphasizing the African American contribution was the festival program book produced by Salaam's Bright Moments company, which included as an insert the "Black River Journal" featuring poetry, prose, and photographs.

28. Salaam, *What Is Life?*, 218–19.

29. Count Basin (SM), "Hail to the Chief," *Gambit Weekly* 27, no. 18 (May 2, 2006): 23.

30. *New Orleans Jazz and Heritage Festival 2006: Official Collectors' Guide*, 40.

31. Regis, "Second Lines, Minstrelsy, and the Contested Landscapes"; Regis, "Blackness and the Politics of Memory"; Michael White, "New Orleans's African American Musical Traditions," 91–93. For an important account of the role of second lining told from the perspectives of club members, see Nine Times Social and Pleasure Club, *Coming Out the Door*.

32. Regis and Walton, "Producing the Folk," 411–13.

33. Regis, "Second Lines, Minstrelsy, and the Contested Landscapes," 481, 497; Nine Times Social and Pleasure Club, *Coming Out the Door*, 144, 148; Regis and Walton, "Producing the Folk," 413; personal communication with Ronald Lewis, Jazz Fest grounds, April 2006.

34. Molotch, "Death on the Roof," 31–34; Dyson, *Come Hell or High Water*, 20–21; Goldberg, *The Threat of Race*, 87–92. For more on neoliberalism and Hurricane Katrina, see the essays in Johnson, *The Neoliberal Deluge*; and Woods, *In the Wake of Hurricane Katrina*

35. Powell, "What Does American History Tell Us about Katrina and Vice Versa?," 865–66.

36. Ibid., 867; Flaherty, *Floodlines*, 59–60; Campbell Robertson, " Settlement over Money to Rebuild after Storm," *New York Times*, July 7, 2011, A13.

37. Le Menestrel and Harvey, "Sing Us Back Home," 180, 195; Swenson, *New Atlantis*, 33–34.

38. Larry Abramson, "New Orleans School Making Progress after Storm," *NPR: Morning*

*Edition,* May 16, 2007, www.npr.org/templates/story/story.php?storyId = 10187992 (accessed May 16, 2007).

39. New Orleans Habitat Musicians' Village, found at www.nolamusiciansvillage.com/about/ (accessed October 10, 2008).

40. Raeburn, "They're Trying to Wash Us Away," 815.

41. Regis and Walton note how the "ideologies" of Jazz Fest, the commitment to "envision creating new social/racial possibilities" have often lost out to "realpolitik, the everyday-ness of doing, the power of the market." See "Producing the Folk," 401. George Wein suggests that he, as something of a financial pragmatist, found himself at odds with the board, which made certain decisions based on a responsibility to the community. One example was the board's refusal to let Brown and Williamson underwrite Jazz Fest as a "Kool" festival because of Kool cigarettes' aggressive marketing campaign to blacks. See *Myself among Others,* 374.

42. Souther, *New Orleans on Parade,* 121; Clifford and Smith, *Incomplete History,* 263–64, 280–81.

43. Regis and Walton, "Producing the Folk," 400, 414–15.

44. Clifford and Smith, *Incomplete History,* 21, 81, 256; Michael Smith, *New Orleans Jazz Fest,* 15. In 1997, according to Clifford and Smith, George Clinton, Earth, Wind and Fire, and Isaac Hayes were scheduled in part to recruit more African Americans into its audience (p. 256).

45. Personal communication with John O'Neal, May 6, 2006; Regis and Walton, "Producing the Folk," 422, 432.

46. The Essence Music Festival was launched as a partnership between Essence Magazine and Wein's production company, Festival Productions, with the encouragement of the Greater New Orleans Black Tourism Network (an offshoot of the Greater New Orleans Tourist and Convention Commission). Although the partnership dissolved after a few years, Wein's company, under the local leadership of Quint Davis, continued to produce the event. Wein, *Myself among Others,* 499–502; Souther, *New Orleans on Parade,* 208; Flaherty, *Floodlines,* 24; Gotham, "Theorizing Urban Spectacles," 233–35.

47. Regis, "Second Lines, Minstrelsy, and the Contested Landscapes"; Regis, "Blackness and the Politics of Memory."

48. Regis, "Blackness and the Politics of Memory," 756; Regis, "Second Lines, Minstrelsy, and the Contested Landscapes," 474, 477.

49. Personal communication with John O'Neal, May 6, 2006.

50. Swenson, *New Atlantis,* 35–36.

51. Holt, *The Problem of Race in the Twenty-first Century,* 102.

52. Flaherty, *Floodlines,* 73.

53. Holt, *The Problem of Race in the Twenty-first Century,* 108–9, 113.

54. Writing about pre-Katrina New Orleans, Regis argues that in this city, as elsewhere, it is clear that "urban [black] underclasses who work in the entertainment and hospitality trades are increasingly perceived by more privileged groups as the sources of crime, which endanger the steady inflow of travelers, jeopardizing their pleasure and business activities." Yet "the cultural productions of urban black working-class communities are increasingly featured as the principal asset distinguishing New Orleans from

other tourist destinations and conference centers." See "Blackness and the Politics of Memory," 753–54.

55. Lowe, *Immigrant Acts*, 86.
56. Regis, "Blackness and the Politics of Memory," 767–68.
57. Saul, *Freedom Is, Freedom Ain't*, 106, 119, 121.
58. Regis and Walton, "Producing the Folk," 407–410, 422–31.
59. BondGraham, "The New Orleans that Race Built," 4, 12–13.
60. White, "The Persistence of Race Politics," 48.
61. Gray, "Recovered, Reinvented, Reimagined," 273.

**SECTION 3**

1. Jon Donley, "Lundi Gras Parade Celebrates Second-Line Tradition," *New Orleans Times-Picayune*, February 3, 2008.
2. Koritz and Sanchez point out that these "asset-based" models of civic engagement are consistent with the philosophies and activism of Saul Alinsky, Myles Horton, and Paolo Freire. See *Civic Engagement in the Wake of Katrina*, 13.
3. Dinerstein, "Second Lining Post-Katrina," 625; Shaila Dewan, "With the Jazz Funeral's Return, the Spirit of New Orleans Rises," *New York Times*, October 10, 2005, www.nytimes.com/2005/10/10/national/nationalspecial/10funeral.html (accessed May 20, 2011); Berry, Foose, and Jones, *Up from the Cradle of Jazz*, 302. Shavers is quoted in Berry.
4. Dinerstein, "Second Lining Post-Katrina," 625, 634.
5. Quoted in "Rebuilding New Orleans: The Second Line Model," transcript from panel discussion at Sound Café, New Orleans, LA, October 25, 2007, www.neighborhoodstoryproject.org.secondline.html.
6. Helen Regis, interview with Ned Sublette, *Afropop Worldwide* (2006), www.afropop.org/multi/interview/ID/90/Helen+Regis+with+Ned+Sublette+in+New+Orleans,+2006Home (accessed July 24, 2006); Adam Nossiter, "Another Social Conflict Confronts New Orleans," *New York Times*, November 26, 2006.
7. Regis, interview with Ned Sublette; Nine Times Social and Pleasure Club, *Coming out the Door for the Ninth Ward*, 223.
8. Berry, Foose, and Jones, *Up from the Cradle of Jazz*, 304, 306.
9. Edwards, interview by Rowell, 1304.
10. Berry, Foose, and Jones, *Up from the Cradle of Jazz*, 303.
11. Medley, interview by Rowell, 1040.
12. Frank Donze and Gwen Filosa, "Bridge March Hails Justice, Voter Rights," *New Orleans Times-Picayune*, April 2, 2006.
13. Roach, *Cities of the Dead*, 2–7.
14. Ibid., 244–45, 261–69.
15. Ibid., 60, 209–11. See also Turner, *Jazz Religion, the Second Line, and Black New Orleans*, a more recent study that builds on Roach's work.
16. Rebecca Solnit, "We Won't Bow Down," *Yes Magazine*, February 15, 2010, www.yesmagazine.org/people-power/we-wont-bow-down (accessed August 12, 2010).

17. Michael White, "New Orleans's African American Musical Traditions," 93.

18. Sublette quoted in Flaherty, *Floodlines*, 8.

19. Medley, interview by Rowell, 1042.

20. Harrison-Nelson, "Upholding Community Traditions," 641–42.

21. Cherice Harrison-Nelson, telephone interview with the author, April 2010.

22. Giroux, "Reading Hurricane Katrina," 175. See also Giroux's *Stormy Weather* for a more extensive discussion of these issues and those that follow.

23. Ibid., 178. Giroux quotes Ojakangas's "Impossible Dialogue on Bio-Power," 6.

24. Ibid., 176–77. As Giroux puts it slightly differently a bit later in the essay, "The state no longer feels obligated to take measures that prevent hardship, suffering, and death. The state no longer protects its own disadvantaged citizens; they are already seen as dead within a transnational economic and political framework. Specific populations now occupy a globalized space of ruthless politics in which the categories of 'citizen' and 'democratic representation,' once integral to national politics, are no longer recognized. In the past, people who were marginalized by class and race could at least expect a modicum of support from the government, either because of the persistence of a drastically reduced social contract or because they still had some value as part of a reserve army of unemployed labour. That is no longer true. This new form of biopolitics is conditioned by a permanent state of class and racial exception in which 'vast populations are subject to conditions of life conferring upon them the status of living dead' . . . largely invisible in the global media, or, when disruptively present, defined as redundant, pathological, and dangerous." Ibid., 181–82. The quoted material is from Achille Mbembe, "Necropolitics," *Public Culture* (2003), 40.

25. Harris and Carbado, "Loot or Find," 100.

26. Flaherty, *Floodlines*, 157. See also page 187 for further discussion of public housing politics in the city as a gender justice issue. Flaherty's analysis draws from the work of the feminist group INCITE! He also notes that a state representative, John LaBruzzo from Metarie, went so far as to propose sterilizing women in public housing.

27. White, "The Persistence of Race Politics," 41.

28. Giroux, "Reading Hurricane Katrina," 189.

29. Breunlin and Regis, "Putting the Ninth Ward on the Map," 761.

30. Katy Reckdahl, "Ruling Clears Way for Lundi Gras Marchers," *New Orleans Times-Picayune*, February 1, 2008; "With Judge's OK, Second-Line Rolls," *New Orleans Times-Picayune*, February 5, 2008. Another member of the organization claims to have received a call from the police suggesting that if they followed through with their plans to hold the unified parade, their own group's parade that August would be in jeopardy.

31. Roach, *Cities of the Dead*, 244, 269, 271–73. It must also be noted that the 1991 municipal ordinance banning segregated krewes from parading put certain elites' interests in opposition to those of the state—at least on that front. Subsequently, three old-line krewes—Comus, Momus, and Proteus—ceased parading. Roach mentions this turn of events on pages 272–73. For a more detailed discussion, see Gill, *Lords of Misrule*, 221–57.

32. Roach, *Cities of the Dead*, 251–52, 271.

33. Regis, interview by Ned Sublette; Larry Blumenfeld, "Band on the Run in New Orleans,"

*Salon,* October 29, 2007, www.salon.com/news/feature/2007/10/29/treme/print
.html (accessed February 15, 2008); Berry, Foose, and Jones, *Up from the Cradle of Jazz,*
290–92; Katy Reckdahl, "St. Joseph's Night Gone Blue," *Gambit: Best of NewOrleans
.com,* March 29, 2005, www.bestofneworleans.com/gambit/st-josephs-night-gone
-blue/Content?oid = 1244049 (accessed June 13, 2011).

34. Nick Spitzer, "Learning from the Second-Lines, " *New Orleans Times-Picayune,* Octo-
ber 11, 2007; Katy Reckdahl, "Culture, Change Collide in Tremé," *New Orleans Times-
Picayune,* October 3, 2007; Katy Reckdahl, "Treme Musicians to Plead Innocent," *New
Orleans Times-Picayune,* October 4, 2007; Larry Blumenfeld, "Band on the Run in New
Orleans."

35. "Second Line Fee Increase Puts Strain on Tradition," April 6, 2006, http://wwozstreet
talk.blogspot.com/2006/05/46-second-line-fee-increase-puts.html (accessed February
5, 2008); "Transcript—Second Line Fee Increase," April 1, 2006, http://wwozstreet
talk.blogspot.com/2006/05/transcript-secondline-fee-increase_02.html (accessed February 19, 2008).

36. Reckdahl, "Culture, Change Collide in Tremé"; Katy Reckdahl, "Permit Fees Raining
on Second-Line Parades," *New Orleans Times-Picayune,* March 29, 2007; Nossiter, "Another Social Conflict"; "Rebuilding New Orleans: The Second Line Model," transcript
from panel discussion at Sound Café, New Orleans, October 25, 2007, www.neighbor
hoodstoryproject.org.secondline.html.

37. Nossiter, "Another Social Conflict."

38. "Second Line Fee Increase Puts Strain on Tradition"; "Transcript—Second Line Fee
Increase"; Katy Reckdahl, "Permit Fees Raining on Second-Line Parades."

39. Regis, interview by Sublette; Reckdahl, "Culture, Change Collide in Tremé"; Blumenfeld, "Band on the Run in New Orleans"; Swenson, *New Atlantis,* 111–13; "Rebuilding
New Orleans: The Second Line Model," transcript from panel discussion at Sound
Café, New Orleans, October 25, 2007, www.neighborhoodstoryproject.org.secondline
.html.

40. Flaherty, *Floodlines,* 157.

41. "Transcript—Second Line Fee Increase."

42. David Kunian, "A Positive, Cultural Thing," *Best of New Orleans,* February 6, 2007,
www.bestofneworleans.com/dispatch/2007–02–06/cover_story.php (accessed February 22, 2008).

43. In retrospect, I think the musicians with the procession probably included members
of the Hot 8, who incorporate elements of "Atomic Dog" and other P-Funk musical
phrases into their tune "Rock with the Hot 8."

44. Flaherty, *Floodlines,* 9. Soulja Slim was murdered on Thanksgiving Day 2003.

45. Spitzer, "Learning from the Second-Lines."

46. Berry, Foose, and Jones, *Up from the Cradle of Jazz,* 310–12; Michelle Nealy, "Living
Legacy—The Shot That Killed Musician Dinerral Shavers Left a Gaping Hole in the
Life of His Family," *New Orleans Times-Picayune,* September 4, 2007; Katy Reckdahl,
"Neighbors Want Answers on the Surge in Violence—Group Plans Protest March"
*New Orleans Times-Picayune,* January 8, 2007.

47. Berry, Foose, and Jones, *Up from the Cradle of Jazz,* 311–13; Swenson, *New Atlantis,* 83;

Reckdahl, "Neighbors Want Answers on the Surge in Violence; SilenceIsViolence website, http://silenceisviolence.org/about/ (accessed August 7, 2010).

48. SilenceIsViolence website, http://silenceisviolence.org/about/ (accessed August 7, 2010).

49. Laura Maggi, "Anti-crime Activists Issue Plea to Cops, Citizens—Murder Victims' Names Ring Out," *New Orleans Times-Picayune,* January 12, 2008; Brendan McCarthy, "Anti-crime Rallies Bring New Orleanians Together—On City Hall's Steps Names of Those Killed in 2008 Are Read," *New Orleans Times-Picayune,* January 10, 2009; Brendan McCarthy, "'Week of Peace, Service' Held in N.O.—Activists Focus on Murder Victims," *New Orleans Times-Picayune,* January 20, 2010.

50. SilenceIsViolence website, http://silenceisviolence.org/ (accessed August 8, 2010).

51. Ramon Antonio Vargas, "Students Join Up to Protest Crime—Weather Doesn't Deter Marchers from Steps of City Hall," *New Orleans Times-Picayune,* March 30, 2008.

52. Laura Maggi and Katy Reckdahl, "A Year Ago Today—New Orleans Residents Outraged by Violent Crime Took to the Streets Demanding Change," *New Orleans Times-Picayune,* January 11, 2008; Maggi, "Anti-crime Activists Issue Plea to Cops, Citizens"; Laura Maggi; "NOPD holds back on Crime Reports—It Limits the Details Released to Public," *New Orleans Times-Picayune,* January 12, 2008; SilenceIsViolence website, http://silenceisviolence.org/ (accessed August 8, 2010).

53. Brendan McCarthy, "Second-Liners March for Understanding—Violence Is No Part of Culture They Cherish," *New Orleans Times-Picayune,* April 6, 2008.

54. McCarthy, "'Week of peace, service' held in N.O."; SilenceIsViolence website, http://silenceisviolence.org/article/171; http://silenceisviolence.org/article/172 (accessed August 10, 2010).

55. Jim Clancy and Wayne Drash, "Crime a Blues Refrain for New Orleans," *CNN.com,* June 9, 2008, www.cnn.com/2008/CRIME/06/09/nola.crime/index.html (accessed August 20, 2010).

56. Flaherty, *Floodlines,* 135–37, 159–76. Quote from page 135.

57. Gillmore, *Golden Gulag,* 245.

58. Van Dyke, Wool, and LeDoux, "An Opportunity to Reinvent New Orleans' Criminal Justice System," 6–9; Flaherty, *Floodlines,* 49–50. Another important antiviolence organization Flaherty discusses is Black Men United for Change, Equality and Justice, which has done significant work around conflict resolution and developing employment opportunities in communities experiencing high levels of violence.

59. Justin Burnell, "The Chasm of Distrust," *Nolafugees.com,* February 15, 2007, www.nolafugees.com/index.php?view = article&catid = 18%3Aprofiles&id = 29%3Athe-chasm-of distrust&tmpl = component&print = 1&layout = default&page = &option = com_content&Itemid = 10026 (accessed June 17, 2011).

60. "Protest Police Abuse at the Sixth District Police Station," SilenceIsViolence website, http://silenceisviolence.org/sharing/304 (accessed August 10, 2010); "Micheal *[sic]* Anderson," SilenceIsViolence website, http://silenceisviolence.org/sharing/297 (accessed August 10, 2010). Michael Anderson was convicted and sentenced to death in 2009 for the horrific 2006 murder of five Central City teens. His conviction was overturned in March 2010 after it was disclosed that prosecutors had withheld evidence

from the defense team and the lead police investigator on the case pleaded guilty to federal charges for falsifying information to cover up police misconduct during the Danziger Bridge shooting that left two civilians dead and four wounded several days after Katrina. Shortly after Anderson's conviction was overturned, the following comment was posted on the SilenceIsViolence website: "The unjust conviction of Micheal [sic] Anderson by a corrupt D.A. demonstrates that 'the status quo' is alive & well, and organizations/groups/clergys are never going to stand up and speak against the injustice carried out by one of your kind!!! And I denounce you all by the very name of your group! . . . Why aren't you all marching in the streets behind this injustice. You marched when you all felt that crime was getting out of control. Or when a father killed his son. Is white-folks off limits to your marches?" Although Anderson was a notorious criminal who later took a plea deal for the murders and other charges that sent him to prison for life, the comment still articulates a reasonable critique of unethical practices in the criminal justice system and the enormous distrust community members feel toward it.

61. Swenson, among others, notes the increase of cross-ethnic musical collaborations in the city post Katrina. See *New Atlantis*, 99.

62. Quoted in Reckdahl, "Neighbors Want Answers on the Surge in Violence."

63. Matt Davis, "TBC Brass Band Protests City's Sudden Enforcement of Controversial Street Musicians Ordinance," *Gambit: BestofNewOrleans.com*, June 17, 2010, www.best ofneworleans.com/blogofneworleans/archives/2010/06/17/tbc-brass-band-protests-citys-sudden-enforcement-of-controversial-street-musicians-ordinance/ (accessed June 22, 2011); Matt Davis, "Glen David Andrews Leads Protest Second Line in Jackson Square, Promises March on City Hall if NOPD Continues to Enforce Noise Ordinance," *Gambit: BestofNewOrleans.com*, June 18, 2010, www.bestofneworleans.com/blogofneworleans/archives/2010/06/18/glen-david-andrews-leads-protest-second-line-in-jackson-square-promises-march-on-city-hall-if-nopd-continues-to-enforce-noise-ordinance/ (accessed June 22, 2011).

64. Trumpets Not Guns website, www.trumpetsnotguns.com/program/ (accessed February 13, 2012).

65. Katy Reckdahl, "Mardi Gras Indians, New Orleans Police Meet to Avoid Conflicts on St. Joseph's Night," *New Orleans Times-Picayune*, March 18, 2011, www.nola.com/mardigras/index.ssf/2011/03/mardi_gras_indians_new_orleans.html (accessed June 23, 2011).

66. Larry Blumenfeld, "Beyond Jazzfest, Ruffled Feathers in New Orleans: Cultural Growing Pains in a Rebuilt City," *Village Voice*, June 22, 2011, www.villagevoice.com/2011–06–22/music/beyond-jazzfest-ruffled-feathers/ (accessed June 23, 2011).

67. "Second Line to Shut Down the Cradle to Prison Pipeline" (event page on Facebook), www.facebook.com/events/64763381645/; Flaherty, *Floodlines*, 78, 138. For a more detailed discussion of Fyre Youth Squad activities and critique, see Simmons, "End of the Line."

68. Jordan Flaherty, "Tamara Jackson, President of the New Orleans Social Aid and Pleasure Club Task Force, Speaks Out for Health Care Reform," *Louisiana Justice Institute*, Thursday, September 24, 2009, http://louisianajusticeinstitute.blogspot

.com/2009/09/tamara-jackson-president-of-new-orleans.html (accessed August 3, 2010). For a brief summary of problems of access to primary and mental health care in New Orleans, see the Amnesty International report, *Un-Natural Disaster: Human Rights on the Gulf Coast.*

69. "UNO Students Stage Second Line," *New Orleans Times-Picayune,* March 24, 2010; "Oil Spill Second Line," *New Orleans Times-Picayune,* June 5, 2010; Cain Burdeau, "Amnesty International: Hurricane Katrina Victims Had Human Rights Violated," *Associated Press,* April 9, 2010; http://louisianajusticeinstitute.blogspot.com/2010/04/hundreds -gather-at-secondline-to.html; "Over 200 Protest Southern Republican Leadership Conference in New Orleans," April 10 2010, http://news.infoshop.org/article.php?story = 20100410184018103 (accessed July 24 2010).

70. Jordan Flaherty, "New Orleans Workers Take to the Streets on Mayday," *Louisiana Justice Institute,* May 2, 2011, http://louisianajusticeinstitute.blogspot.com/2011/05/new -orleans-workers-take-to-streets-on.html (accessed June 22, 2011).

71. "No More War on Drugs," *Women with a Vision* website, http://wwav-no.org/june-17th -no-more-war-on-drugs (accessed June 22, 2011). This event was part of a national day of action, with events held in New York, Los Angeles, Chicago, San Francisco, and other cities.

72. Michael White is among those who have raised such concerns. See "New Orleans's African American Musical Traditions," 99–101.

## SECTION 4

1. Garofalo, "Who Is the World?," 334.

2. Ibid., 326, 332–33, 339–40.

3. Ibid., 325, 328.

4. Ibid., 335.

5. See, for example, McGinley, "Floods of Memory." It further complicates matters that a truly comprehensive account of a post-Katrina soundtrack would also have to consider live concerts (whether benefit or not) in diverse venues, radio broadcasts, and people listening to music on car and home stereos, computers, iPods, and so on, individually or in groups.

6. Simon Frith argues that Live Aid marked a shift in the emphasis of musical benefit events, on the part of musicians and audiences alike, from "a kind of community self-help, doing something about our problems, to a kind of populist noblesse oblige, doing something about them." Garofalo, "Who Is the World?" 334.

7. McLeese, "Seeds Scattered by Katrina," 213; personal conversation with Mark Fowler, April 13, 2010.

8. These comments are informed by George Lipsitz's application of literary critic Mikhail Bakhtin's dialogic criticism to popular music. See Lipsitz, *Time Passages,* 99–132.

9. Masquelier, "Why Katrina's Victims Aren't Refugees," 736–40; Kish, "My FEMA People," 246.

10. Masquelier, "Why Katrina's Victims Aren't Refugees," 738–39. Masquelier says victims rejected refugee status by "asserting one's rootedness in one's native community, while

simultaneously denying that, as a law-abiding U.S. citizen, one's identity could be defined by the mass-mediated images of anarchy, violence and despair that had personified the flooded city during the post-Katrina crisis."

11. McGinley, "Floods of Memory," 57–59, 63–64. McGinley also analyzes Kara Walker's curated exhibition, *After the Deluge.*

12. Brooks, "All That You Can't Leave Behind," 186–92. Brooks also suggests that Blige's performance countered "the erasure of black female artists from rock genealogies [and] the erasure of black female sexual exploitation in rock memory." Yet she is also aware, even in the post-Katrina context, that different iterations of the same song can change meaning as contexts shift. She claims "One" loses its political edge as it moves from the televised benefit concert stage, to album track, to being a standard part of Blige's concert repertoire.

13. Kish, "My FEMA People," 246–47, 250–52.

14. Ibid., 252–63.

15. Leo Sacks, "Home Is in Your Heart," liner notes, *Sing Me Back Home.*

16. "News and Notes: New Orleans Social Club: 'Sing Me Back Home,'" *NPR,* March 31, 2006, www.npr.org/templates/story/story.php?storyId = 5313087 (accessed September 30, 2010).

17. Sacks, "Home Is in Your Heart."

18. "Musicians 'Sing Me Back Home' to New Orleans, Day to Day," *NPR,* April 20, 2006, www.npr.org/templates/story/story.php?storyId = 5353291 (accessed September 30, 2010); liner notes, *Sing Me Back Home.* The liner notes also include "Sing Me Home," a poem by Nikki Giovanni that narrates a collective desire for return, to "Sing a north song on / Southbound trains."

19. McLeese, "Seeds Scattered by Katrina," 217; "News and Notes: New Orleans Social Club."

20. Murray, *The Omni-Americans,* 58.

21. Transcript, interview with the Dirty Dozen Brass Band, *Tavis Smiley Late Night on PBS,* October 3, 2006, www.pbs.org/kcet/tavissmiley/archive/200610/20061003_thedirty-dozenbrassband.html (accessed September 23, 2010); Dirty Dozen Brass Band website, www.dirtydozenbrass.com/catalog/10 (accessed September 27, 2010); liner notes, Dirty Dozen Brass Band, *What's Going On.*

22. Liner notes, Dirty Dozen Brass Band, *What's Going On;* David Ritz, "Marvin's Miracle," liner notes, reissued version of Marvin Gaye, *What's Going On;* Suzanne Smith, *Dancing in the Streets,* 237; quote is from "Marvin Gaye, *What's Going On* Review," BBC Music, www.bbc.co.uk/music/reviews/n825 (accessed June 9, 2011).

23. Ritz, "Marvin's Miracle"; Suzanne Smith, *Dancing in the Streets,* 236–38.

24. Suzanne Smith, *Dancing in the Streets,* 238–39.

25. Dirty Dozen, interview with Tavis Smiley.

26. Frankie eventually got a job as hotel doorman. Suzanne Smith, *Dancing in the Streets,* 237.

27. INCITE! "Statement on Katrina," September 11, 2005. Quoted in Flaherty, *Floodlines,* 102–3.

28. As Jordan Flaherty notes, "New Orleanians can learn a lot from Detroit's experience of

economic devastation." Both cities, for example, experienced the devastating effects of white flight and population loss, and both have tried to jump-start their economies by building downtown casinos. Yet both cities also have made important contributions to American music, and "most importantly, both cities are sites of inspiring resistance." *Floodlines,* 90–91.

29. 2-Cent Freedom Land Project featuring K. Gates, The Show, Young A, Dee 1, Mack Maine, Nutt tha Kid, and Dizzy, "Freedom Land." In Woods, *In the Wake of Katrina,* 371–75; www.2-cent.com/What_is_2-CENT.html; www.2-cent.com/Watch.html; http://current.com/entertainment/music/88798008_2-cent-t-v-freedomland.htm; www.2-cent.com/Watch.html; Flaherty, *Floodlines,* 113–15.

30. Danny Barker recorded these songs for his King Zulu label in the mid 1950s. The performances on *Preservation* may thus be seen as both a recognition of the Mardi Gras Indian tradition and of Barker's role in encouraging it. I thank Bruce Boyd Raeburn for this observation.

31. "Preservation Hall and Sony Red Distribution Announce: 'Preservation,' a Benefit Album," press release, New Orleans, November 11, 2009, www.preservationhall.com/band/press_kit/press_releases/PHJB_Preservation_Benefit_Album.pdf (accessed September 30, 2010). My analysis here is based on the expanded version of the album with a bonus disc.

32. Preservation Hall website, www.preservationhall.com/hall/hall_history/index.aspx (accessed September 30, 2010).

33. Phillip Lutz, "New Orleans Jazz Band Gets in Step with the Times," *New York Times,* January 3, 2010, www.nytimes.com/2010/01/03/nyregion/03musicwe.html?pagewanted = print (accessed September 28, 2010); Ben Jaffe, liner notes, *Preservation.*

34. Mike Greenhaus, "The Preservation Hall Jazz Band and the Essence of New Orleans," *Jambands.com,* www.jambands.com/features/2010/09/21/the-preservation-hall-jazz-band-and-the-essence-of-new-orleans (accessed September 28, 2010).

35. Flaherty, *Floodlines,* 84–86, 100–110, 118.

36. Jaffe, liner notes, *Preservation.*

37. Flaherty, *Floodlines,* 102–5; Luft, "Beyond Disaster Exceptionalism."

38. For more details see the liner notes of *Dear New Orleans,* a 2010 release, discussed briefly in section 1, which includes recordings by musicians who participated in the retreat.

39. "Lenny Kravitz, Mos Def and the Preservation Hall Jazz Band Remake 'It Ain't My Fault' as Gulf Aid Fundraiser," Keith Spera, *New Orleans Times-Picayune,* June 14, 2010, updated June 15, 2010, www.nola.com/music/index.ssf/2010/06/post_8.html (accessed September 28, 2010); Randy Lewis, "Album review: Preservation Hall Jazz Band's 'Preservation,'" *Pop and Hiss, the L.A. Times Music Blog,* February 15, 2010, http://preshall.blogspot.com/2010/02/preservation-review-by-la-times.html (accessed September 28, 2010).

40. Swenson, *New Atlantis,* 3–4, 10–11, 158–61, 217–18, 231–32.

41. A similar, contemporaneous critique is voiced in local musician Shamarr Allen's 2010 recording "Sorry Ain't Enough No More." Joining Allen are Dee-1, Paul Sanchez, and Bennie Pete.

42. Spera, "Lenny Kravitz, Mos Def and the Preservation Hall Jazz Band remake 'It Ain't My Fault' as Gulf Aid Fundraiser."

43. Giddins and DeVeaux, *Jazz*, 588.

44. Porter, *What Is This Thing Called Jazz?*, 287–334.

45. Press release, "Lt. Governor Mitch Landrieu's Office Partners with Jazz at Lincoln Center for Touring New Orleans Celebration," April 17, 2006, www.jazzatlincolncenter. org/about/news/060417-news.html (accessed July 19, 2006).

46. Wynton Marsalis, "Saving America's Soul Kitchen," *Time*, September 11, 2005.

47. Winters, "'More Desultory and Unconnected Than Any Other,'" 457, 472.

48. Washington, "Has Katrina Failed to Blow the Wool from Over Our Eyes?"

## SECTION 5

1. Liner notes, Terence Blanchard, *A Tale of God's Will*.

2. Kirsten Silva Gruesz argues that a Caribbean-centered understanding of creolization potentially elides cultural fusions stemming from networks that exceed that framework. She suggests, for example, that paradigms which connect New Orleans to Caribbean ports and processes of creolization tend to downplay important connections to Mexico and Central America and explore the complicated relationships that New Orleans and other Gulf of Mexico port cities have had to "national interiors." See Gruesz, "The Gulf of Mexico System."

3. See essays in Cohen and Toninato, *The Creolization Reader*, especially their introduction.

4. Cohen and Toninato, "Introduction: The Creolization Debate: Analysing Mixed Identities and Culture," in *The Creolization Reader*, 1–21.

5. Stuart Hall, "Créolité and the Process of Creolization," in *The Creolization Reader*, ed. Cohen and Toninato, 26–38; Jean Bernabé, Patrick Chamoiseau, and Raphaël Confiant, "In Praise of Créolité," in ibid., 82–87.

6. Abrahams, *Blues for New Orleans*, 97–102; Sublette, *The World That Made New Orleans*, 294–311; Jean Bernabé, Patrick Chamoiseau, and Raphaël Confiant, "In Praise of Créolité," in *The Creolization Reader*, ed. Cohen and Toninato, 82–87. More generally, Juan Flores argues, creólité provides a "central reference to African cultural groundings and to the saliency of blackness." See Flores, *The Diaspora Strikes Back*, 29.

7. Abrahams, *Blues for New Orleans*, 102.

8. "The uniqueness of New Orleans," Sublette writes, "owes in no small part to its rapid succession of three distinct colonial eras, each with its own ruling European language and distinct associated African world. The city has superimposed on it in layers different identities that elsewhere remained separate." *The World That Made New Orleans*, 277.

9. Flores, *The Diaspora Strikes Back*, 16–20; Brent Edwards, *The Practice of Diaspora*, 12–13.

10. Flores, *The Diaspora Strikes Back*, 16–17.

11. Ibid., 22.

12. Ibid., 30.

13. Bernabe, Chamoiseau, and Confiant, "In Praise of Créolité," in *The Creolization* Reader, ed. Cohen and Toninato, 83.

14. Lewis, "To Turn As on a Pivot."

15. Allison Graham makes a provocative comparison between the response to the 1927 flood, which was designed to keep African American agricultural workers tied to the land, and the post-Katrina "confinement" of people in the Superdome and convention center, designed to "expedite an exodus" of disposable people at a moment when "the century of black labor was over." See Graham, "Free at Last," 608–9.

16. Michelle Krupa, "Racial Divides among New Orleans Neighborhoods Expand," *New Orleans Times-Picayune*, July 7, 2011, www.nola.com/politics/index.ssf/2011/06/pock ets_of_new_orleans_grow_fa.html (accessed June 22, 2011).

17. Flaherty, *Floodlines*, 90, 117; Finding Our Folk Press Kit, www.findingourfolk.org/pdfs/ FOFPressKit.pdf (accessed June 14, 2011); "National Jazz Museum in Harlem Presents New Orleans Brass Bands: From Second-Lines to Frontlines," *All About Jazz.com*, November 21, 2007, www.allaboutjazz.com/php/news.php?id = 16018 (accessed June 14, 2011); Larry Blumenfeld, "First-Rate Second-Liners: Reinvigorating New Orleans with the Hot 8 Brass Band," *Village Voice*, November 13, 2007, www.villagevoice.com/ music/0747,blumenfeld,78391,22.html (accessed June 14, 2011); "Rebuilding New Orleans: The Second Line Model," transcript from panel discussion at Sound Café, New Orleans, October 25, 2007, www.neighborhoodstoryproject.org.secondline.html.

18. Corrinna Da Fonseca-Wollheim, "The Haitian-Born Rhythm Revolution: An Uptown Concert Celebrates the Tradition That Grew from the Music Exported to Cuba and New Orleans by Freed Slaves," *Wall Street Journal*, http://online.wsj.com/article/SB10001 4240527487048952045753207906086961472.html?mod = ITP_newyork_5 (accessed October 4, 2010); "A Habana | Harlem premiere at Harlem Stage, and part of George Wein's CareFusion Jazz Festival, June 25, 2010," NYC Jazz Festival website, June 19, 2010, http://nycjazzfestival.com/forum/?p = 70 (accessed October 4, 2010).

19. Cherice Harrison-Nelson, telephone interview with the author, April 2010.

20. Flores, *The Diaspora Strikes Back*, 17.

21. Harrison-Nelson, interview with author.

22. Geraldine Wyckoff, "A Blessing . . . ," *Louisiana Weekly*, July 30, 2007. Reprinted at New Orleans Habitat Musicians' Village website, www.nolamusiciansvillage.org/news/ detail.asp?id = 70 (accessed February 11, 2011); Harrison-Nelson, interview with author.

23. Ferguson, "The Lateral Moves of African American Studies," 127.

24. Graham, "Free at Last," 609.

25. Flaherty, *Floodlines*, 215–18.

26. Shana Walton, "Sabor Latino: Central American Folk Traditions in New Orleans," New Populations Project, Louisiana Division of the Arts Folklife Program, www.louisian afolklife.org/LT/Articles_Essays/latinos.html (accessed February 2, 2011); "Five Years after Katrina, New Orleans Sees Higher Percentage of Hispanics," *Washington Post*, August 21, 2010; Michelle Krupa, "New Orleans' Official 2010 Census Population Is 343,829, Agency Reports," *New Orleans Times-Picayune*, February 3, 2011.

27. Walton, "Sabor Latino"; Dominic Bordelon, "'My Way to Show Baton Rouge I'm Here': Latino Music and Dance in Baton Rouge," New Populations Project, Louisiana Division

of the Arts Folklife Program, www.louisianafolklife.org/LT/Articles_Essays/latinosbr1 .html (accessed February 2, 2010).

28. Tomás Montoya González, "Music and Dance in South Louisiana's Cuban Community," with contributions from T. Ariana Hall, New Populations Project, Louisiana Division of the Arts Folklife Program, www.louisianafolklife.org/LT/Articles_Essays/ cubanMusicDance.htm, (accessed February 2, 2010).

29. Ibid.

30. Schmidt Camacho, *Migrant Imaginaries,* 196.

31. Yolanda Estrada, interview with the author, New Orleans, April 2010; Elizabeth Fussell, "Welcoming the Newcomers: Civic Engagement among Pre-Katrina Latinos," in Koritz and Sanchez, *Civic Engagement in the Wake of* Katrina, 140; Montoya González, "Music and Dance in South Louisiana's Cuban Community."

32. Amy Serrano, "From Punta to Chumba: Garifuna Music and Dance in New Orleans," New Populations Project, Louisiana Division of the Arts Folklife Program, www.louis ianafolklife.org/LT/Articles_Essays/garifuna.html (accessed February 2, 2010).

33. Denese Neu, "Honduran Identity within South Louisiana Culture," New Populations Project, Louisiana Division of the Arts Folklife Program, www.louisianafolklife.org/LT/ Articles_Essays/Hondurans1.html (accessed February 2, 2010).

34. Montoya González, "Music and Dance in South Louisiana's Cuban Community"; AsheSon My Space page, www.myspace.com/ashesonmusic (accessed February 11, 2011).

35. Walton, "Sabor Latino."

36. Review of Los Po-Boy-Citos, *New Orleans Latin Soul, OffBeat* (November 2008), 42.

37. Milena Merrill, "2008 New Orleans Carnaval Latino," *Nola.com,* June 17, 2008.

38. Ibid.; Jaquetta White, "World Cultural Economic Forum Begins in New Orleans," *New Orleans Times-Picayune,* October 30, 2008.

39. For more on the Decatur case, see Graham, "Free at Last"; and Redwood, "The Rebuilding of a Tourist Industry."

40. "Latin Star Is That Huge for New Orleans," *USA Today,* April 22, 2010.

41. Liner notes, *Proud to Swim Home.*

42. Ibid.; *The Uptown Cajun All Stars Present an Old Tyme Cajun Fais Do Do!* (IXNAY-18).

43. Harrison-Nelson, interview with author.

44. Ibid.

45. Le Menestrel and Henry, "Sing Us Back Home," 191.

# SELECTED BIBLIOGRAPHY

Abrahams, Roger. *Blues for New Orleans: Mardi Gras and America's Creole Soul*. With Nick Spitzer, John Szwed, and Robert Ferris Thompson. Philadelphia: University of Pennsylvania Press, 2006.

Amnesty International. *Un-Natural Disaster: Human Rights in the Gulf Coast*. Washington, DC: Amnesty International, 2010.

Berry, Jason, Jonathan Foose, and Tad Jones. *Up from the Cradle of Jazz: New Orleans Music since World War II*. Lafayette: University of Louisiana at Lafayette Press, 2009.

BondGraham, Darwin. "The New Orleans That Race Built: Racism, Disaster, and Urban Spatial Relationships." *Souls* 9, no. 1 (January–March 2007): 4–18.

Breunlin, Rachel, and Helen A. Regis. "Putting the Ninth Ward on the Map: Race, Place, and Transformation in Desire, New Orleans." *American Anthropologist* 108, no. 4 (December 2006): 744–64.

Brooks, Daphne. "All That You Can't Leave Behind: Black Female Soul Singing and the Politics of Surrogation in the Age of Catastrophe." *Meridians* 8, no. 1 (2008): 180–204.

Childs, John Brown, ed. *Hurricane Katrina: Response and Responsibilities*. Santa Cruz, CA: New Pacific Press, 2005.

Clifford, Jan, and Leslie Blackshear Smith. *The Incomplete, Year-by-Year Selectively Quirky, Prime Facts Edition of the History of the New Orleans Jazz and Heritage Festival*. Edited by Kevin McCaffrey. New Orleans: E/Prime Publications, 2005.

Cohen, Robin, and Paola Toninato, eds. *The Creolization Reader: Studies in Mixed Identities and Cultures*. New York: Routledge, 2010.

Collier, James Lincoln. *Duke Ellington*. New York : Oxford University Press, 1987.

Cruz, Jon D. *Culture on the Margins: The Black Spiritual and the Rise of American Cultural Interpretation.* Princeton, NJ: Princeton University Press, 1999.

DeVeaux, Scott. "Constructing the Jazz Tradition: Jazz Historiography." *Black American Literature Forum* 25, no. 3 (Fall 1991): 525–60.

Dinerstein, Joel. "Second Lining Post-Katrina: Learning Community from the Prince of Wales Social Aid and Pleasure Club." *American Quarterly* 61, no. 3 (September 2009): 615–37.

Dyson, Michael Eric. *Come Hell or High Water: Hurricane Katrina and the Color of Disaster.* New York: Basic Civitas, 2006.

Edwards, Brent Hayes. *The Practice of Diaspora: Literature, Translation, and the Rise of Black Internationalism.* Cambridge, MA: Harvard University Press, 2003.

Edwards, Louis. Interview by Charles Henry Rowell. *Callaloo* 29, no. 4 (Autumn 2006): 1301–6.

Ellington, Mercer. *Duke Ellington in Person: An Intimate Memoir.* With Stanley Dance. Boston: Houghton Mifflin, 1978.

Faulkner, William. *Requiem for a Nun.* New York: Vintage Books, 2011.

Federico, Brian. *Our Heritage in the Making: The Origins of New Orleans' Greatest Music Festival.* New Orleans: Scriptorium Publishing, 2001.

Ferguson, Roderick A. "The Lateral Moves of African American Studies in a Period of Migration." In *Strange Affinities: The Gender and Sexual Politics of Comparative Racialization,* edited by Grace Kyungwon Hong and Roderick A. Ferguson, 113–30. Durham, NC: Duke University Press, 2011.

Flaherty, Jordan. *Floodlines: Community and Resistance from Katrina to the Jena Six.* Chicago: Haymarket Books, 2010.

Flores, Juan. *The Diaspora Strikes Back: Caribeño Tales of Learning and Turning.* New York: Routledge, 2009.

Garofalo, Reebee. "Who Is the World? Reflections on Music and Politics Twenty Years after Live Aid" (online discussion with Billy Bragg, Tiffiniy Cheng, Susan Fast, Simon Frith, Holly George-Warren, Karen Pegley, and Will Straw). *Journal of Popular Music Studies* 17, no. 3 (2005): 324–44.

Giddins, Gary, and Scott DeVeaux. *Jazz.* New York: W. W. Norton, 2009.

Gill, James. *Lords of Misrule: Mardi Gras and the Politics of Race in New Orleans.* Jackson: University Press of Mississippi, 1997.

Gilmore, Ruth Wilson. *Golden Gulag: Prisons, Surplus, Crisis, and Opposition in Globalizing California.* Berkeley: University of California Press, 2007.

Giroux, Henry A. "Reading Hurricane Katrina: Race, Class, and the Biopolitics of Disposability." *College Literature* 33, no. 3 (Summer 2006): 171–96.

———. *Stormy Weather: Katrina and the Politics of Disposability.* Boulder, CO: Paradigm, 2006.

Goldberg, David Theo. *The Threat of Race: Reflections on Racial Neoliberalism.* Malden, MA: Blackwell, 2009.

Gotham, Kevin Fox. "Theorizing Urban Spectacles: Festivals, Tourism and the Transformation of Urban Space." *City* 9, no. 2 (July 2005): 225–45.

Graham, Allison. "Free at Last: Post-Katrina New Orleans and the Future of Conspiracy." *Journal of American Studies* 44, no. 3 (2010): 601–11.

Gray, Herman. "Recovered, Reinvented, Reimagined: *Treme*, Television Studies and Writing New Orleans." *Television & New Media* 23, no. 3 (May 2012): 268–78.

Gruesz, Kirsten Silva. "The Gulf of Mexico System and the 'Latinness' of New Orleans." *American Literary History* 18, no. 3 (2006):468–95.

Harris, Cheryl I., and Devon W. Carbado. "Loot or Find: Fact or Frame?" In *After the Storm: Black Intellectuals Explore the Meaning of Hurricane Katrina,* edited by David Dante Troutt, 87–110. New York: New Press, 2007.

Harrison-Nelson, Cherice. "Upholding Community Traditions: An Interview with Cherice Harrison-Nelson by Clyde Woods, March 1, 2009." *American Quarterly* 61, no. 3 (September 2009): 639–48.

Harvey, David. *A Brief History of Neoliberalism.* New York: Oxford University Press, 2005.

Holt, Thomas C. *The Problem of Race in the Twenty-first Century.* Cambridge, MA: Harvard University Press, 2000.

Jabir, Johari. "On Conjuring Mahalia: Mahalia Jackson, New Orleans, and the Sanctified Swing." *American Quarterly* 61, no. 3 (September 2009): 649–69.

Johnson, Cedric, ed. *The Neoliberal Deluge: Hurricane Katrina, Late Capitalism, and the Remaking of New Orleans.* Minneapolis: University of Minnesota Press, 2011.

Jones, LeRoi. *Blues People: Negro Music in White America.* New York: William Morrow, 1963.

Kish, Zenia. "'My FEMA People': Hip-Hop as Disaster Recovery in the Katrina Diaspora." In *In the Wake of Katrina: New Paradigms and Social Visions,* edited by Clyde Woods, 245–66. Baltimore, MD: Johns Hopkins University Press, 2010.

Klein, Naomi. *The Shock Doctrine: The Rise of Disaster Capitalism.* New York: Metropolitan Books/Henry Holt, 2007.

Koritz, Amy, and George Sanchez, eds. *Civic Engagement in the Wake of Katrina.* Ann Arbor: University of Michigan Press, 2009.

Lambert, Eddie. *Duke Ellington: A Listener's Guide.* Lanham,MD: Scarecrow Press, 1999.

Le Menestrel, Sara, and Jacques Harvey. "'Sing Us Back Home': Music, Place, and the Production of Locality in Post-Katrina New Orleans." *Popular Music and Society* 33, no. 2 (May 2010): 179–202.

Lewis, Earl. "To Turn As on a Pivot: Writing African Americans into a History of Overlapping Diasporas." *American Historical Review* 100, no. 3 (June 1995): 765–87.

Lipsitz, George. "Songs of the Unsung: The Darby Hicks History of Jazz." In *Uptown Conversation: The New Jazz Studies,* edited by Robert G. O'Meally, Brent Hayes Edwards, and Farah Jasmine Griffin, 9–26. New York: Columbia University Press, 2004.

———. *Time Passages: Collective Memory and American Popular Culture.* Minneapolis: University of Minnesota Press, 1990.

Lowe, Lisa. *Immigrant Acts: On Asian American Cultural Politics.* Durham, NC: Duke University Press, 1996.

Luft, Rachel E. "Beyond Disaster Exceptionalism: Social Movement Developments in New Orleans after Hurricane Katrina." *American Quarterly* 61, no. 3 (September 2009): 499–527.

Masquelier, Adeline. "Why Katrina's Victims Aren't Refugees: Musings on a 'Dirty' Word." *American Anthropologist* 108, no. 4 (December 2006): 735–43.

McGinley, Paige. "Floods of Memory (A Post-Katrina Soundtrack)." *Performance Research* 12, no. 2 (2007): 57–65.

McLeese, Don. "Seeds Scattered by Katrina: The Dynamic of Disaster and Inspiration." *Popular Music and Society* 31, no. 2 (2008): 213–20.

Medley, Keith Weldon. Interview by Charles Henry Rowell. *Callaloo* 29, no. 4 (Autumn 2006): 1038–48.

Molotch, Harvey. "Death on the Roof: Race and Bureaucratic Failure," *Space and Culture* 9, no. 1 (February 2006): 31–34.

Mudimbe, V. Y. *The Invention of Africa: Gnosis, Philosophy, and the Order of Knowledge.* Bloomington: University of Indiana Press, 1988.

Murray, Albert. *The Omni-Americans: Some Alternatives to the Folklore of White Supremacy.* New York: Vintage Books, 1983.

———. *Stomping the Blues.* New York: McGraw-Hill, 1976.

Nine Times Social and Pleasure Club. *Coming out the Door for the Ninth Ward.* New Orleans: Neighborhood Story Project, 2006.

Ojakangas, Mika. "Impossible Dialogue on Bio-Power: Agamben and Foucault." *Foucault Studies* 2 (May 2005): 5–28.

Piazza, Tom. *Why New Orleans Matters.* New York: Regan Books, 2005.

Porter, Eric. "Jazz and Revival." *American Quarterly* 61, no. 3 (September 2009): 593–613.

———. *What Is This Thing Called Jazz? African American Musicians as Artists, Critics, and Activists.* Berkeley: University of California Press, 2002.

Powell, Lawrence. "What Does American History Tell Us about Katrina and Vice Versa?" *Journal of American History* 94, no. 3 (December 2007): 863–76.

Radano, Ronald. *Lying Up a Nation: Race and Black Music.* Chicago: University of Chicago Press, 2003.

Raeburn, Bruce Boyd. *New Orleans Style and the Writing of American Jazz History.* Ann Arbor: University of Michigan Press, 2009.

———. "'They're Trying to Wash Us Away': New Orleans Musicians Surviving Katrina." *Journal of American History* 94, no. 3 (December 2007): 812–19.

Redwood, Loren. "The Rebuilding of a Tourist Industry: Immigrant Labor Exploitation in the Post-Katrina Reconstruction of New Orleans." In *Seeking Higher Ground: The Hurricane Katrina Crisis, Race, and Public Policy Reader,* edited by Manning Marable and Kristen Clarke, 141–50. New York: Palgrave MacMillan, 2008.

Regis, Helen A. "Blackness and the Politics of Memory in the New Orleans Second Line." *American Ethnologist* 28, no. 4 (November 2001): 752–77.

———. "Second Lines, Minstrelsy, and the Contested Landscapes of New Orleans Afro-Creole Festivals." *Cultural Anthropology* 14, no. 4 (1999): 472–504.

Regis, Helen A., and Shana Walton. "Producing the Folk at the New Orleans Jazz and Heritage Festival." *Journal of American Folklore* 121, no. 482 (Fall 2008): 400–40.

Roach, Joseph. *Cities of the Dead: Circum-Atlantic Performance.* New York: Columbia University Press, 1996.

Sakakeeny, Matt. "Resounding Silence in a Musical City." *Space and Culture* 9, no. 1 (February 2006): 41–44.

Salaam, Kalamu ya. *What Is Life? Reclaiming the Black Blues Self.* Chicago: Third World Press, 1994.

Salvaggio, Ruth. "Forgetting New Orleans." *Southern Literary Journal* 40, no. 2 (2008): 305–16.

Saul, Scott. *Freedom Is, Freedom Ain't: Jazz and the Making of the Sixties.* Cambridge, MA: Harvard University Press, 2005.

Schmidt Camacho, Alicia R. *Migrant Imaginaries: Latino Cultural Politics in the U.S.-Mexico Borderlands.* New York: New York University Press, 2008.

Simmons, Lizbet. "End of the Line: Tracing Racial Inequality from School to Prison." *Race/Ethnicity: Multidisciplinary Global Contexts* 2, no. 2 (Spring 2009): 215–41.

Smith, Michael P. *New Orleans Jazz Fest: A Pictorial History.* Gretna, LA: Pelican Publishing, 1991.

Smith, Michael P., and Allison Miner. *Jazz Fest Memories.* Gretna, LA: Pelican Publishing, 1997.

Smith, Suzanne E. *Dancing in the Streets: Motown and the Cultural Politics of Detroit.* Cambridge, MA: Harvard University Press, 1999.

Solnit, Rebecca. *A Paradise Built in Hell: The Extraordinary Communities That Arise in Disasters.* New York: Viking, 2009.

Sothern, Billy. *Down in New Orleans: Reflections from a Drowned City.* Berkeley: University of California Press, 2007.

Souther, J. Mark. *New Orleans on Parade: Tourism and the Transformation of the Crescent City.* Baton Rouge: Louisiana State University Press, 2006.

Sublette, Ned. *The World That Made New Orleans: From Spanish Silver to Congo Square.* Chicago: Lawrence Hill Books, 2008.

Swenson, John. *New Atlantis: Musicians Battle for the Survival of New Orleans.* New York: Oxford University Press, 2011.

Turner, Richard Brent. *Jazz Religion, the Second Line, and Black New Orleans.* Bloomington: Indiana University Press, 2009.

Van Dyke, Nadiene, Jon Wool, and Luceia LeDoux. "An Opportunity to Reinvent New Orleans' Criminal Justice System." In *The New Orleans Index at Five.* Washington: Brookings Institution and Greater New Orleans Community Data Center, 2010.

Washington, Salim. "Has Katrina Failed to Blow the Wool from Over Our Eyes? Why I Disagree with the New Jazz Orthodoxy." *All about Jazz,* November 9, 2005, www.allaboutjazz.com/php/article.php?id = 19625.

Wein, George. *Myself among Others.* With Nate Chinen. Cambridge, MA: Da Capo, 2003.

White, John Valery. "The Persistence of Race Politics and the Restraint of Recovery in Katrina's Wake." In *After the Storm: Black Intellectuals Explore the Meaning of Katrina,* edited by David Dante Troutt, 41–62. New York: New Press, 2006.

White, Michael. "New Orleans's African American Musical Traditions: The Spirit and Soul of a City." In *Seeking Higher Ground: The Hurricane Katrina Crisis, Race, and Public Policy Reader,* edited by Manning Marable and Kristen Clarke, 87–106. New York: Palgrave MacMillan, 2008.

Willis, Deborah. *Reflections in Black: A History of Black Photographers, 1840 to the Present.* New York: W. W. Norton, 2000.

Winters, Lisa Ze. "'More Desultory and Unconnected Than Any Other': Geography, Desire, and Freedom in Eliza Potter's *A Hairdresser's Experience in High Life.*" *American Quarterly* 61, no. 3 (September 2009): 455–75.

Woods, Clyde. *In the Wake of Katrina: New Paradigms and Social Visions.* Baltimore, MD: Johns Hopkins University Press, 2010.

———. "Katrina's World: Blues, Bourbon, and the Return to the Source." *American Quarterly* 61, no. 3 (September 2009): 427–53.

Yudice, George. *The Expediency of Culture: Uses of Culture in the Global Era.* Durham, NC: Duke University Press, 2003.

# INDEX

ASHTON RAMSEY, ARTIST AND HISTORIAN, BACKSTREET MUSEUM, TREMÉ, 2007